CAN ANYONE TELL ME

Diana E. Linn

Linn's Publishing, LLC

DEDICATION

This book is especially dedicated to my husband, Dr. Robert T. Linn. During the months it took me to write this story from life lived in part from experiences and events around my environment that became the theme to share a story with a relavant message. He was my reader, encourager as I passionately wrote on.

Copyright © 2016 by Diana E. Linn

Please Note: Names and places are purely fictional. Should there be resemblances in present or past history, it is purely coincidental.

Diana Linn's Publishing
6398 S. Wheaton Dr.
Tucson AZ 85747

Ordering Information:

For Sale details, contact the publisher at the address above. Copies may be purchased via e-mail: bdlinn@icloud.com

Printed in the United States of America

Category of the Book: Christian Living Mystery. Narrative with a message.

ISBN 978-0-9980819-5-3
Second Revised Edition

FORWARD

A note from the author. Other books authored by Diana E. Linn such as *Abucted and Lost*; is also written with a message. It doesn't matter where we are in our lives we can step out and allow God to help us change our destination.

What If … The Romanov Dynasty a novel as told to the author, is a historical recap in the time when Russian propaganda was at its worst. Research shows that on numerous occasions fact was actually propaganda. Further research shows that the demise of the Romanov Dynasty could very well have become the "Great Escape" of that decade. Thus, the Novel, *What If … The Romanov Dynasty*.

This novel, *Can Anyone Tell Me? is* written with a message. Written so that the reader can experience how God can make the path straight.

.

PREFACE

Can Anyone Tell Me? is a novel written with a distinct message. On the one hand life can lead us down the wrong path because of our choices which tends to have complicated consequences we don't anticipate, yet, still God can deliver. We may have to endure the scars but He can set us free if we resolve to follow Him. Though underserving as we are, yet, if we do a turn away from bad choices\ the impossible becomes the possible. "… *with God all things are possible."*

CONTENTS

Can Anyone Tell Me

Diana E. Linn

Dedication
Copyright
Forward
Preface

Can Anyone Tell Me
Diana E. Linn

Chapter 1

Life Takes a Turn

The sudden sounds and blaring lights woke me, as I lay on my steel framed bed, too afraid to move. I opened my eyes fearing the worst not knowing what had just happened. Hurriedly I slipped through my bedroom doorway hesitating at the top of the stairs, for just a moment, staring into the into the living room. I ran down the stairs stand next to Tim, thinking he should be aware of what had just occurred. Dad must've already contacted the doctor because they both were now standing beside Mother in silence. The deafening sounds of sirens suddenly stopped as the ambulance stopped at our house. It was only a moment before the paramedics burst into our home asking the doctor for instructions. Tim pulled me closer, as we huddling in the corner of the living room behind our well-worn sofa, watching the critical movement of Mother being transferred from her bed to the gurney. The paramedics re-checked for a pulse then quickly hooked up the oxygen tank. "What happened?" one of them asked.

Dad responded, "I don't know but she did say her heart was bothering her and within moments she said she needed to go the hospital. I called Dr. Fields as quickly as she asked."

The doctor said, "She isn't responding anymore and her heart beat is very weak, we need to get her to the hospital as quickly as possible."

Dad's somber countenance gripped my heart while I watched Mother being rolled toward the waiting ambulance but his heavy spirit showed he believed it was over. We stood there watching Mother being taken into the night as Dr. Fields and Dad stepped back into the bedroom talking. When the Doctor left, Dad said, "Go back to bed," yet, still standing in one place, and then as though he had momentarily collected his thoughts, said, "Be prepared to leave in the morning."

All of us were caught unprepared and no one was prepared to ask questions as we climbed the stairs and headed toward our bedrooms. "Where will Dad take us, Tim?" was all that I could whisper.

As Tim tucked me into bed, he said, "We do have relatives. Just go to bed and you'll see it'll all work out."

The next morning, I awoke from a shuffling noise that came from the downstairs kitchen, thinking that morning had come too soon. Tim came to gather me up and to be sure I would be dressed and ready for breakfast. "Are you ready for something to eat, Jenna?"

"I guess so. Tell me, did I just have a horrible nightmare?"

"You mean a nightmare about Mother going to the hospital? No, that wasn't a dream Jenna, it was for real. Let's get downstairs so I can start breakfast."

"Won't Dad make breakfast?"

"You'll like it better if I do it."

We slowly descended the stairs only to find Cam and James sitting at the kitchen table in total silence while Dad was about to pull the frying pan out of the cupboard.

"Dad, let me do that. Mother allows me to do that for her, I'll make breakfast."

Dad gladly handed the pan to Tim since cooking had never been something he did if he could help it. "Where's Pete?"

"He's coming…here he is now. Did you have a good sleep, Pete?"

"I tried, Tim."

"I guess we all tried." For a moment, we all just sat glued in our chairs unable to move. Attempting to break the silence, "We need to eat, so let's do it." Tim wanted desperately to ease the feeling of loneliness.

Pete was always the first to offer help, "I'll help you Tim. Tell me what to do." Cam and James sat there too frozen to talk.

"Just set the table, Pete. I have the rest under control."

I looked over at Cam who was picking at the food, trying to eat, but like me, our throats were too tight to swallow. I knew mine was. All we could do was eat a few bites, hoping Dad would talk first but he didn't. Finally, after a few mouthfuls, Tim asked, "Dad, are we going to Aunt Emily's today?"

"She's just a distant relative of mine, I can't do that. I'm not even sure we're related." He hesitated for a moment and then just said it, "I'm taking you to the orphanage."

"The orphanage?" groaned, Pete.

"Please don't take us there. We've told you the stories we heard at school from other kids," moaned James. Glancing at James, I could tell he had lost all hope and Cam was just plain somber in his silence.

"Can't we stay here and help you? We can make meals," sputtered Tim, "I know how to do all that. It won't be too long before Mother comes home anyhow."

Dad had a nervous cough and the proceeded to say, "You're too young."

"But I'm already twelve."

"That's just too young to take care of everyone. I'd be in trouble if I leave you home alone." Then without another word, "Grab your stuff and let's go. After I take you there, I still have to go to work."

Dad was one of the lucky ones. A lot of men had already gone to war, but Dad, though he signed up for the Draft, didn't have to go because of his large family.

Dad often told us, "You kids need to be thankful for what we have. During *the Great Depression*, there just wasn't any jobs anymore for anyone to earn money. We couldn't even get our own money from our bank deposits because the banks had been "caught short" with too much of their assets in foreign investments. My store had to finally close its doors as well. Then when Mother and I planned to marry, I only had five dollars to my name and I spent two dollars on a marriage license."

I remembered Mother saying, "God was good to us. We were not married very long and found that we had nothing more to eat when I heard a knock on the door. I went to answer it only to find a lady from the Salvation Army with a box of groceries."

Then Dad would add, "Yes, kids, we were one of the fortunate families and since then we have managed to make ends meet. As much as I don't like wars, it provided us with work because most men went to war fighting for our country and freedom. Best we never forget that."

"How come you aren't fighting in the war?" James had asked.

"Our family is too large so we need to produce the war equipment here at home. Your Mother always said like other women she too wanted to join the work force for the war effort. Even she tried to do factory work but her health was never good enough. I don't want your mother to work, I'd rather have her stay home taking care of you kids."

I knew that Dad was jealous more than anything else. He was always afraid of losing Mother and maybe she might talk to some other man. Mother was more sociably adept than Dad had ever been, so he wasn't about to watch her talk to men. Somehow that was supposed to mean something bad would happen to our family. That part I didn't understand. But then, we were glad that Mother was always at home waiting for us.

Then reality set in once again, "James…" Tim's voice followed him running up the stairs. "I want you to help me clean the breakfast dishes so they aren't dirty when Dad gets home tonight."

"I'll be right back. I'll just take a minute." Like he said, it was only a minute before he was back standing next to Tim but I could see in James face that he wanted to complain about having to help. My mind said *why should we clean up*? Especially, now since we were being taken away. But if James didn't do what Tim asked, Dad would *throw a fit*. That could make it worse and give him cause to hate us even more. If Dad loved us, he'd never do this but there was just no reasoning—it was now over.

I was going to miss our home. Both our parents complained that the rent was way too high anyway but they needed a home large enough for five kids with room for us to play. Our house even had a couple of bathrooms, an unusual feature for an old house. I always wondered how Mother kept it so clean. Just thinking about it, Mother had always cleaned and then painted when cleaning didn't do the job anymore since she couldn't stand anything that didn't look nice. She even did the decorating with the mauve curtains being her specialty, handmade with her foot pedal sewing machine. Not only that, she loved making clothes for me since I was her only girl. She always said, "Boys clothes are no fun to make."

Thoughts of the good times were all I wanted to remember. I wanted to remember the pulley Pete and James made to pull things across the back yard pretending they were sending secret messages back and forth and even the half-built play house my brothers made in the back yard for me. Mother always told us to be careful, it might fall over but Dad reassured her that it was safe enough. Now, that seemed to be all over.

I just had one problem, why wouldn't Dad allow us to go to Aunt Emily's even if she was a *shirttail* relative of his? Yes, we always knew he was uncomfortable when we visited with her but thought that maybe her way of getting preachy and personal about whether we were attending church or not, was just too overwhelming for him. Aunt Emily always had a special peace about her that I would yearn for. Our family just couldn't have that, I never quiet understood why. Then I thought maybe it was Mother that was unhappy because she would tell us stories about when she was young and how hard it was to leave her home and family in Russia.

I'd ask, "Do you ever get homesick?"

"Yes, I do."

"Wouldn't you like to go back?"

"I can't, Jenna. I can't."

"Just once and see things as they were?"

"I can't. That can never happen for me."

"Why?"

"If I did, they'd never let me come home again alive. You just have to know it can never happen."

I thought she meant her health wouldn't allow her to do that. "Well, Mother, you at least have Grandpa."

"That's right, Jenna, I at least I have your Grandfather and your Dad. Don't forget, I have you and your brothers as well."

Those thoughts faded as Dad began ushering us out the door.

Chapter 2

The Lady in Black

We were hesitant to move, so Dad started pushing us through the front door, and that made me feel we were being herded like cattle. Down our front stairs, I stumbled but continued the half block toward the bus stop, no one said a word. We lined up behind the two-other people, who were also waiting for the same bus that arrived within minutes. They boarded and then it was our turn. The next thing we knew we were headed for that forbidden house that I just knew would become our home.

It was only a matter of minutes and a few miles from our home at the edge of town when fear gripped my heart again knowing a fate almost worse than death was about to face each of us. Everything familiar had slipped from view as the bus continued on its route toward the orphanage. I was scared into total silence as I watched, staring out the window. Soon we were at that *other* part of town that everyone called *the dirty section* because people threw their garbage in the street. No one seemed to care about how things looked. My brother's friends from school told us stories of what happened behind closed doors inside that orphanage. Now we were going there and for the first time saw the gray oversized structure we'd only heard about.

The building was too gray for me, a solid stone structure that looked ice cold, to be exact. When I looked up I could see the barred windows and thought, I'll bet no one ever escapes that place, even if they wanted to. There had to have been a courtyard in the middle of somewhere because I could hear the shouting of children's voices echoing in the distance.

Our feet were once again on the sidewalk following Dad to the front of the building. Tim tugged on my arm to help me up the steep stairs. Dad pulled opened the steel double doors as we sheepishly entered that cold stone building while our eyes were adjusting from daylight to the weakly lit room. Most of the light came from the outside, filtering through the gray curtains that hung stiffly on their rods.

Immediately we heard, "May I help you, Sir?" As my eyes adjusted, I saw the voice was coming from a very stern looking woman dressed in black, seated behind a huge desk.

"I've come to get help for my children," Dad told the lady.

"Before we discuss your children, let me take them to another room while we talk." Immediately, we were ushered into, what I supposed looked like a *pretend* play room, and then I heard a heavy clunk as the key turned in the lock. We scrambled to find chairs for fear we might have to sit on the cold cement floor.

"This place looks like the Vet's office, a place they keep dogs until the owners come to pick them up."

"Pete, stop that nonsense. Can't you see this is a play room?"

"Come on, Tim. A play room should look inviting. A place you enjoy being in while you wait for your parents to come get you."

"We aren't waiting for parents, guys. We are waiting for strangers to come take us away and that's only if we're lucky. Otherwise they house us here with other kids that don't have parents."

"Cam, don't talk like that, this is all very temporary. Mother will be home soon and then we'll be gone from here."

"You're living in a dream-world, Tim."

"Why, James? What do you think?"

"It doesn't matter what I think, it's what Dad thinks."

"I know he plans to come get us soon. You'll see this is just going to be for a very short time."

"Tim, I hate to inform you but if you can't figure it out, I'm not saying anything more."

I didn't have a clue what my brothers were talking about and I didn't need to hear all this stuff. Finally, we just sat there in silence, staring at one another, refusing to talk for fear of tears. None of us dared move knowing our future was uncertain in the hands of a Dad who dared to bring us here.

My gaze wondered from one end of the room to the other. Pete was right that this place looked more like a Vets office. All the toys were stacked neatly on shelves with a place marked out for each, not even a whisper of something out-of-place. I just knew no one would have dared play in this room.

"I have an idea."

"What's that Pete?"

"Let's do what no one else dares to do. Play with the toys and then put them where they don't belong. Do you think anyone would notice, James?"

"I'm not going to do it. Get yourself in trouble if you want. You can clearly see this room really isn't for playing."

I couldn't help but ask, "If it isn't for playing, why are there toys?"

"To make parents feel they are doing the *right* thing and that their kids are going to be just fine here."

"Stop that nonsense, Pete. Play if you want to."

"Then why don't you play with the toys, Tim?"

"Not in the mood, you guys go ahead."

James became adamant, "There is no way I'm touching anything."

"You're just making something out of nothing," Tim said more sternly, very unlike him.

"You really think so, Tim?" I asked.

"I do, Jenna. I also think everything will be fine, you'll see."

I glanced over at the others and only Cam and James were motionless. I just knew they had to know something none of the rest of us did. No one talked anymore, we just waited. We were there at least thirty minutes from what I could see of the clock on the wall but it seemed like hours of waiting until the lady in black finally appeared in the doorway alone.

Tim proceeded to ask, "Where's our Dad?"

"He left. I thought it was best that way. A couple of families are interested in taking you and they will be here shortly. Continue to play and I'll be back."

She left, relocking the door.

"Can't we get out of here, somehow?"

"Pete, we can't because the door is locked. Anyhow, if we could, where would we go?"

"Tim, we have relatives even if Dad isn't fussy about Aunt Emily. He's not the one that needs a place to stay," Cam protested. "Doesn't she live a little north of here?"

"You guys are all crazy. We need to do what Dad wants," insisted James."

"Why? You know we're never going home again," spouted Pete.

Tim persisted, "I don't agree, Pete."

"Pete's more right than wrong, Tim," but even as James spoke, he looked very nervous.

"Let's just wait and see," by now Tim sounded like he had a frog in his throat.

Arguing began erupting between James and Pete with none of us being able to hear the other talk. Maybe it was best that way because it was all I could do to hold
back the tears as I looked at Tim.

"It'll be okay Jenna, it will work out in the end, you'll see." He was forever reassuring me.

Suddenly, the door opened again. The lady-in-black began speaking, "We've been watching you through the window…you couldn't see us, but we could see you. I have a couple that will take…let's see, Jenna, Cameron and Timothy. The others will go into separate homes. The three of you need to come now."

The three of us were ushered out through the large doors, back into the office where a man and woman stood to greet us, "You three will be coming with us. This is Bob, my husband. We want to be your new parents. My name is Nettie and you can call me Mother, Aunt Nettie or even just Nettie. I really don't mind. Come with us."

We were leaving the orphanage now but my heart was heavy realizing that James and Pete were not coming with us, they were still locked up in that so-called play room. I looked at Tim but saw how sad he looked, so I turned away watching Cam to see if at least he was able to handle all of this.

"Just so you children understand what's happening, let me explain. We will be driving a few miles north from here to our home. It is very large with many rooms so I know you will be very comfortable— you'll see." With that we were ushered down the stairs, out the door into an old Sedan.

"That's a 1924 Nash 694, made by the Nash Company. I've only seen pictures of those cars," Cam knew every car ever made. Mother had started a collection of toy cars that he guarded with his life. He said they were only for looking at, not to be played with. "They don't make those cars anymore because people want them to look fancier these days." He definitely knew cars and he wanted everyone to know it. As he continued talking, "This one has room for all of us, even a partition between the front and the back. I didn't know the Nash Company made these cars that way."

"They did on some, on special orders only, Cameron."

"Does that mean we can't hear you from the back seat?"

"See this button in the front in the middle of the dashboard? If I press that, the speakers are opened so we can talk back and forth. But, unless you see the light in the back, it wouldn't be on." Our *new parents* were silent for the rest of the ride but grinned that Cam would know so much about cars.

As we sat in the car, once more I slipped into that hopeless feeling of the unknown and I could see the terror stamped on our faces as we drove on to our new home. We had no idea who these people were that we were assigned to live with since Dad hadn't bothered to explain anything to us.

Chapter 3

Finding Our Way

———————————

Pete and James were terrified as they looked at one another, "They're sending us somewhere else separately," whispered James.

"Quiet, they didn't remember to lock the door."

"But they said they could watch us through that weird window."

"They'll be too busy sending the others away, let's go!"

"Run away?"

"Yeah James, what else can we do? We have no choice."

"I just don't think this is the right thing to do."

"You heard them James, both of us are going to be separated. There just is no other way!"

"You could be right, let's do it." For James, who always wanted to do what was right, his heart felt torn to shreds.

They both used their bodies to push against the heavy door as it creaked, giving them barely enough space to slither through the gap.

"Okay, James, follow me," whispered Pete, "there are stairs at the end of the hallway, quick, we can do it."

James still wasn't sure that he should be doing this but what had he to lose? They had already lost their Mother, their Dad and now this split up.   All he could think was that Dad had abandoned them so why not run away? "Let's go, Pete, we gotta' get outa' here, like now!"

"I'm coming! We should have a head start before they'll even notice us because right now they're busy sending Pete, Jenna and Cam away."

They were half way down the fire escape when they could hear the echo of scrambling above them and a muffled scream that sounded like the lady-in-black, "Where did the two boys go?"

"My heart is in my mouth. She knows we're gone!"

"Don't think about it, James. My heart is pounding too and I feel like my feet are made of iron, but we have to keep running."

Pete was convinced there had to be an answer somewhere. He wasn't about to be stuck in an orphanage when there were relatives that could have taken them. They kept running as fast as they could. Neither of them spoke as they made their way into the street.

"Which way do we go James?"

"I'm supposed to know?"

"You're the smart one, I'm the brave one—the risk taker, remember?"

"Between the two of us, Pete, we should be able to find our way."

"I feel so lost even though I know we can figure it out. I feel like we've been thrown away. We aren't even good enough for our own Dad."

"Shut up, and keep running."

They ran as fast as they could, still hearing the pounding of running feet behind them—yet, too afraid to look back. "Let's duck into this alley. Hey, Pete, there's a bush! Let's hide for a while." They slipped through the alleyway and then into the underbrush not far from the orphanage.

"James," whispered Pete, "this is a blackberry bush. Look at my scratches all over my arms!"

"Just eat the blackberries and be quiet. It's food, you know. Hey, there they go past us. Yeah, I've got tons of scratches too."

"Maybe if we slither out, we won't get any more scratches?"

"Do you think we made it?"

"I think so, Pete. They've gone by and no one is following as far as I can tell."

"Won't they come back this way?"

"Sure, but we're close to town. We can run into the shops so they won't see us. You have to know the lady-in-black will try to find us but the guys chasing us have never seen us before. They don't even know what we look like."

"You are the smart one, alright. I would never have thought about that. I'll bet we are the first to have ever run away from that orphanage under her rule."

"I doubt that, although that might be the reason a person like her is in charge, as the lady-in-black, *the mighty one*. Not only that, she's so proud that she won't call the cops on us because she doesn't want to get into trouble either. That would scar her record."

"We'll have to be very careful. She could have *stooges* looking for two kids that don't know what they're doing."

"That's it. Let's be careful and stay safe, look out for each other."

"Yeah James, we'll look after each other, alright, losing our parents is enough. They might abandon us but I wouldn't do that to you. When we get this, all figured out, we have to start finding out where the others are."

"Pete, *first things first* or we will get ourselves in bigger trouble."

"Let's go, they're gone."

"What's that smell, James?" as Pete crawled out from behind the bushes.

"Don't look now but let's get outa' here, like now!"

"Why, what is it?"

The wind blew a musty rotten smell their way. Again, Pete asked, "What is that, James?"

"A Hobo in the brush!" The boys ran but the hobo began to follow after them. Pete and James kept running toward town determined to lose the old man.

Pete was puffing hard, "I think we've lost him for now. It's not enough that we should have to hide from the people of the Orphanage but now a Hobo who just wants something to eat. They don't get to bathe very often so of course they smell. He probably came after us to see if he could get money." That's what's going to happen to us, isn't it?"

James was as tired as Pete yet, he desperately wanted to stay positive, "Let's try to find our way before we worry about it."

"I thought Dad said there weren't many hobos around anymore. Didn't he say a lot of them joined the army?" Pete was remembering.

"Yeah, he did but we still have some, probably the ones who got used to being a bum. Don't you remember the time we had one in our home to join us for dinner. We didn't even have enough food for us but Mother couldn't refuse to feed a hungry person. You remember that, Pete?"

"I guess I do."

By now they had run at least a mile from the orphanage toward town.

James started thinking, "We had better slow down before we are seen running. That could tip somebody off."

"I'll bet you're right but I'm famished and scared, James. Are we going to die of starvation?"

"I hope not."

"We have no money and we're too young to work," Pete was beginning to feel the fear.

"Dad always let me keep the money I got from people for doing odd jobs. When Dad said, he would take us to the Orphanage, I remembered the money hid in my drawer. When we were at home and I was supposed to help clean up but I ran upstairs? I grabbed what I could and stuffed in my pocket. That's also why I knew we had to get away from the Hobo. It's all the money we have."

"So that's what you were doing. Come to think of it, Dad never let me keep anything."

"That's just not so, he never took any of *my* money."

"Stop that James! I know what *I* got to keep."

"You're lying and you know it."

"No way am I lying! I knew he liked you better than me! It might even be because you were older but I didn't get a choice. After what happened I'm not sure you can believe anything he said to us."

The arguing was about to get feverously persistent when James came to his senses and said, "Let's not argue or we'll get ourselves caught, let's go see what we can buy."

"Should we just take the fruit from the stands and run? No one will be able to catch us—you saw how fast we ran from the orphanage."

"I don't think so. That's all we need to attract attention. Then for sure the cops would come after us. We'd be sent back to the orphanage without even the help of the lady in black. That's exactly what she's hoping we'll do. If we buy the food, they'll just think our parents gave us some money and leave us alone."

"Okay, but I'm hungry for meat, even a can of sardines would be good about now. I used to go to our corner store to buy those for Mother and they only cost a little, like nine cents a can. That's why she wanted them, it was about all she could afford.

"I guess we could do that. There has to be a store like that somewhere."

They wondered down the main street and soon found a small corner store just a few yards ahead of them. "This is it, James. Let's see if we can find a can."

"How're we going to open it?"

"Remember, they have a kind of *key* on the can that the lid gets wrapped around?"

"Oh, yeah, I remember. I even opened a few for Mother."

The store clerk asked, "Can I help you boys?"

Both James and Pete jumped back a step.

"Sorry, is something wrong, boys? I didn't mean to startle you."

"No, we were just looking for a couple cans of sardines."

"They're over here on the left of this row. Close to the bottom, you'll find them."

"Thanks." Pete and James walked over and whispered to one another, "How about a loaf of bread?"

"Good thinking—and a quart of milk?"

They brought their purchase to the counter, praying James would have enough money for all that stuff.

"Okay boys. Let's see what you have. It comes to seventy-five cents."

James put a one-dollar bill on the counter.

"Here's your change. I've never seen you around here before— did your family just move here?"

Pete knew how to answer as James swallowed deeply. James had a hard time making up stories. "Yeah, we just moved here. Our parents sent us over to get a few things they forgot to buy."

"Hopefully, we'll see you again then."

"I'm sure."

As they left the store, "Pete, how could you lie like that?"

"James, you need to get a grip. We've run away and bought food. We didn't steal anything. We need to eat before we start on our way to Aunt Emily's. I don't want to go hungry and I don't want them to know that we've run away, either."

"Okay, but I'm scared. I have a hard time making up stories."

"Just follow me. I pretend it's all a game and that means I'm just telling stories."

"You and your big ideas, Pete, you always have an answer for everything you do."

"Okay, James. You keep us out of trouble if you don't like what I'm doing."

"Fine, I'll do whatever we have to if it means we'll survive."

"You got that right. We made the decision to run so now we have to figure out how to survive. I'm hungry, so where do we eat the stuff we just bought? Mother used to always say, don't argue until you eat something. Maybe it's just a little food we need to keep us sane."

"Let's go to the park and eat, it can't be more than a half mile away by now. Do you think we can carry all this stuff and make it there?"

"Yeah, let's do it. That way people will just think we're having a picnic. Nobody will question us."

When they reached the park, and sat on the grass between two large trees for shade. Both James and Pete were anxious to get some food into their famished bodies. They didn't talk until they had swallowed a few sizeable bites.

"Oh, oh, Pete, it looks like we might get the summer rain, again."

"Well, I hope it holds off until we find our way," as they lay there, James began talking, "You know Dad said that Mother was dying, don't you?"

"No, James, he didn't say that to me."

"He said it to Cam and I, that's why he took us to the orphanage. He said the doctor told him not to count on her coming home anymore."

"I wondered what the doctor told him when he and Dad went back into their bedroom to talk just before he left, I guessed as much. I didn't think Dad would unload us if it was a temporary situation. Still it would have been nice to at least have a Dad."

"We still do have a Dad."

"Oh yeah, then why didn't he say good-bye to us? That sucks."

"It does hurt I know, Pete, but I have to believe we will find Dad and our brothers." James turned to look at Pete, realizing his face had turned bright red.

"What's with you, Pete? You aren't going to get sick, are you?"

"No, I'm just really mad. I wish I could go up to Dad and just say, "How dare you give us all away and don't even say good-bye!"

"I'm hurt too and I'm really sad but I still don't think that Mother is dead."

"Oh yeah? How will we ever know?"

"Once and for all, Pete, we have to decide that we will find out about Mother, how, I don't know, but we have to keep trying. I have an idea, James. Both of us know where we live from this park. Do you think we could sneak into our own house when Dad's at work?"

"I must admit it would be easier than finding Aunt Emily, although, from our house I could find it, Pete."

"Let's get cleaned up in the park bathroom over there. Then we'll feel a little better and think clearer so that we can figure out our next move."

By now they were racing to see who could get to the bathrooms first. It wasn't more than a few yards, when they looked at one another and James said, "We'll sneak into our house and when Dad comes home, we'll just ask him where Mother was taken, he'll know."

"Fat chance he'll even let us stay with him, James! He'll just unload us again and if you talk to him, don't tell him I'm with you. I'll see what he does with you but I'm not going back. I bet he doesn't even care the least bit about us."

"Stop it Pete. I don't know what made him do what he did but let's you and I survive."

"I hate him. How could he leave us even before Mother died?"

"She's not dead, Pete!"

"You keep saying that so prove it! What do we do, find the hospital and go see? Who's going to let kids in a hospital anyhow?

"We could sneak in and find out?"

In an attempt to change the subject, James said, "The sardines weren't what I would've wished for but I'm at least full."

"So am I. Let's throw the leftover food to the birds. They'll like it and then tomorrow we'll starve."

"But keeping the leftovers would go bad and make us sick anyhow. Enjoy the food, birds!"

"Let's find our house and see what happens."

The boys were walking fast trying to reach home before the rain clouds would release its summer furry.

"It does make for a beautiful rainbow, though."

"Like you said, James, we'll argue later but now we need to go home before Dad gets there and look, the sun is going down. I get scared when it gets dark."

"Pete, that's our house!" They just stood there staring as though they had just seen a mirage.

"You're right, it's our house!"

The neighborhood was still quiet, still too early for workers to arrive home from work. The gas station across the street had a few cars getting gas and repairs although they were getting ready to close shop. It almost seemed busy yet the town had very few twenty-four-hour service stations because not everyone owned a car.

They walked through their front gate when Pete asked, "How do we get in?"

"We'll try all the doors, and maybe even the windows."

"The house is all dark, that means Dad isn't home yet. Good, maybe we can get in before him. Let's try the door knob."

"Sorry Pete, it's locked."

"Try the side door that we never use and then the back door. Let's try those."

Within minutes, they discovered all the doors were locked.

"We're back to square one. Any idea what time it is James? You think it's about the time Dad usually comes home?"

"That's what I'm thinking."

"I'm wondering if I stood on your shoulders, maybe I can reach a window. I'd rather be in the house when Dad comes home than out here waiting for him where we don't want to be seen."

James hoisted Pete up on his shoulders to reach the front bay window.

"Locked, now what?"

"Let's try the back windows, something has to be open."

They made their way around the back but nothing was open.

"Everything is locked, James, what do we do now?"

"I don't know."

"We can't stay in the back yard because if we do, we won't to be able to sneak in behind Dad when he does finally come home."

"So, we wait in the bushes in the front?"

"What else can we do?"

"He shouldn't be this late, James, something isn't right. What if he doesn't come home at all?"

"I guess we sleep out here."

"But it's wet. It might not be raining now, but it did." Soon they leaned against a rock behind the bushes, resting. Pete started spouting off about Dad again.

"I'm still mad. Who in the world does Dad think he is? He has five of us, not because we asked to be born but because that's what he wanted and now we're an inconvenience. How sweet of him to care about us. What does he think about? Himself, of course, that's what matters most."

"I'm just as mad as you. Like I told you, he said Mother was dying and would be dead by morning, so this is what we get, sorry Pete. All I want to think is that when things get settled away for him, he'll want us back."

"You want to believe that? Is that fantasy or what? All he ever thinks of is his own needs. I'm not sure what they are but to him, he comes first. You see how jealous he gets about Mother."

"Yeah, I guess I know that too, Pete. How could I help but know that, he's always been afraid she wouldn't come home if she goes out without him."

"Are parents always that bad? If so, I don't think I ever want to get married."

"Pete, you know you'll get married. I've seen you watch girls and if they're pretty, you look twice at them."

"You do the same think, James. Don't tell me you think you don't."

"I want to get married someday. Let me tell you, I'll never do to my wife what Dad does to Mother, no way. My wife will be free to be whatever she wants. She'll have to love me because she wants to."

"Don't you think they love each other?"

They hesitated for a moment, "Quiet. That sounds like Dad's voice, but he isn't alone." James whispered, "Get back in the bushes, Pete. No one will see us."

"We've done this once before and still have the scratches to show for it."

"Don't make jokes now, Pete."

Chapter 4

Fearing Foster Care

———————————

We were in the Sedan driving past everything only vaguely familiar to us. I couldn't remember if I had ever seen this side of town before or I'd just forgotten.   Like Cam said, it was unusual to have a partition between us and our hosts but this car was more like a limo, a car we were only acquainted with during funerals. In a whisper, I asked, "Tim, why didn't they take all of us? Aren't we going to miss James and Pete? Why didn't these people take them too?"

"I don't know, Jenna. I wished they would've but they're saying five was too much."

Everything we ever knew from the past was now fading. All I could think about was, would Mother get well again and would we ever be able to go back home? We had lost a home, possibly a Mother and now Dad who had given us away. He didn't even say goodbye. Within minutes we felt shoved in, packed up and tossed into the care of strangers. I didn't think these people had any intention to take all five of us in the first place. They had an agenda I couldn't understand.

It felt dreadfully wrong, that someone else should be assigned to care for us. We had relatives that could *pitch-in* for a few weeks or maybe even months. Did Dad think this was forever? Tim was always reassuring Cam and I that everything would work out, yet, I just knew not even Tim was sure anymore.

The shock was beginning to filter through my brain as the driver drove us down a bumpy gravel road, swerving to miss angry potholes. Finally, we were about to approach a yard that had a six-foot green hedge blocking the view of the house. As we came closer the driver stopped in front of large wrought-iron gates that without hesitation swung open. The partition between us and our hosts suddenly opened as well.

I looked at Tim, "Have you guys ever seen grass as green and as beautiful as this?"

"Nice," was his only response.

"Would you look at that blanket of grass? Smooth…would I ever love to run on it."

Our host turned to us, "You children will. Once we get everything together and you guys situated, you'll have time to do a lot of things," Bob turned to his wife, "Isn't that so, Nettie?"

"Surely, we want you to love it here and treat it as your own home."

Even the trees looked planted by a master artist. The car now slowed, pulling to the curb by the house when it came to a stop.

"Would you believe that, a red brick house? I love it! Don't you Cam?"

"Yeah, I guess so."

"Children, stay in the car until I come for you," the driver advised.

Suddenly two large reddish-brown doors swung open wide with a tiny woman appearing in the doorway waving for us to come. We anxiously stepped out with the driver at our side, together making our way up the cement stairs, still trembling.

"Ms. Nettie and Mr. Bob, you didn't bring all five children? You told me there were five."

"Three children are enough, Marie. That's more than enough for you to handle and us to care for."

"I said I'd do it already, I told you before you left."

"Five is too many children for us."

"What did they do with the other two?"

"The lady at the orphanage said they were sending them into separate homes."

"I'm so sorry. Just seeing them now I know I will like them very much."

"The other two were restless and fighting with each other."

Cam whispered in my ear, "They don't even like us, or they would've taken James and Pete, you can see that."

"Not so sure, Cam."

Tim couldn't help but hear our whispers, so turning to us he said, "Stop it, we'll talk later."

We were beckoned by Marie to sit on the sofa in the living room for a moment. Then Nettie announced, "I'm going to my office for a bit so if you need me Marie, that's where I'll be."

Marie turned to us and said, "Go ahead and sit on the sofa while I make sure the upstairs is ready for all of you children," Marie quickly climbed the stairs and was out of sight in an instant.

The three of us just sat there, stiff as boards, afraid to move.

Marie just as quickly returned down the stairs, then turning to us, "You do as Ms. Nettie says, and you can stay as long as you like, she is a good lady. She has a big heart and since they have no children of their own, if you behave, she'll want to keep you." Then Marie headed for another room, likely the kitchen.

I took one look at Tim when he spoke, "Don't worry, Mother will be home soon and then we will all go home again."

Cam finally spoke, "I thought she was dying? That's what Dad said."

"Mother's dying?" I gasped in a whisper.

"Mother is not dying. Don't say that and don't even think that. We will be home as soon as the doctors say she can come home," Tim now talked in a stern voice. He wasn't about to accept hearing anything like that and didn't like talking about death.

"But why did Dad…"

"Cam, Dad is very afraid and he feels helpless. All he knew to do was to get help for us. You heard him say he couldn't leave us home alone without getting into trouble…quiet, here comes Marie."

Just then, Nettie was back as well, "Okay, kids, come with me. Marie tells me she has all the rooms ready for the three of you. You will have the whole third floor for everything you might want to do. Come."

We climbed the stairs to the second floor where we could see rooms with closed doors and a sitting room open to the stairway. Then up another flight of stairs to the third floor and by now I was gasping for air as usual. I stopped for a moment, seeing such a spacious open room. This really looked like a play room, nothing like the orphanage! Then to the sides I could see other rooms that I imagined would be the bedrooms and bathrooms.

"Let me show you everything. By the way, if the stairs get too hard to climb, we have an electric chair that can be turned on and will bring us up or down. See this?" Nettie showed us how the chair could be laid flat and the switch turned on with a lever.

I said, "Oh, that's good because Tim has a lot of trouble with his knee."

"We know that, your Dad told the lady at the orphanage. Bob and I feel we might be able to make a difference and help you both, Jenna. We have the best doctors."

"Actually, Jenna is the one you need to worry about," Tim answered trying to get the attention off himself.

"Oh no, don't worry about me, I'm okay."

James insisted, "She has lung problems," he wasn't about to let the subject go.

"We know that too but you'll find that every room in this house is allergy free, you might just feel really good here. Later when you are all settled, Marie will be up to help you with your schedules like when we eat and what we eat."

Nettie left and headed down the stairs, I assumed to her office, as we started looking around at our new surroundings. "I really miss our brothers, and Mother, I even miss Dad."

"I guess we all do, Jenna. All the money in the world can't replace our parents."

"Oh yeah, Tim, this isn't half bad."

"Stop that Cam."

"Why should I? Dad said Mother is dead and then you saw what he did…he gave us away."

"I understand but that isn't right."

"I know, Tim. But if you can get the medical help you need, wouldn't that be good?"

"Sure, Jenna, though, I'm not sure it would be any different from the medical help our parents can give me because there isn't any cure for what I have."

Cam responded with, "But our parents can't afford the help you and Jenna need, you know that."

"Yet, we always get the help we need in the end."

"That's just what you think but I know we don't," Jenna argued.

"Cam and Tim, stop talking like that." Trying to comfort Tim further, I continued, "There isn't any cure for me either, you know."

"Just a little different, though."

"Well, if that's so, don't you just have to believe?"

"We do. You're right, we just need to believe," answered Tim.

"What are you guys talking about? Believe what?" Cam questioned.

I answered, "I don't know, but Mother always said that, Cam. There must be something to it."

"Oh, there is, guys." Tim answered, but before Tim could settle in to talk with us about what he knew in regard to believing, we were ushered together by Marie to help us settle in.

"Do you have questions?" asked Marie.

Cam just wasn't done yet, he wasn't accepting the fact that Pete and James weren't with us. "Will we ever see our brothers again?"

Chapter 5

The Pub

———————————

A cloud of loneliness hung over Edgar's head as it was all he could do to make it through the day working the heavy machinery. His job could be very dangerous if he was careless but thinking about his wife and kids wasn't going to make it any safer. The end of his work shift finally ended.   As his mind kept spinning, he decided that maybe a beer at the local pub would relax him enough to sleep this first night alone in such a large house. He reflected at the worst shock of his life when the paramedics took away the love of his life. The doctors had always warned him that there could be that last heart attack and this must've been it. Was he to blame for her illness? Did she have too many kids to care for? She was pregnant but just thinking about it made him feel like his heart was breaking. How could anyone say he should know what to do in times like these? Had this happened before? Heart attacks yes, but death? His wife, Tasha had always been in charge of the kids, what they wore, their discipline and education. Virtually everything was in her hands because she just knew how to handle things without losing control. Edgar knew only too well, he tended to panic, making the wrong decisions and losing his cool. Now she was gone, and so suddenly with no time to prepare.   To take charge of his children was more than he could handle, he felt it was not something he could do.

Once inside the door walking toward the bar, the loneliness began to fade from his countenance. He was among people now, not people he knew but just people. Some wobbled into the corners of the pub with a drink in hand, as if becoming invisible. One drink was never enough for most people. Could it wash away their sorrows? Would it wash away his? Edgar knew the rules of the road and that the next day he would get to pay for the drinking with a blinding headache. He knew only too well the headache always came with an attitude making him even more miserable. The pounding headache would feel like the rushing falls of Niagara, a direct result from indulging too much. Why would Edgar come here? To avoid losing his senses, he needed people around him even though once he left these surroundings he would have to face his loneliness once again.

"Haven't seen you around here, are you new?"

"No, I've been in and out."

"What can I get you?"

"Just a beer will be good enough for me."

An older red headed man stepped forward facing the bartender, "Come on, Jake, you call yourself a bartender? Bartenders are supposed to recognize everyone. I've seen this guy before. Not often, but he's been here before." Turning to Edgar, "Don't you work at Vancouver Construction?"

"Yes, I do."

"I know you don't know me, but I work at the other end of the building in the Parts Department. You must be a machinist? My name's Dan."

"Hi, Dan, and yes to your question."

"You look tired. What's up?"

"Oh, just stuff going on." Edgar wasn't about to unload anything to a perfect stranger and about stuff he didn't yet know how to handle. With his chin hanging low he responded, "That obvious, eh?"

"You do look like you need a friend."

"I must look really bad."

"I know a couple of girls that always cheer me up. Actually, when my wife divorced me, these girls kept me going. Meet Wilma and Thelma. Thelma's my girl." That last comment was meant for Edgar but he already knew better than to interfere in another man's love affair.

"Hi, there handsome, what are you doing tonight? What's your name?" Wilma was right in there to make her move.

"Edgar."

"Where have you been all my life?"

Edgar had used that phrase enough times himself on women.

"I know just the prescription for you. Why don't we go hang for a while at the night club down the road? There's a show I'd like to catch with Dan and Thelma. Would you like to join us?"

"Oh, why not, can't hurt."

The two couples walked the few blocks to the nightclub. The bright neon sign lit up the night sky so people could read, *The Pink Flamingo is Always Open*. Everyone knew they no longer honored the all-night call because of the rowdy younger crowd who couldn't hold their liquor but would try for one more drinks and then a fight would ensue. It was easier just to close earlier than to charge someone for damages, knowing full well the owner would have to foot the bill himself. At that, losing clientele was costlier on business than the cost of damages, so it just made more sense.

As they opened the doors to enter the night club, they found themselves walking into a blast of shouting and dancing that sounded like the clanging of drums. The band was loud and noisy, hearing only the sharp sounds of the symbols that didn't always fit the rhythm of the music. Edgar already knew it was not for him. He couldn't hear himself think, but maybe thinking wasn't the thing to do right now, anyway.

Dan took one look at Edgar, "You're not doing too well, are you? What's with you anyhow, can't take the night club scene?"

"I'm just too busy to be carousing at night."

"You mean you're too good for people like us."

"I didn't mean to insinuate that, Dan, I just merely get too busy with life."

"So, what's really up with you?"

"Not a lot."

"Spying on someone?"

"Not me, I just work where you work, that's all."

"Who are you, really?"

"You already know."

"No I don't, tell me."

By this time, Dan had too many drinks to concentrate, so Edgar sidestepped his questioning and made his way further into the crowd of people with Wilma. He wasn't sure that Dan wasn't up to a fight for whatever reason. He knew some people could drink and joke around while others literally became violent. Edgar was here to bury his sorrows but instead he found himself trying to stay away from Dan and at the same time fighting off an almost crippling headache. Somehow, he had to make distance between him and Dan quickly.

Almost instantly, Dan managed to find Edgar, yet again, "There you are, Edgar. Trying to hide from me, are you?"

"Leave the man alone, Dan. Can't you see he's hurting?" Wilma protested.

"If he thinks he can spy on me, I'll put a quick stop to that."

Thelma got into the mix, "Stop the nonsense, Dan. I'm taking you home with me before we get thrown out of here."

Dan was about to take a swing at Edgar when Wilma tugged at Edgar's arm pulling him back into the crowd of people. "Let's go."

Edgar pulled Wilma over, "I'm sorry Wilma, I've got to get out of here, my head is killing me and I have no idea what Dan is up to. I just know when I drink too many beers I get a severe headache, so I think I just need to hit the sack."

"Can I come with you?"

"Oh sure, why not come, there won't be anyone else waiting for me." Once again, his mind was on his family and he knew full well that it was he who sent them all away.

As they walked together Edgar blurted out, "Where do you live, Wilma?"

"Oh, if I have to, I have a room above the bar." Wilma was stumbling over her own feet by now, a little too drunk to stay steady.

Edgar thought under his breath, *if you have to*, I'll bet.

Wilma continued, "Don't get to sleep until about two in the morning when the bar closes, though. But, hey, I don't go to work until five at night anyway and I can't complain about that. The way I have it figured, if I did complain, no one's listening."

"I'm listening but I think you've just had too much. Let's just keep walking if you can."

The two walked to Edgar's home in the dead of night now only hearing the echo of the few sleeping birds that were disrupted as they passed under the tree branches. It didn't take very long since the night club wasn't far, just a couple of blocks.

Edgar turned to face the house. "This is it."

"Oh, I like your house. Do you own it?" Wilma was now desperately trying to stand still.

"No, just rent."

"I don't believe it, a white picket fence? How nice. Big house, you must live with other people?"

"No." Edgar knew at least this part was true. He reminded himself again, that his children and his wife were gone. Even when he answered Wilma, his heart ached from loneliness. Edgar was never the guy to live life alone, even the very thought frightened him and that was why he brought Wilma home with him.

"Why the big house, Edgar?"

"Probably the only house I could get at the time."

"What's that noise? It came from the bushes?"

The bushes moved back and forth for a moment and then they were still again.

"There're always noises around here, it's probably just another stray cat after a mouse in there. That would make the bush move. A day doesn't go by that this place is full of noises, believe me."

"Didn't sound like a cat to me."

Chapter 6

Hiding Inside

———————

"Stay behind the bushes! Dad sounds drunk," whispered James.

"Can't be him, he never gets drunk but that lady sure is."

"Quiet! We can't let them hear us."

"I wish I knew a few bad words and I'd use them right about now," Pete was still whispering.

"Stop it!" James commanded in a barely audible voice.

"I'm getting all scratched again from these bushes."

"So, am I, but be quiet, or we go back, remember?"

"I hear you, James. I'm not going back to that orphanage!" With that, Pete missed his footing and slid into the mud. "I'm full of mud!"

"We'll get cleaned up later, Pete, it's been drizzling most of the day. We should have remembered this low spot here."

"What a mess." Pete hesitated for a moment. "Who is Dad with?"

"Never saw her before. We need to be careful or we'll get caught. Somehow, we have to get into the house without Dad seeing us and before he locks it, again," was James only remark.

"But if he locks the door when he goes in, how do we get in? Besides, I have to get in to get this mud off me."

"Don't talk. They might hear us, Pete."

———————

Edgar and Wilma approached the stairs while Edgar fumbled in his pocket for the key to unlock the door, "Oh, here, I found the key."

"I hear more noises loud and clear, Edgar, what was that?"

"Like I said, there must be something in the bushes, it has to be a cat after a mouse or maybe even a rat."

"You have cats?"

"There're always stray cats around the house, too many." As Edgar pushed the front door open, a white Persian cat rubbed up against him.

Wilma stooped down to pet the cat. "Beautiful, isn't she. What's her name?"

"Whitey, her name is Whitey."

"Ooh, Whitey, you're adorable. You mean to tell me that it's just you and your cat in this big house?"

"At least it's something."

"I guess." Wilma stumbled behind Edgar as they walked through the door. Then she hesitated for a moment, "Just one question, Edgar. If you always hear noises, why didn't you lock the door behind you, all you did was close it?"

"Just before I hit the sack, I make sure all the doors are locked. It's the last thing I do. I know I shouldn't but I'd dare anyone to mess with me."

James and Pete sat in the bushes as they watched their Dad walk into the house with the strange woman.

"You must admit she's cute," whispered Pete.

"I think she's ugly, she's not our Mother."

"I know that, James, but apparently, Dad doesn't care."

"He thinks Mother is dead, that's what he told me. He'd never do that unless he thought that."

"Dead, did you say dead again? You keep saying that. I thought we talked that we were going to find Mother. You just have to stop saying or even thinking that." Pete insisted now. "What exactly did Dad say at breakfast to you and Cam?"

"He said the doctor told him she wouldn't make it this time. It's a miscarriage, you know and all Mothers don't make it."

"Let's stop right here. First of all, I don't believe Mother is dead and neither do you. We already talked about finding her."

"It didn't take him long to find another woman. I've seen him flirt with women and then he's jealous of Mother. I'll bet it's because he's afraid she'll do the same."

"Stop that Pete. He doesn't flirt with other women."

"Where have you been? Haven't you ever seen him flirt?"

"Dad doesn't flirt with women, where did you get that idea?"

"If you watch the older kids at school flirt with the girls, you know what Dad does is called flirting. I've even heard our parent's friend's lots of times whisper to each other about Dad flirting."

"Who said that, Pete?"

"For instance, Aunt Emily, you've even heard her accuse him. Come to think of it, I bet that's why Dad wouldn't ask her to take us."

"That's not true. He doesn't flirt, my Dad just doesn't flirt. He doesn't like the Christian stuff Aunt Emily talks about. Besides, when she gets started she never stops talking about God and the Lord. He just hates that."

"If we keep arguing out here, Dad will come out and he can tell you himself whether or not he flirts. Just ask him, if he loves women. Besides, someday we'll be just like him and we'll like it too. Isn't that what men do?"

"Pete, stop it. We're supposed to be hiding and figuring out what to do next, like how do we get in the house?"

"I don't know. If he stays in there, do we sleep out here?"

"But, Pete, in the morning he goes to work and then he'll lock the door for sure."

"Let me try the door. Maybe he didn't lock it."

"Wait just a minute! I think you're right about him not locking it, I didn't hear the click of the lock you're supposed to hear, did you?"

"No, but give them a few minutes, Pete, he probably plans to take the woman home soon anyway."

"Oh, I hope so, I don't like her."

"You just said that."

"I know, but I meant it." James and Pete sat in the underbrush hiding but now Pete was even more restless. "Can I try the door now?"

"Why don't we? But we have to be sneaky if they're in the kitchen. We'll slip by them and go up to our rooms. Like I said, and I'm saying it again, we have to do this all in the dark, you understand, Pete?"

"Yeah, yeah, I know."

"Hey, it's open."

"Be careful." They pushed their way in, pulling the door closed behind them, but it creaked. Knowing they had to have been heard, they cowered under the staircase in the darkness.

"What was that, Edgar?" Wilma started for the front door.

"Come back, I doubt it was anything, Wilma."

"I heard that as clear as a bell, don't tell me it wasn't anything."

"It wasn't anything, just drink the tomato juice to sober up. I always hear noises but it's always nothing."

Wilma seemed to accept that explanation as she followed Edgar back to the kitchen. "Show me where you keep the coffee, Edgar. I could use some right about now. You do have coffee, don't you?"

"Could be just tea?"

"Tea drinker, are you, eh?" Wilma opened the fridge door, "You don't even have a can of beer in here, Edgar."

"No. I guess I ran out."

"How long have you lived here by yourself?"

"Oh, Wilma, I don't know." Edgar was trying to forget, not to resurface all the events of the most horrible day of his life. He had been up most of the night with the doctor and the paramedics while they were working on Tasha. Now this woman wanted to know details and details would only bring back the fear and sadness. He tried hard just to forget since he felt his whole life had just collapsed and he still didn't know how to handle it.

"Let's go, Pete…take your shoes off," whispered James, while he was in the process of removing his own shoes. With each step, they took, they could hear the squeaking in the stairs. "I think I hear the radio on, the noise from there could save our hide for now." Both Pete and James hesitated at the top of the stairs, straining their ears to listen, hoping to hear what Dad was doing.

"I'm going back down to tell that woman to leave Dad alone," whispered Pete.

"You can't do that. We were supposed to be with other people in another home, remember? Anyhow, I thought you said if I said anything, you wanted to be left out of it!"

"I didn't know about this woman. Who does she think she is?"

"Maybe, Dad told her Mother was dead," snapped James.

"And maybe she is, but we are going to find out, right?"

"I don't know, Pete, but we'll figure it out because I'm not going to let that go. I have to know if Mother is dead or alive."

"Let's try to hit the sack and figure out tomorrow what to do next." They finally settled into their beds trying to sleep, dirt and all.

"I'm not undressing in case something goes wrong."

"Pete, don't worry about it. We'll be alright. Let's get some sleep."

"But I can hear them talking."

"I can, too."

____

"What can we make to eat, what do you have, Edgar?"

"Don't remember, Wilma, take a look around for yourself. You can have whatever you find."

"You don't remember? Do you eat out every day?"

Edgar grinned, "Sounds like a good idea, doesn't it Wilma?"

"Good to see you can smile, now and again."

Wilma scrounged up enough food to make a quick sandwich with a quick cup of tea. "Where is your bedroom, Edgar?"

____

Unable to sleep the boys lay awake, listening, "It's a good thing they talk loud enough for us to hear them. James, what are we going to do if they come up here?"

"Pete, just be quiet. Dad has a bedroom downstairs. He isn't going to come up here."

"I think you are wrong, James, I can hear them coming up the stairs. Probably Dad won't want Wilma in Mother's bed, that means he cares for Mother."

"I hate to say it, Dad's afraid she'll see all of Mother's stuff. Think about it. That would be a dead give-a-way, besides he probably didn't clean it up since Mother was taken away."

"Pete, under the bed now and don't say dead again, to me."

"You think they'll come in here?" Pete wasn't moving yet, he wasn't convinced.

"We can't take a chance since they don't know we're here, remember?"

"Oh, yeah, you're right."

"And what if our room is their room of choice?"

———————————

"Which room, Edgar? You have a lot of rooms up here and you live alone? Not sure I believe you."

The sounds of footsteps were coming closer.

"Pete, under the bed now, they're coming in here!"

As Pete slid under the bed, hoping they hadn't seen anything, the door swung open.

"We can use this room."

"It's a mess, Edgar. It's just got two single beds."

"We can push them together. I can do that."

James was under one and Pete was under the other. Edgar pushed the beds as the boys crawled along their bellies trying desperately to stay under the beds to avoid being seen.

"Aah…" Almost a sneeze as Pete squelched the sound of it.

"What was that?"

"Nothing but the cat, she's curled up in the corner of the room.

"You know what, Edgar, you need a maid. Why don't you hire a maid? A machinist earns good money. You can afford it. You don't have anyone but yourself to care for, which reminds me again, why the big house? What were you thinking? You need to move out of here into something smaller."

"I'm sure I will, Wilma, but houses are at a premium these days. Not easy to find anymore, you know."

"Who says you need a big house? You could rent a room. If you do that, though, make sure you can have overnight visitors, first. Even an apartment might be better."

This was not what Edgar wanted to hear. If anything could put him into a sour mood that would be it. He didn't want to hear those words of not having anyone but himself. Both of them sat at the foot of the bed for a moment when Edgar said, "Wilma, I don't know if this will work. Maybe tomorrow would be better."

"Oh, Edgar, I just want to make you happy."

"I'll walk you home."

"What was it I said? What ticked you off? You don't have to take me home, just call a cab. Suppose I'll ever see you again?"

Chapter 7

Another Night

———————

By now Pete and James were exhausted.

"I'm so tired, James. Do you think Dad will want our room again tonight?"

"Hopefully, he won't. We were lucky Dad called the cab for Wilma and maybe that means now that she's gone and he'll use his own downstairs bedroom."

"It sounds as though his downstairs bedroom door just closed, it should mean he'll stay there for tonight."

"I need to get out from under this bed and get cleaned up."

Still under the bed, afraid to move, "Sorry, Pete, you have to wait until the morning when Dad goes to work."

"Why?"

"Think for a minute. How do you suppose you can let the water run without him hearing us?"

"This is horrible, I can't stand myself. You at least didn't slide in the mud, James."

"Yeah, well, here we are in our home, not in somebody else's. Just think we could've had a nice bed where the lady-in-black wanted to send us."

"Don't try to be funny. I'll bet she would've split the two of us up as well."

"That's exactly what I heard her say, Pete."

"I hate this whole situation, what with Dad giving us away. I don't even like the thought of running away, it scares me as much, though you must admit, it's quite an accomplishment. That part makes me feel good but I hate that looming feeling that this all might come to an end and we go back to worse circumstances."

"I wouldn't be surprised, either," was all that James dared to whisper quietly.

"Though I'm grimy from the mud I slid in knowing I have to wait to wash for a few hours to get cleaned up yet if we were in a foster home, you have to know that not every foster home kid get sent to is good. Remember those two brothers at school? They're always coming to school with bruises. They always say they fell or use some other lame excuse. You have to know it can't be all good out there. Man, I really hope they are treating our sister and brothers better than that."

"I wouldn't worry about them, Pete. Those people would probably have been good for us too. Besides, Cam and Jenna are younger, so with Tim to help them from getting home sick, it was good they kept them together, that's probably why they did that."

"Listen James…do you hear anything? I don't. Dad must've gone to sleep in his own bed. That's cool. We can get out from under here and at least sleep on the top part."

The house was quiet now but they dared not make another move. Soon the boys were sound asleep.

Finally, morning came. "The sun is shining, where am I?"

"Pete, you woke up because Dad just left the house, I heard him leave. Let's get cleaned up before something else goes wrong."

Pete lay there trying to remember what just happened. "Was this a dream?"

"I wish it was."

"Why are our beds together, was there an earthquake?"

"Pete, I wish this would have all been a dream but it's more like a living nightmare."

"Oh, yeah, I remember. Dad and his girlfriend came in here to sleep. Something Dad didn't like and he said good-bye to her."

"Pete, we can't take any chances that Dad doesn't bring Wilma home again. We had better use Tim and Cam's room tonight."

"How do you know they won't change to one of the other rooms? Somehow, we have to stay out of their way. I don't know how long we can get away with hiding here. I hate to change the subject but not only am I hungry but I want to finally get cleaned up."

Pete was in the shower by now while James was busily washing up when. James started recalling the events of the past day, "I keep thinking, don't you remember Mother being in the hospital before? She's always come home the next day. This time seems different.

"Why—what do you know that I don't?"

"I know that she was pregnant again. I overheard the doctor say that she couldn't carry this baby. Something like they have to abort it."

"What does that mean, James?"

"I'm guessing we won't have another baby in our family. Mother can't do that anymore."

"This isn't the first baby that she lost."

"I know. The other one she lost was before Cam was born, and then she had Jenna."

"Mother and Dad said Jenna just replaced our sister."

"They always say, kind of like she came back again. Can that happen? Wouldn't she be older than Jenna?"

"That can't happen, Pete. It's just that both of them look so much alike. I think it just makes them feel better. Maybe, like they can think about life instead of death, at least that works for me."

"I don't know, James, too many people die in our family. Maybe we should've stayed at the orphanage. That might have been a place where people don't always die every time you turn around."

"If I remember our Sunday school teacher, she said that there would be no more dying in heaven, and that's a good thing, don't you think?"

"But you have to die first to know about that. What good is that?"

There was no answer for that comment. The boys finally finished bathing and were finally cleaned up. Descending down the stairs, the phone began to ring.

"Pete, you answer that. It could be Mother."

"Okay, but why can't you answer that?"

"Just answer it. You need to change how you sound and I don't know how to do that, remember we aren't here?"

"I get it." Pete answered with a deep muffled voice, "Hello."

"I need to talk to Mr. Nedder, Please."

"He isn't available at the moment. May I take a message?"

"When will he be available?"

Pete didn't know how to answer so he dropped the receiver back in its holding cradle. "Whew, I didn't know what to say. I'm sure it was the lady-in-black asking for Dad. They must be looking for us."

"You know they have to be looking for us."

After breakfast both James and Pete headed back to the park and tried to play for a while.

"Let's get some ice cream. Can we afford that James?"

"I think so, but you're going to owe me big time."

"How could I get any money?"

"You can give me some of your allowance."

"You're dreaming James. I don't get money."

"Let's not argue about the money. Enjoy the ice cream and then we better head home before Dad gets there."

"You're right James. I wish that woman would leave him alone but she won't because Dad's too lonely." They walked into their quite dark house. "It's almost scary to be here alone. Mother was always here when we came home from school. Come to think of it, we've never been left alone, that makes this even scarier!" Pete couldn't stop thinking about it.

"While we wait to hear Dad come, we could listen to some of our favorite radio stations. Superman usually comes on later when Dad's home, but Fiber McGee and Molly would be on."

"Yeah, I miss hearing that program. Our Miss Brooks comes on early enough, though. She's good."

"She's funny and about now we need some of that. I wish she was my teacher."

"She's only make-believe, Pete."

"I know."

"Captain Midnight is on at 5:45. If Dad first goes to the bar to get Wilma, he won't be home as early. Have to keep our ears open for his coming, though."

"Captain Midnight might get us spooked."

"Come on, Pete. We need to get scared over other people's problems for a change so that ours won't seem nearly so bad."

"Good thought."

"Let's listen to the *Shadow*. Oh, listen, the announcer just said it's called, *The Cat that killed*. Let's listen:

"If we find the tug boat captain, we have a good chance of winning the game tomorrow."

"Yes.

Then Pete asked, "That was a fog horn, James, did you hear that? You can hear it in the background."

"Shush, I want to listen."

"I can't say that this is my favorite part of town. It gives me the willies."

"The water front's always like this."

This time James interrupted, "It's too quiet, Pete, there isn't anything—makes it sound like looming darkness."

"You're making it sound spookier than it is, James. Stop that!"

"It's so quiet. Not a soul for blocks around. Look at how the fog seems to wrap itself around the warehouse, like a …"

"A ghost?

"Yes…No! Don't mention ghosts around here, please!"

"Just what I need to hear, Pete, the ghosts are beginning to scare the woman they call Margaret."

"What's the matter Margaret, you're not afraid? …"

Then an eerie sound came screeching through the fog.

"What's that?"

"I don't know but it …came from the roof of that warehouse."

"Wait for me here, Margaret."

"Did you hear that, Pete? The investigator is asking Margaret to wait in the foggy darkness by herself while he goes to check on what they see."

"Oh no, you don't, I'm coming with you!"

"You can't keep up with me."

"You can't lose me"

They listened intently like there would be no tomorrow. Pete jumped when he heard a sound from outside their house, "What was that, James?"

"Oh, oh, that must be Dad at the gate, turn it off! Let's hurry and use that other bedroom before the rest of our lives fall apart. If we're quiet, we can play with the stuff in that room. Hopefully they won't change their minds about where to sleep tonight." Quickly they ran up the stairs, "You can see Dad won't take Wilma into Mother's bedroom. That part makes me happy."

"Yeah, that's a good thing. I still hate him for bringing Wilma here, though."

"I do too, Pete, but we can't talk to Dad and you know he'll do exactly as he pleases anyway, but it would be nice if Wilma wasn't with him tonight."

James and Pete's problems hadn't ended there, when Pete perked up, "Oh, oh. I hear two people talking now."

"Sounds like Wilma with Dad, alright, they came in together. We need to be quiet."

"We know that only too well!"

––––––––––––––––––

"Okay, Edgar. How about doing something profitable this weekend? Like say, we look for an apartment?"

"Would you live with me, if I did get a smaller apartment?"

"Are you asking me to move in with you?"

"If you think this house is too big and we get an apartment?"

"I do. I think you are wasting your hard-earned money. Besides, you could spend some of that on me."

"I suppose, that could happen."

"Like a ring?"

"We'll see how that sounds to me in the morning, let's hit the sack for now."

"Shall we use the same room, Edgar?"

"Yeah, that should work for us."

––––––––––––––––––

Pete whispered with a raspy voice, "James, did you hear that?"

"Yeah, what're we going to do? Where do we stay if they do that?"

"Forget about us, Pete, Dad's talking about buying a ring for Wilma? I hate that. What are we going to do now?"

"I don't know, but we have to find Mother!" Pete was adamant and wanted to scream a resounding *No!* It could only be a whisper.

"What if Mother is dead? What will we do then?" whispered Pete.

"Dad must believe that she's dead or he'd never do that. I still don't like it."

"Then what do we do, James?"

"Try to sleep right now, tomorrow we can figure this all out and that's when we have to find Mother."

With the urgency in their hearts to locate their Mother, both James and Pete lay on the beds tossing and turning in a restless attempt to sleep until they finally dosed off.

Chapter 8

Adoption Option

It was hard enough to be separated from James and Pete. We didn't even know how they were doing or where they were sent. Cam was always insistent about wanting to know their whereabouts and why they couldn't be with us.

"Marie, please can't you bring James and Pete back to live with us? There's lots of room in this house for them."

"I'm trying, Cam. Somehow I think that it will happen." Marie promised that Bob and Nettie would look into getting them to stay with us. She was even excited about the possibility of that happening.

It should've been a rainy summer day but instead we had sunshine today. I awoke early. I had left my window curtain separated to allow the sun's rays to brighten my room. My health was great since we had come and I couldn't help but think of all the fun we had together just playing, being kids for a change. Even Tim went up and down the stairs using the electric chair—it seemed to stop him from hurting so much. Bob and Nettie had given Cam a whole set of toy cars so he was happy and delighted to have so many not only to play he could name the make, even the model of each one without reading their tags.

"Read to me Tim, I love to hear the stories. Can you read one of *Uncle Wiggley's* books for me?"

"I can, Jenna, but for Cam, let's read something about Dinosaurs. You'd like that, wouldn't you, Cam?"

"I can help read that, couldn't I?"

"Yeah, and maybe even help me read that *space stuff* about the V-2 rockets, eh? Imagine rockets that are unmanned."

"What does that mean, unmanned?"

"They've discovered how they can send bombs in flight to fight instead of using people. Only problem is, the wrong people are using it. I wish it was us so the war could soon be over. If we had that technology, it certainly would be. Wouldn't that be great?"

"We should send our spies in to find out the technology."

"Smart thinking, Cam, I wouldn't be surprised they try that every day."

"How come Dad didn't have to go and fight in this war?"

"Our family is too large. That's another reason we need to have the war stop soon, Cam. When they need more men, it keeps getting closer to his turn. So far five kids are too many."

"Didn't he sign up for the Draft, Tim?"

"He did that to be able to have a choice of jobs they could ask him to do. But, so far, he can't qualify."

"What will happen now that we aren't with him?"

"I just don't know that answer, Jenna. But let's get into reading some of these books. We didn't have any of them at our house, so let's enjoy them."

I could see Marie, grinning while we sat there reading with Tim. She would straighten up our rooms for us and let us enjoy ourselves before the rest of the family would be ready for morning breakfast. We were already calling Bob, *Uncle Bob*. Usually he would be gone before we would come for breakfast. *Aunt Nettie* had her office in the house, so she would eat with us at the kitchen table while Marie would serve the breakfast. We always asked Marie to sit with us after everyone else left. It was good to have her just be with us.

"You know what, Marie?"

"What, Jenna?"

"We like having you sit with us at breakfast. That way you remind us of Mother. Do you know if Mother is ever going to come for us?"

"I don't know that, Jenna."

"Yeah, Marie, you are fun to have around."

"Thank you, Cam. I like being with all of you kids, it keeps me young."

"Oh, Marie, you aren't old! Our parents are much older than you are."

"Are they?"

"We like how you listen to us and let us tell you about everything."

"Yeah, you treat us like adults, like we know what we are talking about."

"Jenna, you are so sweet. I enjoy being with you and you know you are my family now."

Following Tim sit on the electric chair was fun, while Cam would come running behind because none of us wanted to be late, especially in this house. We followed the aroma of the food from the hallway but I was surprised to see Aunt Nettie and Uncle Bob both sitting at the table. Usually, it was Marie that greeted us after Uncle Bob had left for his office.

"Hi guys. Marie has prepared a very special breakfast for us because we are going to celebrate.   We have a surprise we hope you'll like."

I asked, "What's the surprise? Everything is so much fun and nice here, how could there be anything more?" I asked.

 Cam asked, "A surprise? Are you taking us to the park?"

Tim was quiet. I could tell that he was still wondering about Mother. I knew he was hesitant to ask.

"You'll want to know that we have contacted the orphanage and asked their permission to contact your Dad so that we can adopt all of you."

"What about Pete and James?" Cam asked with a crack in his voice.

"Marie tells me that you want your brothers together so I've asked the orphanage to allow us to pick them up as well." Bob hesitated for a moment. "They are trying to locate Peter and James as we speak. How would you like that?"

"Doesn't the orphanage know where they are?"

"I asked that same question, Jenna, but the woman at the orphanage assured me that wouldn't be a problem, just a *snag* in the system. She said she would call us with directions. As soon as we hear, we will pick them up and bring them here. Then if you like this arrangement, we will call your Dad and ask his permission. He will still be able to visit with you children any time he wants."

Then Tim asked what I knew he would, he couldn't stop himself, "But what about our Mother? Does she know this? Does she want to give us up?"

"The woman at the orphanage said your Dad reported her as dead."

Grief gushed over my heart feeling the pain like that of a sword stabbing into the very core, it was excruciating. Why hadn't we been told when she died? I couldn't talk any more, I just hurt.

Tim asked, "When did she die? We weren't told."

Surprised, Bob said, "The woman said she died the night the paramedics came for her."

"She wasn't dead then. She was losing her baby which apparently caused her heart to act up—she even told me she was coming home—I talked to her before the doctor or the paramedics had come while Dad was away in the living room calling for them. She even gave me instructions on caring for the house, what to do to make it easier on Dad when he'd be coming home from work. Then, as soon as she was taken in the ambulance to the hospital, Dad told us he was taking us away. In the morning, he informed us we would be going to the orphanage because he couldn't leave us home alone."

"Was she still talking when the paramedics came, Tim?"

"No. By that time, the doctor was there as well. I think it was then she had her heart attack."

"Sometimes children, things don't go like we would want them to. Maybe your Dad knows more about what happened at the end than you might guess. It could very well be that things went bad later, but I'm very sorry."

Tim still held to his opinion, "Somehow, I just don't think Mother is dead, I feel it in my heart."

"Is your Dad prone to quick judgments before he has all the facts?"

I spoke up, "He always jumps to conclusions. Like the time he just knew it was Pete that broke the front window. Dad went into a rage over it and just before he hit the ceiling in venting his fury, the neighbor came by to apologize for his kid's football that came through the window. Did Dad tell Pete he was sorry for accusing him? He never apologizes, like he doesn't have to because he's the parent and has to be the *tough guy.*"

"What do you kids do when your Dad does things like that?" asked Nettie.

Cam spoke up, "Stay out of his way. When he plays the *crazy man,* what can you do?"

"We didn't know any of what you said about your Mother, but we will find her doctor who will be able to tell us. Would any of you know her doctor's name?"

Tim answered, "Dr. Fields. He's the family doctor. I've been to his office a lot."

"Where is his office?"

"On Robson and Ross, it's a tall building on the corner, right down town."

"We had no idea that your Dad might just be assuming the death of your Mother, and like we said, the woman at the orphanage assured us of the information. After we've made contact with your mother's doctor, we'll call the orphanage. We still have to find Pete and James and rest assured, we will."

"The lady-in-black doesn't sound too smart to me," Cam insisted. "She was strange to begin with."

"I think Cam is right. She didn't even have enough time to write anything down in the thirty minutes we waited until you came for us. Dad probably was busy flirting with her, who knows."

Soon Tim had enough, "I've had it with this gossip, don't talk like that. Dad may have his mistakes but he is our Dad."

Cam continued, "It's that lady-black I'm mad at. She locked us up in a room where she said she could watch us through a glass window. It must've been a one-way window because we couldn't see her. She couldn't possibly have known everything."

Then Jenna asked, "Wouldn't Dad even allow us to go to Mother's funeral if she had died?"

"The lady-in-black was too busy being snoopy without finding the facts," Cam retorted.

"Come on, guys. We don't know anything for sure and Aunt Nettie and Uncle Bob have been so good to us, let's not be unappreciative," Tim turned to face Nettie and Bob, "We do thank you both for your care. With all the stories, we hear in our school about foster parents, we are grateful for both of you as well as Marie."

"Thanks. Tim. You're very thoughtful. I have never seen such delightful children. I'm sure James and Pete are wonderful too."

Cam had a grin on his face, "We think so, because they're our brothers."

"I know. Jenna, as to your question about attending funerals, sometimes parents won't allow their children to attend funerals. Maybe he thought that was best."

"All of us, but Jenna, were at Josie's funeral. So, that doesn't make any sense," Cam snapped.

"Take it easy Cam. We are all trying to understand what's going on here," Tim was desperately trying to calm his brother and sister.

"Who is Josie?" asked Nettie.

"We had an older sister who looked exactly like Jenna but thirteen years older. She died and then Jenna was born that same year. Our parents always say she was Josie's replacement," responded Tim.

"We are so sorry to hear about your sister but just so you know, every parent will say that about their children when they die. Don't take that part personal, they desperately want to hang onto life. I think both Bob and I are beginning to understand you guys just a little bit better. In spite of all this, we do love you. If your Mother is dead and your Dad says he'll release you to us, we want to be your parents, if you will allow us that privilege. Now, more than ever, we want to do that."

With that, Bob excused himself and left for his office in town.

"Don't worry about any of this. None of us knew anything about what you just told us. Whatever happens, and I'm beginning to wonder with the information you have given us. No matter what, we want to keep in touch with you. Even if you get to keep your own parents in the end, which is always the best, we will be happy for you. We would count it a privilege if you all allow us to be a part of your lives. Would that be okay?"

"Surely, we appreciate everything you are doing but right now my heart is breaking. I don't know what to say or think. If it does happen that we really don't have a Mother or she can't take care of us, it would be great to be a part of your family, Aunt Nettie."

"Why, Tim, thank you."

Cam didn't know whether to smile or cry. Parents are parents, good or bad, and he wanted his parents. I could see it in his eyes even though he enjoyed the luxury of his new home and then he said, "But Pete and James would have to be with us."

"Of course, we would want that too." That was all that Nettie had to say for now before Nettie retreated to her office.

We were back upstairs just sitting there, afraid to talk, "I have to break this silence. Tim, you said yourself, Mother is not dead. I don't think she is either, you'll see."

"How can you be so sure?" asked Cam.

"I guess I know it in my heart."

Tim looked broken to me, resigned to accept reality, "I guess I've given you guys the wrong hope. I just knew we would be going home."

"Tim, we are going home."

"Jenna, how would you know? Dad even told James and I that she died,"

Chapter 9

Looking for Hope

———————

Nothing had changed much for James and Pete. Though free to find their own way, yet trapped in not knowing what to do next, they couldn't speak to anyone about their location for fear of facing even worse circumstances. Their chosen path had kept them captive from themselves and everyone dear to them. This day of trauma was about to open up much like the last, awakened by the same creaking noises but still too tired to stir. There was nothing unusual about noises for them but in this situation, they knew they must ever stay alert.

The night was restless, tossing and turning in a semi-conscious stupor the entire time, so when the sun began peeking through the curtains it pierced like a knife. There was just no way either of them could sleep in.

"Is Dad gone, yet?"

"I think so, Pete. I heard him leave. I don't sleep too well anymore."

"I don't either."

"We have to do something about the mess we're in. I've been thinking Pete, why don't we do something today?"

"Like what?"

"Find our Mother."

"How're we going to do that?"

"Grab the phone book, look under hospitals and start calling."

"But, James, they'll know we're kids and won't tell us anything."

"Let's first find the names and phone numbers of all the hospitals. Write them down and then see what happens."

"I'm hungry, we need to eat first. Let's get dressed and see what Dad has left in the fridge. We've been able to keep our secret this long so let's not get sloppy, we need to keep everything where we find it."

Opening the fridge door, Pete said, "Look, there's still some, milk, eggs and bread—I'll fry the eggs that should keep us for a while. We can come back later for more." They finished eating and then sat there for a moment, feeling too stunned to move.

"Are we ever going to get over this frustration, James?"

"If we can ever work our way out of this jam we're in."

"Did we make an awful mistake by running away?"

"Pete, you need to stop regretting the past. We can never change the past, we can only do something about the future."

"You're just too smart. Are you always like that or does God give you the wisdom when we need it most?"

"Maybe it's because of necessity. Yeah, we didn't have to run away from the orphanage and I'm not sure I'd want to do it again, but with Dad saying Mother died and then he just flat out gives us away without even as much as a promise of coming for us when things get better and on top of that, he couldn't even bother to say goodbye. Just maybe that's why God cares about what happens to us."

"I may not be as smart a thinker as you James, but I just know somehow God cares for us no matter what we do, even in our foolishness."

"Come to think of it, that's what our Sunday school teacher used to say, like God cares for us all the time. He even knows what we're doing right now."

"Shouldn't we pray, then?

"We probably should but how do we do that? Isn't He away up in heaven?"

"Yeah, James, how do we do that when He's away up there?"

"Just don't know that. Maybe someday we'll find out. The problem we have is that Mother and Dad and everyone else thinks that somehow, we just know, like we are born with the truth or whatever it is we're supposed to believe. They think God will just fit into whatever it is we're doing."

"But then they put us into circumstances like this. Shouldn't we just be kids? How does that even figure?"

"Pete, like they say, *go figure.*"

In a rambling stroll, they headed for the living room, satisfied with the food they had eaten, James reached for the phone book pulling it off the shelf where it was perched on the wall by the phone. He started thumbing through the pages, "First we need to find all the hospitals around here. It looks like there is about one or two near enough to us. Pete, I've written the phone numbers down."

"Do you know where they are, James? I don't recognize any of them since we've never been to them."

"That's okay, let's call and find out. We only need one. Like you said, it'll be the closest one to our house. Here, you can call, you're the impersonator Pete, go for it."

"Me?"

"Yeah you, Pete, the only one person I know who is good at it. You're always cutting up and pretending, so go for it."

"Okay. If I remember, Aunt Emily calls Mother Tasha, right? We're asking for Tasha Nedder."

"We know that Dad's name is Edgar because of that Wilma he's now hanging out with, and that's what she calls him. Funny thing, we didn't even know our own parents first name. Is that odd, do you think?

"Probably, but okay, James, here goes. Let me try these two hospitals. I think I'll just muffle my voice and make myself sound important. How's that, what do you think?"

"Whatever works, Pete, you're the master here."

"But what'll I say?"

"Just ask if they have a lady by the name of Tasha Nedder who was admitted…what was the date…Monday?"

"June 10. Okay, here goes nothing." Pete dialed the phone and waited for someone to answer as he felt the knots form in his gut.

"Hello, I'm looking for a lady by the name of Tasha Nedder. Yes, she was admitted on June 10. No? You don't have anyone by that name." Pete hung the phone back on its cradle.

"Sounds like that didn't work, but go on, keep trying. What's the next hospital? Here, try this one."

"Here goes nothing again. "Hello, do you have a lady by the name of Tasha Nedder? Yes, uh, a patient. She was admitted on June 10." There was a lengthy hesitation and then, "You do?"

"I'm a relative? Yes, I am." No one talked for a moment. "Do I want to talk with her? That won't be necessary, but when does the doctor expect to release her? Saturday, do you mean this Saturday? Thank you so much." It was all Pete could do to contain his composure to get through the inquiry. He hung up the phone, "Oh, James, I thought I would die! I almost shouted."

"Pete! What did they say?"

"She's Alive! She's Alive!"

"Pete, when is she coming home?"

"She's Alive! She's Alive!"

By now Pete couldn't contain himself. He jumped up and down, running down the hallway, still shouting, "She's alive, James! She's alive."

"Stop that Pete, when is she coming home?"

"Saturday, she's coming home Saturday! We'll have our Mother back on Saturday!"

By now they were beside themselves—should they shout or jump with joy? They hadn't expected to find out so quickly. This was better than one of their wildest dreams.

"At last things will be back to normal, James."

"Oh yeah, really, is that what you think? I'm glad that's how you feel, Pete."

"Instead of worrying, let's go out and celebrate, James."

"How shall we do that?"

"I don't know. Is there money in the house?"

"I still have some."

"I wouldn't mind getting a Neilson Chocolate bar, how about you?"

"Isn't that what Dad always bought for you because it's your favorite?

"Sure is. I'd love a *Neilson* chocolate bar right about now. How about you, what's your favorite?"

"I'll stick with ice cream. That's always been my favorite."

"James, don't forget we need to find a key. Every day we go out and come back before Dad but when it comes to be Saturday, we might have a problem. By the way, how do we tell Dad that Mother is supposed to come home on Saturday?"

"How would I know?"

"Wouldn't she call home? She doesn't know about Wilma, I'm sure. Dad isn't about to tell her since as far as he is concerned, she's dead."

"Pete, don't forget that Saturday is the day when Dad was going to go look for an apartment and buy Wilma a ring."

"I hate that man even more. He might be my Dad but how could he do this to our Mother? We won't know what to expect on Saturday so we have to find a key. We need to be here when Mother calls or comes home."

You know what, Pete? Doesn't Aunt Emily always put her key under the mat at the front door?"

"But this isn't Aunt Emily's, James."

"Let's see if Dad does that," both of them ran to the door, searching for a key that could be stashed anywhere. "There has to be one here, somewhere. There's none under the mat."

"Did you look under the flower pot or even in it?"

"Nothing, that's just like Dad. No key for anyone to find. Let me stand on the stair railing where it is flat. I'm light enough James, help me keep my balance."

"What are you doing, Pete. There won't be anything there. We checked everything when we first came home from the orphanage."

"We have to try, James. I'm checking the top of the door on the ledge."

"Find it?"

"Nope, it's not there. Where could he…might not be one after all. Oh, look, the corner of the bay window behind a slat. Dad must've put a nail there to hide it. How cool, is that?"

Walking back into the house, they started discussing plans for their Mother's home coming. "So, James, what's our plan for Saturday?"

"We can go over all that tonight. For now, let's lock the door and go get our treats to celebrate."

"That sounds good to me, James, it sounds like a plan."

They headed back to the store they had stopped at when they ran away from the orphanage. "Hi boys, haven't seen you for a few days, how are you? What did your parents ask you to get this time?"

"We're fine but we're just here for a couple of treats for ourselves. We came for a Neilson Chocolate bar and James wants an ice cream cone."

"Sure, here let me get that for you." The lady behind the counter brought the *goodies* to the front, counted them up with the cash register and said, "That comes to twenty cents." James put the money on the counter, and was about to leave when a lady from the back room came to greet them as well. "Are you by any chance, Peter and James Nedder?"

Pete had to think quickly, "Actually, I'm Jeb and this is George, like we said earlier our parents sent us over. But our last name is Lester, Jeb and George Lester. Who did you say you were looking for?"

"A couple of men came by and said we should be on the lookout for two boys who had run away from the orphanage."

"We live on Third Avenue and our Dad works at Dominion Bridge. That isn't us."

"I guess not. They left me a phone number, so I'll call them and tell them you are the wrong kids."

Pete and James quickly walked out hurriedly and then a half block down the road, they ran all the way until they reached home. Pete was gasping for air when he said, "We made a mistake," he was still trying to catch his breath, "we gave them too much information. Let's get in the house and keep the doors locked. Don't answer the phone, the door or anything!"

In moments, they unlocked the door and ran in the house, "Check to see that all the doors are locked, we can't be careless this time." Pete quickly checked everything and then pulled the curtains closed and dropped on the couch. "Where's your ice-cream James?"

"I took a couple of bites but lost it running."

"Here, have some of this *Neilson* chocolate bar. It has to be the best." As they split the chocolate bar, James sprawled out on the sofa, desperately trying to relax. "I'm so happy that Mother is coming home, yet so afraid that those men will come after us or worse yet, find our Dad and tell him we ran away."

"Don't forget, they could try to break into our house, since we told them where we live…how could I do that?"

"Easy. This time I'm on your side because I wouldn't have done any better. You tried to be honest, hoping they would realize we have a home and a family. The store ladies believed us but then they were going to call those guys and tell them what we said. They will know our address from Dad and then it'll all click with them that we really are the kids they're looking for."

"We better pray, James. Isn't that what you always said?"

"I did, but like I said before, I just don't know how to do that."

"So, you don't know what you're talking about?"

"I guess you're exactly right, you hit the nail on head. We talked about that before. We're just supposed to know everything by osmoses, right?"

"I'm asking God to help, even if I don't know Him. Oh, God please help us now."

"Parents are just plain weird, we know way more than they could possibly imagine, but we can't tell them that. They'd have a cat if they found out what we understand. Mother forgets we grow up. If she'd have her way, we'd always be her little boys."

"You're right again, Pete. Let's head for our room. I've had enough excitement for one day. Tomorrow's the big day we have to be afraid of and hopefully, those guys won't try to come for us tonight."

"If they see Dad, there isn't any way they'll tell him we've run away since we're supposed in be their custody."

"You're so right, and he's due home soon unless he heads for the bar to get Wilma tonight."

They soon settled onto their beds in Tim's room and started dozing but in a fidgety mood, every move or noise awakened them. Suddenly they were aroused by the jerking of the front door knob. "That's not Dad, James."

"No, I hear that, it can't be! It has to be those guys coming after us. What do we do?"

"James, let's look through the front window from upstairs. See if we can see them."

Gingerly, they made their way to the window. "I can almost see them. They backed off the door and now they are looking around."

"Pete, do you see them? Don't you recognize them?"

"Should I?"

"Yeah, they are the same guys that wander around the school all the time. Mother told us to be sure to stay away from them and not to trust them. They must work for the lady-in-black."

"I'll bet you're right."

"Oh, God, please save us from those men. They're not here just to take us back to the orphanage, I'm sure of that now. I'm so glad we ran away. We would've been in worse trouble. Oh, God, please, please save us!"

The two men tried the front door and then they headed to the side door. "I just hope that door can hold its own. We never use it, James, how good is it anyway?"

"Do you hear that? They're jerking the side door now!"

"Pete, see them? They left that door and now they're coming back to the front."

Chapter 3

The Hospital Visit

———————————

Tasha was resting. It had been a hard few days for her since she had just lost her baby and suffered a heart attack. Unable to forget the trip to the hospital, she couldn't stop thinking about how her children were coping. Edgar wasn't good at handling situations much less emergencies. She worried most of all about Timothy and then Jenna. Would they be okay without her? Timothy had recently been diagnosed with bone-cancer for which the doctors said there was no cure. Jenna had a poor set of lungs and the Canadian Prairies was not the place for people like her.

Nurse Julia walked into Tasha's room, "Good morning Tasha. How are you?" The head nurse loved to have an upbeat sense of humor hoping it helped her patients.

"What do you think, Julia, am I getting better?"

"Certainly, a lot better from when the paramedics brought you in. But I have a visitor for you. Are you ready?"

"You mean my husband has decided to come after all?"

"No, I don't think so. But he says he is related."

"Related? I don't have any relatives here. Who is he?"

"I'm hoping you know each other. Let me get him."

Tasha couldn't imagine who this visitor could be, let alone a relative. She didn't even know if Edgar had told anyone she was in the hospital.

The she heard that voice, she knew she was supposed to recognize it, "Hello, Tasha?"

"I'm sorry, your voice is almost familiar but I don't know who you are."

"I guess it's been about twenty years since we left our home?"

"I still don't know who you are. I was born in Russia and left there twenty or more years ago, you must be mistaken. I'm not even a Canadian except by marriage to my husband. You can't be looking for me, I'm the wrong person and I don't even have any relatives in Canada outside of my own family."

"You don't remember, do you? I'm Alexis, your brother."

Tasha stared for a moment. "Oh, my God, how can that be, they told me you died!"

"They told you that because we were always together and they couldn't ever keep us apart. We'd always worry about each other wondering if we would get to see another day. I heard our Dad tell Uncle Abram to take you back with him and make up a story so that you wouldn't worry about me anymore."

"Alexis, this is a dream, it can't be you. Uncle Abram," then Tasha chuckled, "that was so long ago and all these years I've called him Dad, but I remember he came back from the Palace and said you had died. I knew the country was in such a chaotic uproar yet none of our cousins wanted to talk about it when I asked them what was going on. I think it was too terrifying knowing that any one of us could lose our lives. Our Father was busy leading his army, and come to think of it, I thought it was funny that he couldn't even come to have your funeral. When I asked about that, Uncle Abram said the ground was too frozen to even dig a grave so we would have to wait until spring. That didn't even make any sense because I was told they were also running for their lives. I just had to cast off the idea since Father's absence was all too common. I decided to accept whatever, him being the Czar of Russia, priorities were different. It had to be that way since I knew that he took his position very seriously. Then, just as suddenly, with the country being in such turmoil, Uncle Abram said we needed to leave our home immediately because our lives were in danger. We packed up what little we could and left."

"You might not have realized, but Uncle Abram was in serious danger because of you."

"I'll bet you're right about that."

"Did you say they call you Tasha, now?"

"Yes, they do, everyone calls me that."

"That's close enough. Call me Alex."

"We're still on the run then, eh?"

"Not so much running but staying hidden. I go by Alex Roman. It reminds me of who I am but doesn't identify me."

"What has happened? How did you even find me?"

"I've been in Toronto practicing law. It was Father's last wish to find you, he begged me but it was tough. Father told me that he had arranged for you to come to Canada through Uncle Abram's church. The last he heard, you were in St. Petersburg and from there you were to get passage to Canada."

"We did. It was supposed to be Uncle Abram, Tina and me. We had all the paperwork and then Tina didn't pass the physical exam. She was supposed to stay back in Russia until she could get clearance. Uncle Abram had to get me out of the country, so he said we couldn't wait for her. That was so out of character for him, to leave anyone behind. He would've brought even his mother and wife had they not died. He was devastated to leave Tina behind. He would have brought all of them if he could and yet we left with just him and me. I still haven't gotten word whether Tina is ready to come yet. I do hear from her from time to time."

"In a nut shell, that was our past, Tasha, we're going to have to get together again and talk about all that. But to find you, I checked immigration which showed that you were slated to come to Winnipeg. As an attorney, I was able to find all that stuff through public records. It showed that you married Edgar Nedder. I was even able to visit with the pastor that married you and Edgar."

"You talked to Pastor Peters? I haven't seen him for a long while since Edgar isn't crazy about going to church these days."

"Well, Pastor Peters gave me your address you used to have. I checked with the Post Office. You'd be surprised the information I got from them. They have you living on Ross Avenue so I called you at your house but there wasn't any answer. I went over to your house and was able to talk to one of your neighbors who told me that you had been taken by ambulance to a hospital. This was the closest hospital to your house. When I told the hospital staff I was your brother, they gave me the information about you having had a heart attack."

"You are my brother, alright. Do you live here now?"

"No, I flew in from Toronto to come see you."

"You came from Toronto just to see me?"

"You're my only living relative now and my only sister."

"What happened to everyone else? Did our parents die?"

"After the fighting broke out in Russia and after they sent you away with Uncle Abram's family, we were told that the new government needed a portrait of our family for the records before we would sail to France to live in exile. Remember how Dad always had that powerful telescope we always liked to look through? He had it to check on the safety of the Palace, you knew that."

"We used to stand on the chair to look through it."

"Well, being as he fought with his troops, he wanted to know if anything was going wrong. He was waiting for the photographers to arrive so that we could be ready for them, so he watched through the telescope. He also knew that times weren't safe anymore so watching wasn't uncommon. He spotted them looking through the telescope and realized instead of the photographer coming, it was the death squad because he recognized the leader."

"How did you get out of that situation?"

"You knew we had a tunnel that used to lead to the hospital? You remember they bombed the hospital but the tunnel was still assessable. In fact, as it turns out, the tunnel went much further and brought us all the way to the sea port. Anyhow, Dad was able to convince the servants to trade clothing in a ploy to stall the assassins.

Dad didn't know what the tunnel conditions would be like, for my health, so he asked Rasputin to take me with him. No one worried about him because he was the self-proclaimed preacher that prayed healing for the sick but then caroused with any good-looking woman he could find. *The crazy man,* remember? No one cared that I was with him because I had a blood disease that would kill me anyhow. Still, I was disguised as one of the servants so that we could slip past the guards. We made my bed to appear as though I was sleeping and told them we had to get medicine for me. You have to know, good ole Rasputin put me on the ship to France from Estonia and disappeared. Dad had given me plenty of money as well as Rasputin to keep the both of us for quite a while."

Alex shook his head for a moment, "That Rasputin was one weird man. I have to admit, when he prayed though, I would get better."

"He was weird, very weird as I remember."

Dad had given me a letter of reference for our relatives we had in France. But enough of me, what happened to you?"

"I lost a baby for the second time and had a heart attack. You remember how it was with me."

"Tasha, I think it's all a nightmare. How could any of us have survived?"

"I've been so home sick sometimes. My daughter Jenna asks me often if I wouldn't like to go back to visit our home in Russia but I just tell her I can't. You haven't yet told me about our parents and how they are now?"

"Mother got a heavy case of the German measles and complications set in. She didn't get better and finally died. Father did fairly well, but his spirit had been broken for so many years that when *his Alice* died, you remember he always called her *Alice?* He just started to exist. I was getting letters now and again, telling me about our family. I wanted so badly to visit with them but I knew it would have been taking a chance to try to move around in Europe so I never went back. Dad would write and tell me how people were suspicious of who they really were. He even caught a couple of guys sneaking around their house trying to take pictures. To go shopping, they'd have to wait until the snoopers left. They kept to themselves and were using aliases. What else could they do?"

"It was horrendous for all of us and the risk of being found and tortured isn't worth all the money in the world."

"I can't stay much longer, Tasha. Visiting hours will be over in a minute and I have to catch a plane back to Toronto. You need to hang in there."

"Will I ever see you again?"

"Yes, I promise. Just so you know, I'm still not open about who I am. I suppose you aren't either?"

"You can say that again. Not even Edgar knows. He couldn't keep a secret if his life depended on it. Before you go, I forgot to ask you…our sisters, how are they?"

"They didn't make it very long after they arrived in France since they got Typhoid. It took its course, and one by one they died. Before Father died, like I said already, he begged me to find you. By the way, I'm thinking of buying property in the greater Vancouver area. I should have that all wrapped up soon. Here, take my card and don't lose it. Stay in touch. Like I said, I have to fly back to Toronto tonight on the ten o'clock flight. I will do anything I can if you will just let me know what it might be. How is your financial situation, Tasha?"

"We're as poor as *church mice* because of all the hospital bills. Edgar works but we have a big family. We'll make it—we're a proud people, right?"

"We are, but I want you to touch base with me when you get home. I have to know how you are doing"

"I will."

"Call me collect, and remember you have five children and a husband to care for. They need you and I want my sister to live. We have to get together again and talk about what happened to us. Your husband, Edgar, he's been to see you?"

"No, but you just have to understand Edgar. We lost our oldest daughter a few years ago. He never did get over that so now he hates hospitals."

"What happened to your daughter?"

"My doctor wasn't too sure but he expected she might have had a brain hemorrhage. She screamed for six weeks and then died on Mother's Day."

"How awful that must've been for you! Isn't that all the more reason Edgar should be here for you?"

"I wish he would be."

"You had a heart attack and lost your baby and he can't come to see you? Something doesn't make sense."

"Yeah, I don't understand him either. But that's how he is."

"I really do have to go." They hugged until nurse Julia returned to check on Tasha.

"I'm gone. Love, you!" With that he left.

The nurse noticed how peaceful Tasha looked, "Was that a good visit, Tasha?"

"It was but now I want to go home. When can I go home?"

"Your Doctor is due to come by in just a few minutes. You can check with him."

Tasha's mind was in a whirl. Did she just wake up from a dream? Was it really Alexis that had come to see her? She just couldn't get over that he was alive in spite of all the years she was led to believe that he had died.

A moment later, Doctor Fields walked in. "My, you look good, Tasha. You look as if you've seen an Angel. What happened?"

"I want to go home, when can I go home?"

"I think you could go home by Saturday since you've made such an improvement. Has Edgar been by to see you, yet?"

"No, I don't know why my husband doesn't come. I think he gave me up for dead. I know he hates hospitals."

"You were a very sick lady, even I had some doubts. You've improved so much already. I'm going to release you Saturday. Your nurse will go over everything you need to do."

"Doctor Fields, I've been thinking since you are my family doctor and you know my son Tim has bone cancer. You also know that Jenna suffers with Asthma, what if we were to move to Vancouver?"

"What a splendid idea. If you can pull that off, it'll be one of the best things you do for Jenna. You might want to know that Tim confided in me when I asked him if he had one last wish. You know what that was?"

"No, what is his last wish?"

"He wants to see the west coast. He said he wanted to be able to see the Rocky Mountains and then the Pacific Ocean." The doctor looked at Tasha as if to be studying her expression. "Do you think that you can actually make that happen for him?"

"I think I'm going to try to convince Edgar that this would be a good move for us."

"If you do it, I have references to give you for a doctor there. They have the best cancer specialists in Vancouver, so for that reason it would be good. I'll give that information to the nurse for you. I wish you the very best, I hope you can do what you want. It would be a good thing and you have my blessing."

"What about me, my heart condition?"

"Let me tell you something. You are going to have to live with your heart condition. You have two choices, either you live in spite of it or you succumb to the pain of it. We can give you all the medicine in the world but somehow you have to plan for the future or you'll be planning for your funeral. You have to learn to live."

"I appreciate all you do Doctor Fields. Until I get situated, if we do go to Vancouver, can I keep you as my doctor?"

"I'll help you through the situation but you will need to have a doctor there. I'll give you the names of who I recommend. Don't worry about it, do what you can." He hesitated for a moment, "You're okay to go home Saturday." And moments later the doctor left Tasha's room.

"Good news, isn't that Tasha? I'll get all the instructions from Doctor Fields and have it for you on Saturday before you leave. Glad to see that someone really does care about you, Tasha. You are going to be just fine, hang in there." The nurse was about to leave Tasha's bedside when she made an about turn, "The man that just left, he is a relative of yours, right?"

"God sent him to me…he was a messenger directly sent from God."

"You sure made a turn-around after that. Have you always known him?"

"I have. Like I said, he was like an angel God sent to me. He told me that I needed to hang in and live because I still have five children and a husband to care for."

"Do you see him often?"

"No. this was the first time in years. I didn't even know he was alive."

"Is he an old boyfriend of yours?"

"No, more like an angel."

"Somebody really does care about you. You do have an Angel watching over you, for sure."

"I know for sure that God is watching over me but I still have to figure out that husband of mine."

"He'll be here to get you on Saturday, I'm sure."

"I'll call him and tell him."

Chapter 11

The Phone Call

———————————

"Oh, oh, do you see what I see? Those men saw Dad coming!'

"He's with Wilma and look again, James, those guys are running through the side gate. I wonder if Dad saw them. Thank you, God, you must've heard us when we prayed."

"Now we better stay quiet for the night and remember, tomorrow is Friday only."

"I'm so glad this will soon be over."

"We need to whisper if we're going to talk, because it isn't over until it's over."

"Oh, I know, James. Why don't we just admit that was a God thing, even if we don't understand anything about God."

"You know you have to be right, just like He's always there hovering over us."

"Yeah, but let's get some sleep."

Sleep came quickly for James and Pete, having had enough for one night. This time it was pure exhaustion but soon the night faded into morning meaning they had another day to endure before everything could reveal itself for when it would be Saturday that Mother was scheduled to come home. The only ones that knew it was them.

The night passed with Wilma & Edgar in the upstairs bedroom with little more excitement. The usual conversations but James and Pete were too tired to hear anymore or maybe they didn't want to hear the plan their Dad was falling into.

"Ooh, am I awake, James? Just think, we made it to Friday—do you think we can endure one more day?"

"I sure hope so but how are we going to use up our time until tomorrow without getting caught?"

"Let's Just keep going to the park to play and get back before Wilma and Dad get here. As long as they don't change their minds about which bedroom to sleep in, we'll be okay."

"Yeah, James, I think the hardest thing is to stay quiet. You know how we like a good scuffle."

"You do, I don't."

"You do, too. Don't tell me you don't like to play fight."

"Pete, we're going to really fight in a minute if you keep this up and I'm just too tired to get into anything. Probably too worried, also."

"Why would you worry about Mother coming home, shouldn't we be more worried about Dad?"

"It's like this Pete, if Mother finds out about Wilma, do you think she'll still come home?"

"Oh, James, don't say that! She'd never give us up like Dad did."

"You want to bet? When Dad says to her he took us to the orphanage, she'll think we're still there."

"Mother would come get us, wouldn't she?"

"Pete, if she has nowhere to go, why would she come for us? Besides, she won't know we aren't being cared for."

"James, don't tell me we have to give ourselves up after all this?"

"We should be prepared to."

"Before that happens, I will find Mother when she comes home and tell her I'm here, even if you won't because I'm not going back to the orphanage. I'll just run away again."

"Suit yourself. We'll need to do what we need to do when the time comes."

After the boys conjured up breakfast, they both just sat looking at one another when Pete said, "I'm too scared to go back to the park with those guys after us. They already know where we live."

"Good thinking, why don't we just stay around the house and rest. Tomorrow will be our tough day and we have enough games upstairs as well as a radio we can listen to."

"Yeah, James, as you know we'll have to watch our every move."

It was soon the afternoon when once again they heard the struggle with the door knob.   Pete, whispered, "They just won't give up. From upstairs, we can watch them easily like we did yesterday."

Walking over to the upstairs window they stood watching, "They're leaving again. I guess they're hoping we'll go outside, I think we need to be very careful from now on."

"You know what I think, James? I think they want us to believe they're gone.   They think they can grab us if we go outside. No way! I'm staying put for today."

"So am I. I am away too afraid to get caught!"

James and Pete played a few games, found a few snacks while listening to programs on the radio. However, it didn't take too long for them to become mentally and physically exhausted from the fear of getting caught by strangers. They were also afraid of the next day when they knew their whole world would either come together or fall totally apart. Fortunately for them, the exhaustion of fear, soon gave way to the need for sleep.

"I don't know about you, James, I'm exhausted. I'm not even hungry anymore, just tired."

"Of course, you're not hungry—we've been eating snacks all day. Yeah, I'm tired too, why don't we give it up for tonight?"

"Sounds like a good idea, especially since I hate having to worry about our future so much. We're just kids and we have to have the mind of an adult. Oh, well, we're learning for our future even though I say it's just not fair."

"Well, Pete, life is never fair anyhow, that's what Dad and Mother keep saying."

"We'd better be quiet with Wilma and Dad downstairs. If Dad was really listening, he'd have found us by now."

"You're probably right, James. As a matter of fact, I'm sure you're right but why isn't he checking? Do you think he's grieving for Mother?"

"Nothing would please me more but since when are people so easily replaced?

"Almost like replacing a cat or dog because you hurt from the separation. Sorry, Pete, I don't know the answer, either."

"I just have to get some sleep."

Rest was difficult at best, tossing and turning but too tired to stir. Soon it was Saturday morning as the sun's rays made it in through the drapes while Pete lay there unable to move. "Are you awake, James?" he whispered.

"Yeah, but I don't think Wilma and Dad are though."

"We need to quietly sneak out. We have a key now so we'll come back when we know they've left."

"I don't think that'll work, Pete, those guys are still after us."

"I'm so excited about Mother coming home that I almost forgot about those men."

"It's better to let Dad and Wilma leave first. Listen, they just went downstairs. Remember, they want to go apartment shopping today. Besides, Dad doesn't know yet that Mother is supposed to come home today."

"Dad was going to buy a ring for Wilma today, right? I wish the walls would be sound proof so I wouldn't have to hear that stuff. It just makes my blood boil."

"We have to know what's going on, Pete. Let's hide at the top of the stairs so we can hear and see everything that's going on."

"Grab a pillow. It makes more sense to wait for them to leave the house first, hopefully they'll talk about their plans so we can know what to do next."

"We can't forget, James, we can't be too careful of those men who are looking to catch us. We're safer in here unless Dad leaves the door unlocked. Maybe if we listen, we can lock it for him when they leave before any of them can get in."

"Here's another plan, Pete, after they've gone, we go out and wait somewhere we can see when she gets home. Then beg her to let us go to Aunt Emily's. She just might do that and then maybe we can wait until Mother can take us back."

"But those men…"

"Yeah, you are right, we can't leave. I keep forgetting that we're in trouble on both ends, in here and outside as well. We have to survive, Pete, we have to!"

"Even so, somehow we have to talk to Mother. At least we could stay in touch. Mother would stay in touch with the rest of our family and that way we could even visit once in a while."

"The best thing to do now, Pete, is to let everything play out and see what happens. We gotta pray. God answered our prayer already once, so I know God cares even when parents get all messed up."

"You think?"

"I don't just think God cares, now I know, Pete. You have to believe. You have to believe."

"How do I do that?"

"I don't know, but you have to."

––––––––––––––––––

"Edgar, what was that noise?"

"There you go again with your noises. I told you there are always noises around here that don't make any sense. Maybe it's good we are going apartment shopping. We'll finally get rid of all that nonsense."

Wilma and Edgar were already in the kitchen when Wilma said, "This time you make the breakfast."

"You expect me to make breakfast?"

"This is your house. You need to make it, since you don't have to work today."

"That's true, I don't have to work, but I don't prepare food either."

"That isn't fair."

"I gave you a bed to sleep in."

"What's that supposed to mean, Edgar? I don't need your bed. I have my own place, remember? Who's been taking care of you before?" Wilma started browsing around, looking to find food that could be appetizing. "Who's been in this kitchen, anyhow? That's not where I left the cereal…and look—someone moved the milk in the fridge—that's not where I put the milk!"

"Oh, come on Wilma. What is this, *The Three Bears*? Goldie Locks stole your porridge? I'm just going to the corner store to get some fresh cream for the cereal and the newspaper while you make breakfast. I'll be back in a minute."

"While you're buying cream, why don't you bring back some coffee? Maybe we could have coffee for a change. Then don't forget, Edgar, today's the day we also get my ring." Edgar left and Wilma continued to grunt and groan as she prepared the greatest breakfast they had smelled in days.

"Not fair, I'm hungry," whispered Pete. "Sounds like Dad just left, can you imagine he wants cream for cereal and all these years, you and I just got milk? Like I said, I'm hungry."

"We have to wait," whispered James. "Oh, oh, the phone's ringing. Will Wilma answer that?"

Wilma stumbled over to the phone, muttering to herself, "I'm making breakfast why should I answer the phone? Edgar should've stayed to answer his own calls. Oh, what the ... "Hello. Edgar? ... Who is this? You say you are Edgar's wife, Tasha…and what? You're coming home? The hospital is discharging you at three this afternoon so you want Edgar to come for you? For your information, my name is Wilma and no, I didn't know he was married!" There was a pause, and then, "What, five kids? He didn't tell me that either. He didn't tell me any of that! ... What am I doing here? You can forget about me, 'cause I'm outa' here! But you want to believe I will tell him you called and you need him to come for you. This ought to be good and I want to hear his excuse!" Wilma dropped the receiver, letting it hang, hoping Tasha would stay on the line until Edgar came home.

It wasn't about breakfast anymore, but more about who Edgar was. Wilma was furious and wasn't about to leave without venting her angry opinion.

"Move it Pete, back to our bedroom!" They ran across the hall in stocking feet grabbing the pillows, hoping they hadn't been seen.

Wilma was up the stairs in less time than it took her to drop the phone, still talking to herself in anger, "There are those noises Edgar keeps saying don't exist. This is all too weird for even me." She gathered her belongings and was about to descend the stairs when Edgar returned with his newspaper and pint of cream.

Edgar looked around the kitchen, hearing the frying pan sizzle he turned the stove burners off. "Where are you, Wilma? Breakfast will burn if you don't take care of it…" he turned, now facing Wilma standing at the kitchen entrance when he noticed she was carrying her overnight case, "why are you packed Wilma? We're only going to look at apartments, we're not moving in yet."

"Edgar, you get in here, right now! And don't give me any excuses."

"What's with you?"

"Well, let me guess, you have a wife and five kids? I understood we were on our way to buy an engagement ring! Just who do you think you are?"

Edgar was in shock. How could she know that? Should he deny all of this? "Who told you that?"

"Who told me that? Can you believe it could just be your wife?"

"My wife talked to you? I thought she died."

"Oh, you wish she was dead but I bet you wish it was you who died, now. Is it Tasha? Well, I'll have you know she just called. Do I tell her she is dead, or do you?" Wilma walked over to where the phone was dangling. "Oh, no, it's too late. She hung up." Wilma headed for the door, "Don't bother to call me ever again! I wouldn't suggest you're seen in the pub, either. If you do, everyone will know you are a pervert. You will pay! By the way, unlike you, I'm honest and I told her I would tell you to come for her at three this afternoon."

James and Pete were now standing at the top of the stairs, hidden in the darkness of the hallway, watching and listening.

"James, did you hear that?"

"I'm hearing that. I can't believe my ears."

"It's just like you said, Dad thought Mother was going to die so he gave us all away and started getting on with the rest of his life. No thought for us."

"Take it easy, Pete. He still doesn't know we heard all this. He doesn't even know we are here, or I should say, I hope he doesn't."

"I wish we had snuck out earlier so we wouldn't have heard any of this."

"We did hear them. For now, we just need to stay put, play it cool, maybe God is fitting everything together for us, for us Pete."

"So, we wait…Wilma runs away and Dad goes to bring Mother home? James, how do we live through all of this?"

"Pete, we just keep praying and tell God to keep our secret."

"And like Dad, we go on with the rest of our lives?"

"What can I say?"

"We stay here until Mother comes home. If she doesn't come home, we find our way to Aunt Emily's, is that what we do?"

"That's what we'll have to do. It isn't a choice anymore."

"We could go to see Aunt Emily already and tell her what Dad did to us."

"Pete, you know very well if we do that, we will be back at the orphanage. No one wants kids from a family in a *fix* like ours. The best we can do is to pray that Mother comes home and when she does, she finds us here."

"You know James, I'm not even hungry anymore, just mad. Why don't we rest until Dad leaves, then get breakfast for ourselves?"

They were in an emotional upheaval, too exhausted to move but crept back to their bedrooms. Lying on their beds, dozing off was a rare situation for boys on a Saturday morning.

"There goes our plan of wanting to live with Aunt Emily now. That's the end of that idea."

"We still may get the chance but we just need to wait and see. We'll pray that she has mercy on us if that's our only choice."

Chapter 12

An Angel or a Man

———————————

"Who is that talking? I hear Dad talking to someone, James, but I don't see who he's talking to. It startled me when I heard Dad talking."

"We just dozed for a few minutes but I hear him too. Let's sneak to the top of the stairs."

"Is he talking to those men that were after us? I'm scared James, we're going to get ourselves caught, they know we're here."

"Quiet, Pete, look."

From the top of the stairs, James and Pete watched in silence as they saw Edgar on his knees with his hands on a Bible.

"What is he doing, James?"

––––––––––––––

Edgar knelt in silence. His heart was heavy and he knew immediately that he had committed the most unforgivable sin of his entire life. He had broken the heart of the dearest person in his life, Tasha. How could anyone understand his loneliness when he was sure that this time she had died? The doctor had told him as much. He had said, "Edgar, you must realize, she may never come out of it this time, you shouldn't count on it."

He prayed out loud, "Lord please forgive me. I know I wasn't supposed to jump the gun and make such an awful assumption. I was lonely, and yes, I know I could've come to you but I didn't. Jesus, I have my Bible open to 1 John 1:9 and it says here, *if we confess our sins, you are faithful and just to forgive us our sins, and to cleanse us from all unrighteousness,* please do this for me." Then he became silent and just bowed his head. It was almost ten minutes before he finally got off his knees.

––––––––––––––

"Do you pray aloud, James?" whispered Pete.
"No."
"But you pray?"
"I do, Pete, when I need something from God."
"Shouldn't we pray aloud like Dad did?"
"I don't know, I think God hears us anyhow."
"I sure hope so. What did he mean about forgiveness?"
"I don't know. If Tim was here he would know."

––––––––––––––

Finally, Edgar got off his knees, checking his watch, and began to ready himself to leave for the hospital to bring back his wife. Almost, instinctively, Edgar looked over to the left of the couch, hesitated and then lifted a candy wrapper into his hand. For a moment, he held it and then put it in his pocket. He took one last look around glancing in every direction but didn't seem to pin point anything.

––––––––––––––

"Pete, did you...? ...Did we forget to...?" James whispered. He continued, "We were running from those guys, remember? We were exhausted and all we had left was that one chocolate bar that we ate while we sat there trying to catch our breath."

"Now Dad found it, but I hope he thinks Wilma dropped it and I know for sure he wouldn't want Mother to find it when he brings her home. He might even think it was there from before or he would've checked around to see if we were here, right?"

"I hope you're right, Pete, which reminds me, we can't leave the house, today because those guys are still after us. We need to be sure the doors are locked."

"Hey, Dad just left, see, he just went out the door. Let's check the doors and windows."

They checked every door and window that could be reachable from the first floor of the house. "Good thing we have the hidden key, so they can't find that one. If they break a window and get in, we have to phone the cops."

Pete just couldn't get the scene he had just witnessed out of his mind, "Tell me, James, I've never seen Dad pray before, have you?"

"No, but Mother used to say that when they first married they always prayed together and then somehow they just didn't anymore. When he was praying this time, we heard him ask God to forgive him for what he did to Mother."

"Even if God forgives him, will Mother?"

"I don't know, Pete. Would you?"

"James, I want them together and all that, but how do you forgive Dad?"

"I don't know. God promises, I think, to forgive, but I don't know what we do."

———————

Edgar realized he needed to be at the hospital. Grabbing his hat, he left through the front door in a rush, almost in a sprint to catch the first available bus since he'd have to be committed to a bus schedule. What was his excuse going to be this time for Tasha? His heart was in turmoil because he knew what he had done was unforgivable yet the loneliness he felt was just too consuming for him to take. He'd have to face the beating of the drums but just the thought made him ache even more. The right thing to do was to ask to be forgiven even though he had no excuse for anything he had just done. With her weak heart, if she didn't die now, it would be a miracle. Edgar walked those dreaded steps into the hospital as he begged God's forgiveness over and over again. He felt God would forgive him but how could Tasha—he didn't even expect her to.

With his heavy aching heart, he walked stair by stair, praying, "Oh God, please forgive me." Now he must endure the pain that could easily make Tasha walk away from him. She had every right to.

At the nurse's station, Edgar hesitated, "What room is Tasha in?"

"She's in Room 21. You are?"

"I'm her husband. I've come to take her home."

"You are her husband? Just so you know she missed you terribly and never stopped talking about her children. The good part was that she had a phone call from a family member and then a man she knew stopped by to encourage her. I think that's why she did so well. You will have to ask her about all of that."

Puzzled by, "…a man she knew…" He pushed that back into his mind for the moment for now it was time to face the music. As he approached her bedside, before he uttered any words, he could see it coming. The signs were there, the anger was on her face, yet, she voiced only one question, "Who was that woman, Edgar?" as quietly as she dared speak.

Edgar didn't answer for a moment as his mind was now on *the man* the nurse said had stopped by to see Tasha. How dare she know *another man!* Why should he have to feel guilty? He just wasn't sure any more. Then he decided he would confront her later about this other *man*. He turned to face Tasha, saying, "Woman? Oh, her, she was just a cleaning woman." Edgar knew that was a blatant lie but as he thought for a moment, he felt he had to mentally justify what he had done. It would hurt even worse if he were to admit the truth. How could he do that to the woman he loved more than anything in the world. He did what he did out of pure loneliness, not out of hatred for his wife but he couldn't bear to have Tasha suffer anymore.

Then he thought again, *that other man* that came to see her? It would have to be later but he decided he certainly would be sure to ask Tasha what business she had to visit with another man.

The bus ride would be especially long for Tasha. She couldn't let this *Wilma* go. "Wilma didn't talk like a cleaning woman to me. She was too surprised when she heard my voice and found out we have five kids. Who was she? What did you tell her?"

"I don't have any idea what she was talking about."

"Oh, you don't, eh? If she was a cleaning woman she wouldn't have dropped the phone in a huff and told me, you said I was dead!" Neither one of them spoke anymore. Sitting on the bus in total silence, abiding the time to reach their house.

Finally, they arrived at the entrance to their house as Edgar opened the door for Tasha but immediately Tasha realized the house was empty even though they were only at the bottom of the stairs to the front door.

"Edgar, where are the kids? What have you done with them?" Now Tasha was yelling, "What have you done with my children?"

"They're coming home as soon as we can go get them. I took them to the orphanage because I couldn't leave them here alone knowing I had to go to work. We can go pick them up any time you want." Then he thought again, if he had half a mind he'd find out about that *other man* right at this juncture.

All Tasha could do was, head for the front door when she hesitated. By this time, Edgar knew he'd better follow. Edgar hailed down a cab, since there was now no sense to enter the empty house. More, he didn't want to endure the absence of their children and the hostility of Tasha any longer than possible. If she just saw the kids, she would melt again and be his wife. Edgar thought to himself: I've never done anything as stupid as this, but Lord, you have to believe me, my loneliness was more than I could handle. Please forgive me, though I know Tasha may never, but I will always love her no matter what. Still I need to know about *this other man*.

It took a good thirty minutes to reach that old gray stone building of the orphanage. As they entered through the same front door, Edgar remembered very well when only a week ago he had brought his children here, the familiar lady-in-black still sat behind the desk as though she had never moved.

"How can I help you? Oh, Edgar! We've been trying to reach you. We called your home and someone picks up the phone. I say who I am and the receiver slams down."

Staring straight ahead at the lady-in-black, Tasha demanded, "What's wrong with my children?"

"Timothy, Cameron and Jenna are fine. They are staying with a family just a few miles north of here. As a matter-of-fact, those people want to adopt them, if they can. Best of all, they want your other two boys as well, Edgar." The lady-in-black ignored Tasha's presence.

Before Tasha could open her mouth again, the lady continued, "They are aware of the medical problems your children face and want the privilege of giving them the best care available. That is certainly good news, isn't it Edgar?" Then turning to face Tasha, she asked, "You said, your children? Who is this woman you brought with you, Edgar?"

"This is my wife, Tasha."

"You're wife? You said she died!"

"These people want to adopt my children?" Tasha turned to face Edgar, "Where are the others? You mean you separated them?"

To Edgar's defense, the lady-in-black, answered, "We had to. The other two were fighting when the couple came to pick them up. That's when I suggested they only take the three of them."

"How could you separate my children? Don't you realize the trauma they were going through when they saw me being wheeled off into an ambulance?"

"Lady, you have to understand."

"I don't have to understand anything, Lady. You're here to provide a service which you failed to do. Now where are the other two boys?" demanded Tasha.

"Well, that's just it, we don't know."

"How could you not know where they are, and then just say you don't know? Did you call the police?"

"We don't like to do that. It gives us a bad name. This has never happened to us before. None of our children have ever run away."

By now Edgar was stepping in. "I entrusted you with my children! You find them or we sue, do you hear?"

"Yes, sir, I'll contact the police as soon as you leave."

"You will contact them right now before we leave!"

"Okay. Here Ms. is the address of your three children. I will let them know you are coming for them. Here are the directions to their house."

"Edgar, let's go. I will find the other two."

"How can you do that, Tasha? You have no idea where they went but I think I know where they might be."

"Then where are they?"

Ignoring Tasha for a moment, Edgar continued, "Let's just go get Tim, Cam and Jenna first."

"Then you better show me where they are."

"You'll see."

Back in the cab, Tasha handed the directions to the cab driver. "Okay, that's easy enough. I've been at that end of town before." With that, they were off to pick up Jenna, Cameron and Timothy.

It was only a short distance to the better part of town and now they stood at the door frantically ringing the doorbell. A voice from behind the door, nervously spoke out, "Oh, we didn't expect you just yet—we just got a phone call saying you were coming for the children. Marie will be with you shortly." The man made his way to the back of the house.

"Who was that?"

"He might be the gardener but I've never been here before. The lady at the orphanage told me to leave so I didn't even get to say good-bye to the kids and I didn't even know she separated them."

"I can't believe you. Edgar. You let that woman do that to you? What do you suppose the kids think of you now?"

"Not good, I'm sure."

"You have a lot of living down to do, you know Edgar."

"I know. I just hope you can forgive me."

Once the kids saw Mother and Dad, there was no stopping them. "Mother, Dad, where have you been? We missed you so much!" Tim was beside himself, it was an emotional outburst for all of them. "I told Jenna and Cam that you guys were coming and it wouldn't be very long."

"It seemed forever," Cam sputtered.

"Mother," was all that Jenna could say.

Nettie stepped in saying, "We've enjoyed your children very much but I know you're all anxious to be together. We know you are facing health issues so would you allow us to help you financially? Here's our phone number, you know where we live. We would love to stay in touch."

"Thanks, Nettie. I know we need the help, but now is not a good time."

Within minutes they were back in the cab heading toward home. "Aren't we going to pick up James and Pete, Mother," asked Tim?

"Later," Dad said with a trembling voice.

"Pete, those guys are here again. I thought they would leave us alone since they saw Dad and Wilma."

"The doors are locked, right?"

"All of them are locked, but I'm scared, I just don't trust these guys."

"Look, James, they're leaving again. They're just playing games to see if we'll weaken."

"I told you Mother told us never to trust them, Pete."

"I know. I guess all we can do is to keep the doors locked. We've got to get some release from this fear we have. We can't just sit here and do nothing. We need to do something different. Maybe if we listen to our favorite programs. There has to be something on this Radio—somewhere on the dial."

"Oh, listen, *Calling All Cars.* It's about thieves."

"That's a re-run, because I remember they leave boot marks found at the scene of the robbery."

"James, isn't that how they identify them?"

"Yeah, and they kill the Marshal when they run after the robber."

"The Sheriff tries to finish the job."

"That's it, Pete. I remember, let's listen to it, okay?"

They listened for an hour. "I'm scared and I feel like we're locked up, James. Can't we just open the back door a little? We could just sit on the porch. If we see them, we run in and lock it."

"Not a good idea, but let's do it anyhow, we need fresh air."

Edgar and Tasha sat in the cab while they drove on and soon came to their house with the white fence. Dad gave the cab driver the fare leaving the family to stand at the gate of their home. Then, at the door, it was Dad's turn to sputter, "The house is a mess."

"So, she wasn't the maid, after all."

Not another word was spoken about the situation, but would time heal the heart—who would know the answer anyway?

Edgar pushed the door open, "That's weird, Tasha, the door isn't even locked any more, and I locked it when we left to go to the orphanage."

"Listen, Edgar. Do you hear that?" Turning to face Tim, he said, "Keep the kids out of the house until we tell you it's safe in here."

Turning to Cam and Jenna, "You heard Mother, let's stand at the gate where we can see everything and run if we have to."

Standing at the open gate, "I'm scared, Tim, what's wrong?"

"I don't know, Cam."

"Is there a fire?" I asked.

"I don't think so, Jenna. If there was, we'd smell smoke."

Cam couldn't help himself, "There's a robber in our house and they could have guns."

"Don't say that, Cam. We don't know what's going on yet."

———————————

Edgar and Tasha quickly entered the house, finding two men trying to tie up James. Pete was already tied to a chair as he struggled to free himself. "What do you think you're doing to my kids? Those are our kids you're tying up. Get out of here now! I'm calling the cops," as Edgar reached over to the phone on the wall.

"We don't want any trouble. These kids ran away from the orphanage and we were hired to bring them back. They fought us off, so we were tying them up to take them back with us."

"Get out of my house, now!"

The men left in a hurry, passing the others at the gate. Tim, Cam and Jenna came running in, "What happened, what happened?"

"Your two brothers ran away from the orphanage. I didn't really know for sure they were in the house but I heard noises. Today I found this wrapper on the sofa," Edgar reached into his pocket, "I knew Pete had to be here somewhere." He pulled out the wrapper of a Neilson chocolate bar. "I knew, who else but Pete, the Neilson chocolate lover. You are some brave kids. Did you know those two men were after you? How did they get into the house?"

"We got in with the key you had hidden. Today we had *cabin fever* so we went outside for a minute to play and when we came in to listen to a radio program I forgot to re-lock the door. They surprised us and snuck in while our ears were *glued to the radio*. The man with the beard grabbed us, tied me up, and while one guy was tying up James, the other went to check the front door and unlocked it. Probably because I told them that you, Dad, were on your way home. We said we were living with you and you were due home any minute.

"Those are the same men at the school grounds I always tell you to stay away from."

"Tasha, those are truant officers for the school. That's why you see them there. They're actually there to keep the kids safe and to stop kids from skipping school. Most schools don't do that yet, but Kits does."

"You think the lady-in-black hired Truant officers? She hired two crooks, Edgar."

Edgar, felt he had to change the subject and focus on his wife, "Tasha, I still want to know who that man was visiting you in the hospital—the nurse told me about him!" Edgar was readying himself to get into a fit of anger.

"The only man I saw was an Angel from God. He said I needed to live because I have five kids and a husband that need me." Tasha thought to herself, I can never tell him.

Edgar wasn't about to quit stewing over *the other guy*! An Angel sent from God—he would eventually get to the bottom of it, somehow. There was no such thing as an Angel. How dare Tasha think he shouldn't have been with Wilma!

Chapter 13

Driving Snow and Dusty Winds

Fall arrived with the furry of winter just around the corner soon here to stay as the dusting of snow settled sparsely on the ground. It had only been a few weeks since our reunion as a family but winter had finally locked its clutches on Winnipeg. It was cold and the lake had already frozen over. This year the cold would be on us before winter would be official but that was only a date on the calendar anyway. Liking it or not, it was here to stay for the next five months. Except for skating on the frozen lake, kids would be house bound in the early evening while winter tightened its jaws on everything.

"The News just forecasted another *Whiteout*, Tim. I hope your Dad gets home before it happens."

"Mother, didn't he say he was working a double shift?"

"He is and isn't due home until morning. I packed him extra food so he would be okay but sometimes when the weather is bad they quit early. That's when I worry he won't make it home before the bad weather."

"I thought it wasn't that far from home where he works."

"It isn't but he sometimes doesn't come straight home."

"Would he stop at the pub when it's dangerous?"

"I pray he won't."

For an awkward moment, everything was quiet. Then I looked over and saw Cam busy on the glass drawing.

"Look, I just drew a picture in the ice on our window."

"You did that Cam? I bet I can do that too. Let me try."

"Cam and Jenna, stop that! It's too cold to stand at the windows. Your hands will freeze. Leave the windows alone and whatever you do don't put your tongue on that ice! It will freeze to the window—Cam you didn't! Don't move. I'll have to pour water on your tongue until it loosens."

Cam's tongue loosened and he was sore for days, but okay. "I'll bet you'll never do that again!"

"I guess you're right, Jenna."

"Come into the kitchen where it's warmer. There isn't enough coal in all of the Prairies to get the furnace hot enough for the ice not to form on the inside of the windows," Mother continued, "I'll make lunch for everyone and then we'll head over to the stores."

"But Mother, you just said there was a *Whiteout* warning."

"Oh Tim, that's not until this evening, we should be okay for a couple of hours yet."

"Are we Christmas shopping, Mother?"

"I just need to get a few pieces of clothing for your brothers. They've already outgrown their jeans."

Even if we weren't going Christmas shopping, it would be fun. As we walked the blocks to where all the stores were lined up in a row, we could pick and choose which ones we would go into. We could hear the carols as they rang out from each department store we passed. "I love looking in the windows, Mother. Cam, look at the trains going around the Miniature Mountains and the Christmas trees decorated with all the bright lights in the store window."

"Mother, can I have a train for Christmas, please?"

"We'll just have to wait and see what Christmas brings."

"Maybe you don't have to worry about that, Mother. Couldn't Santa bring that?"

Cam sneered, "Jenna, do you honestly believe there is a Santa?"

"Well, no. I was just hoping there was. Dad can't afford the train and the dolls I'd like to have. So, believing in a Santa, could that help?"

"Get a grip, Jenna. Santa just isn't real."

I turned to Mother trying to ignore Cam, "I love this, Mother, that guy playing the violin. Isn't he good? Can we stop and listen?"

"Those are Hobos. They're homeless and begging for money."

"Don't say it like that, Cam. I like watching them—look, the monkey is dancing while that man turns the handle on the box."

I said, "Minstrels are everywhere. Those people need money too, don't they?"

Mother answered, "Being homeless can't be any fun, Cam and Jenna. I'm sure they need money. That's why there are places to go to like the Salvation Army."

Christmas was coming alright, whether we were ready or not. Ladies and men dressed in blue suits with the *big S* on their collars wearing their hats proudly, standing at every entrance to all the major department stores. They rang the Christmas bells next to a pot hoping it would soon be full of money. Mother turned to us and said, "Here, Cam and Jenna, put those coins in the pot." We gladly did it. "They've helped us when we needed it."

"What did they do for us, Mother?"

"They gave us clothing for all of you boys and a couple of dresses for you, Jenna. You kids are still wearing some of them."

Trees for sale everywhere, some would be silver tipped trees and others just green. There was always that ugly tree that made you wonder, who on earth would buy such a tree? Some people would wait until Christmas Eve and grab the unsold trees as the gates were left open with a sign, "Free Trees for all."

Soon we were home again, out of the wind and into the warm house being heated by coal and wood. "Boys, help me stoke up the stove so that we can get warm."

There it was our tree, green as ever, preserved by the winter weather. Mother would decorate it and soon put each of us to work in making decorations. It was a messy bit of fun but we were enjoying ourselves, always an early Christmas treat.

With the war in action, decorations were scarce, so Mother became innovative. "Here kids, let's make colored chains to put around the tree. Tim and James, you two can cut the strips—Cam and Jenna can glue the chains together like this," Mother seemed to be as excited as we were. "Pete, you can pop the popcorn and then we'll put a thread through and make a long chain that way. After we get it all done, let's have some hot cocoa."

"We are going to have Cocoa?" Cam was eager.

We ate the left-over popcorn and enjoyed our cocoa. "It tastes good, doesn't it?" After all that we had been through, we loved being together as a family again.

"I'm making eggnog, anyone want some?"

"Yeah, are you going to make that pudding cake, too?" asked Cam.

"If you want me to, *Christmas Plum Pudding*, is what it's called."

"We do," Pete answered.   "That must be Dad I hear, coming up the stairs, he is home early." Pete ran to the door, "Dad, we're glad your home."

"Why, what's wrong?" He was almost afraid to ask.

"Oh, we were worried about the forecasted *Whiteout* tonight."

"I didn't know that, now I'm glad I came straight home because I have so much work to do in the basement."

Dad was also busy getting ready for Christmas. Every night he would come home and right after dinner disappeared to the basement working on his secret Christmas projects we all knew about.

I asked, "What is Dad doing in the basement, Mother?"

"He's making something for the house for Christmas so he doesn't want any of us to see it until he's done."

Then it finally came, it was now Christmas morning. None of us really believed Santa would come since toys for us were very scarce. Dad brought up his special project, "Here kids, I hope you enjoy my hard work."

"Dad, the cars—the wheels even go around. Thank you," Pete and Cam jumped for joy. There were toys enough for all of us to play with. Here's a wooden doll for you, Jenna. Look, its arms move."

We were engrossed with our playing when suddenly we were startled by the doorbell ranging. "Who could that be? No one said they were coming to visit us and besides, it's Christmas morning so everyone would be with their own family. Edgar, were you expecting anyone?"

"No, I wasn't but maybe it's one of the neighbors?"

"Mother, can I answer the door?"

"Jenna, let me get it." Mother opened the door, "Strange, no one is here," turning to look around, oh, my, there's a box—help me bring it in, James." The box lay propped up at the foot of the stairs, in the snow like it was anxiously ready to spring into the house.

"Santa came, didn't he Mother?" I asked.

"Get a grip, Jenna, there is no such thing as Santa," Cam scoffed.

"Then where did the box come from?"

James and Dad pulled the box into the living room through the open door. "Close the door before it gets too cold in here. Hey, here's a note, I wonder what it says?" Dad asked.

"Let me have it, I'd like to read it," Tim said. "It says, 'Merry Christmas. Enjoy the few things we were able to give you. We are praying for you and the offer still stands.' What does that mean? Here's a phone number on the note. That's the people we stayed with, right?"

"They want us," Cam said in a complaining voice.

Mother took the note from Tim, "No, no. That's an offer to pay for Tim's medical expenses." Then she turned her face to the ceiling as if looking straight up to God, "Thank you, dear Jesus."

Dad immediately broke that bit of hopefulness over the news Mother was enjoying, "We don't need their help but we'll talk about that later. Let's see what we have here, if anything is any good." Almost sounding like Dad could be jealous of good will but he still allowed us to open the box as the toys began falling everywhere on the living room floor. It was one of our best Christmases.

———————

Time didn't stand still for any of us and soon spring was in the air after the thawing of the snow. Now we had to face the coming dust bowl with the hot, humid weather that would faithfully follow. It did every year and this would be no exception.

"Tim, what's bothering you?" I asked.

"My knee is sore and my leg is so swollen, I can hardly put my pants on anymore, Jenna."

"Does mother know that it hurts you that much?"

"She does and I think we are going to the doctor today."

"You will be alright because the doctor will know what to do, Tim."

"I hope so."

"I'm really sure, Tim."

―――――――――――――

Soon after that, Tim was admitted to the hospital.

While Edgar was away helping, Tim gather the few belongs he might need during his stay in the hospital, Mother pulled out the scrap piece of paper she held so dearly in her purse, she kept it with her other card that Alexis had given her, making sure she would always have them. Nervously, she called the number on the paper knowing if she was to call, she'd need to do it while Edgar was busy. Finally, the phone rang and then someone answered, "Hello Marie is it possible for me to speak with Nettie, please? Thank you." There was a short pause, "Hello, Nettie, I just wanted to let you know we are taking Tim to the hospital today. Since you are interested and asked that I let you know how things are going, I thought I would call you. I'm not calling because we need the money but Tim is going to be admitted in the hospital today so if you did want to visit him, he will be in Town General." Tasha hesitated just for a moment and then continued, "Thank you so much Nettie, I know he'll be excited about your visits. He always reminds me of the good times he, Cam and Jenna had with you and Bob. I couldn't be more pleased with your care for them. Thank you again, and I must go, Edgar is coming. I can't let him know I called. Bye for now."

A moment later, Edgar was downstairs again, eager to leave for the hospital, "I think we have everything we need. Should we call a cab or take a bus, Tasha?"

"That's a wonderful idea, Edgar."

Tim knew this was expensive for them, "Please don't do it on my account. The bus is just fine for me."

"Are you sure you would be okay with that?"

"I am Mother, save the money."

After the tedious bus ride, Edgar, Tasha and Tim arrived at the hospital, now standing at the admittance counter knowing they were to pay upfront before the doctors would help their son. Edgar nervously spoke, "I have some of the money, Tasha. I hope they will accept what we have and maybe we can pay a little at a time."

Tasha gave a sigh, "I've been praying they will."

Tim stood next to them in silence but Tasha could see the pain in his eyes. Pain killers were not enough anymore for what he was experiencing.

"Can I help you?" The lady at the desk, asked.

"We're scheduled to bring our son in today."

"Give me his name, please."

"Timothy Nedder."

"Okay, I have the information right here. It looks as if everything is set up for him. The nurse will be right out to get him."

"What about the payments," inquired Edgar?

"That was all taken care of, don't worry about a thing."

"Is this something the doctor is doing for us," Edgar asked?

"I'm not sure of who or why, but just that it's all taken care of."

They moved back to sit in the lobby to wait when Tasha could no longer stop her emotions, "Thank you, Jesus! Edgar, just thank God."

"None of this makes any sense because no one does anything for us."

"God always does things for us."

Sarcastically, Edgar said, "Whatever you say, Tasha, you know best, I'm sure."

Days became weeks and soon it was a month that had gone by. Everyday Mother made her way to the hospital to visit Tim while Dad was at work. One day, I asked Mother, "When will Tim come home?"

Cam interrupted, "Tim isn't coming home is he, Mother? He's going to die in the hospital. Everybody that goes to the hospital dies there."

"No, not this time," Mother answered. "Our prayers have been answered and the doctors are hoping for this surgery to be the cure. Tim has been in rehabilitation but the Doctor said he should be coming home on Saturday."

The house was in disarray for a few days as Tasha, James and Pete made preparations to ready a room on the main floor so that Tim wouldn't have to climb the stairs unless he wanted to. Mother finally said, "There, it should all be ready for Tim."

"Won't Tim ever be able to come up the stairs to play with us in our rooms?" asked Pete.

"I'm sure he will, but I want him to slowly get used to doing what he can."

I could hardly stand it, "I'm so glad Tim's coming home. I just need to have him around."

"We all do, Jenna. Tomorrow's the day when Dad and I go to bring him home."

"Okay, guys I need you to behave while we go for Tim. We won't be long, so keep out of trouble and I mean, I don't want a messed-up house when we get back with Tim."

It wasn't long this time, when Mother and Dad brought Tim home from the hospital and I understood, seeing him use his crutches, since now he had only one leg. He said he had no more pain though he couldn't run like James, Pete and Cam but I couldn't run anyhow, so we hung out together a lot.

He liked watching his brothers' skate down the hill, seeing the dust fly. James and Pete would roller skate down the hill while Cam would roll his wagon down, but it was always something they did, never us.

––––––––––––––––

It was a hot dusty summer day like always but the only thing Edgar wanted after a ten-hour shift of hard work was that one glass of beer and Wilma wasn't totally out of the picture either. In his heart, he'd accepted that the man at the hospital who came to visit Tasha, was an Angel sent from God but in his mind, it was more like, how dare a man visit my wife and who was that guy for real? That meant he was justified in seeing Wilma now and again.

"I thought I told you never to show your face here again, Edgar."

"Stop arguing with me, Wilma. I'm tired and I need a break—I work hard, you know that."

"I suppose you think I don't, Edgar?"

Edgar could tell by the glow in Wilma's face that she enjoyed just being with him. She nudged her way closer as she spoke in a whisper, "So what are you up to now? What secrets are you going to keep from me this time?"

"You know all there is to know, I just need a break from life."

"What, you want me to give you a break after all the lies you fed me?"

Chapter 14

Boxes & More Boxes

Tasha couldn't help herself from remembering all that had happened to her in the past. Now she was about to face an uncertain future for her and the kids. Would Edgar agree to follow her decision to travel to the west coast and live where Uncle Abram resided? Her heart was aching. She knew she had to follow that decision not only for her children but now it was about herself as well. The Doctor's confirmation had set her into motion since Edgar's past actions were less than acceptable. She was about to become a woman of action knowing once her mind was made up there would be no stopping her. Then why not, Alexis was moving there too. She had to see him, her only living relative. She remembered her scripture as her Bible fell open to the marker, *"For I know the plans I have for you, declares the LORD, plans to prosper you and not to harm you, plans to give you hope and a future,"* Jeremiah 29:11. Thinking to herself, 'I really love what I feel God is telling me to do. This time I will follow Him.'

Then out of nowhere, Pete walked in on her, "Mother, what are you doing?"

"I didn't know you were there. Where are the others?"

"They're outside playing with their roller skates. I was thirsty, so I came in for water, but what are you doing?"

"I'm reading the Bible and I'm asking God so I would know if we should move to the west coast. It's Tim's last wish and I want him to have that. Then, Jenna needs the mild climate to survive. Most of all, it would be thrilling for all of us."

"Oh, really? I'm going to tell the others." Pete was about to run out.

"Stop, Pete, not so fast. I need your help and I don't want you to talk just yet, but I have some questions for you. When I was in the hospital, the nurse said a relative called for me to see how I was. Do you know anything about that?"

"That was me, I disguised my voice so they wouldn't ask me if I was a kid."

"Didn't you know I would be coming home? I told Tim to take care of you guys until I got home."

"Tim wanted to but Dad told James and Cam that you wouldn't come home anymore. I didn't know that at first but when everything seemed hopeless, I convinced James to run away from the orphanage with me."

"Was that when you found out you were being separated?"

"It was. We just felt in our hearts that you were still alive so we called every hospital we could to find you."

"So, when you knew I was coming home, you just stayed in hiding?"

"We did, trying to be as quiet as we could. We even prayed you wouldn't leave us like Dad did. If you would've abandoned us like Dad we knew our goose was cooked forever."

"I'm not like that, Pete. I would never do that and I'd find a way to keep us together."

"Let me ask you, when we came home and found you and James tied up, Dad said that he thought you guys were there because of the candy wrapper he found but didn't pursue it since he was coming for me. When I called, how come you didn't answer the phone instead of Wilma? Did you know about Wilma?"

"Yeah, we did. We couldn't pick up the phone because they didn't know we were there, in the house, or so we thought." It was quiet for a moment, "Dad had to have picked Wilma up at the pub because she was drunk when he first brought her home. Mother, Dad wasn't drunk, just Wilma. We were waiting outside, hoping we could sneak in when Dad came home."

"So, she was his girlfriend?"

"They were going to go apartment hunting and go shopping to get an engagement ring for her when you called. We were upstairs trying to figure out what to do when we heard the phone ring. Another thing about Dad, he wouldn't take Wilma into your bedroom but instead he brought her to ours. When we realized that they were coming up to our room, we quickly slid under the beds. I almost gave it all away when I was about to sneeze. That's when Dad spotted the cat in the room. They didn't sleep together the first night, Mother, if that helps." Pete caught the look on his mother's face. He quickly started talking about their capture. "We knew the orphanage was trying to find us and with all the wrong steps we made in hiding we realized there were two men coming after us. We couldn't do anything but wait inside the house. It still makes me mad to know that I forgot to lock that back door. We just had to go out for air and play. It's hard to be hiding all the time."

"It is okay, Pete, I would've done the same thing. Don't blame yourself and besides, we got there on time."

"Are we moving to the west coast with Grandpa? Will Dad be coming with us? Are you mad at Dad? Are you going to leave him?"

"Whoa, Pete, not so fast, I didn't say any of that. I just decided that we are going to move to where our uncle..." Tasha hesitated, she knew Uncle Abram had to be the kid's Grandpa, she could never admit anything different. "... Grandpa is. I plan to tell Dad. He will have a choice to make. It would be a good idea if you just let Dad do that. He can decide if he wants to stay with us or go after Wilma. I want to give Tim his desire and I want to know what Dad wants. He can stay or come."

"I'm sorry, Mom. He's absolutely awful but isn't he our Dad?"

"He is and I want him to make his own decision. You understand I can't make it for him."

"Where will we live when we get there?"

"Your Grandpa will let us stay with him. If Dad decides to come, we can rent a flat in Grandpa's building. We'll be okay, no matter how it goes."

"I guess now I don't feel like telling any of this to the others. They'll have to figure it out on their own."

"I'm sure they will.

Pete was about to run and play with his brothers when he turned to face his Mother again, "Mother, will you leave Dad?"

"It won't be me leaving him, rather it'll have to be him staying behind because he doesn't want the responsibilities he's had up to now. I can't help him with that, he'll have to decide."

Pete slowly walked into the backyard, his thoughts still totally engrossed on what Mother said.

"What's wrong, Pete?"

"I don't know, almost feel sick, Tim."

"I can tell, Pete." Tim could easily read Pete's mind. He was just so predictable. There were no secrets with him. "I bet you told Mother what you and James told us about Dad."

"She knows, Tim, but I'll be okay."

A few uneventful days went by but Tasha knew she had to face Edgar with her plan. Tasha had a hearty breakfast ready for Edgar when he arrived home from graveyard shift. Tasha decided it had to be now, to ask him, "Hi, Honey. Are you ready for your bacon and eggs?"

"I'm famished. It was a very busy night but I'm glad to be home."

"It's early, the kids aren't up yet and I have a question for you. You know how Tim wants to go to the west coast so badly? Well, you know the doctor says he hasn't any more than a year left at the most, possibly only six months. Well, I wrote Abram about coming and he says we can rent a flat in his building or stay with him."

"Tasha, how will I ever get a transfer at such short notice?"

"Edgar, I've done a lot of praying and I have to do it. We can go on ahead and when it works out for you, join us later. If you really don't want to, I'll understand. It is a decision you have to make but either way, I'll understand. I have to know you want to come, not that you have to."

"You haven't forgiven me."

"I've forgiven you, but I don't need to be a rocket scientist to know you see Wilma sometimes, so I need to know that you want your family."

Edgar's countenance changed instantly. He thought that was his secret but Tasha knew, she could tell. He desperately wanted to storm out in anger and deny all of it. That wasn't going to work this time, he knew Tasha had decided, there was no turning back. He also knew that he really loved her. This time he had to stand and take it. He had to make that decision. He didn't yet know if he was willing, though.

Tasha continued, "You'll have the chance to prove what you wish. Eat your breakfast, get some sleep and then we have the evening if you want to talk. I'll take the kids out to the park during the daytime when they get up so that it's quiet in the house. We won't bother you."

Edgar had to blurt out, "How can you accuse me of seeing Wilma?"

"Don't argue with me, get your sleep. We'll talk when you're ready, about the move."

Edgar knew from experience, what Tasha had decided would happen, so that meant she and the kids were moving. She was determined and this time she would leave him. Was this what he wanted? Did he want his freedom to join up with Wilma? He was sure that Tasha couldn't know that he saw Wilma at the pub on the way home from time to time, but how in the world did she guess? This life changing event would be a tough decision for him to make. He had enjoyed that time of 'freedom' while Tasha was in the hospital. He had a taste of freedom from responsibilities, so he thought. The next hours of sleep were not too kind to him as he tossed and turned restlessly, finding no peace.

Edgar heard Tasha and the kids return from the park, "Would you please tell the kids not to make any noise? I'm trying to sleep."

"Okay kids, please go outside and play while I make dinner. It's already 4 o'clock so it'll just be an hour."

Soon, Edgar was yelling again, "Stop making noises with those pots and pans!"

"I'm making dinner, the kids are outside and you just need to get it together. Get down here and talk or quit the yelling!"

For the next half hour, all was quiet. Finally, Edgar appeared in the kitchen. "How can you ask me to move with you and the kids to live with Abram? How am I supposed to make that change?"

"You know what I want and you know why I want this but if you don't I'll spell it out. Is that what you want me to do?"

"It's so Tim can have his last wish! What about me and my job? Where do I come in?"

"This time it's about whether you want your family. Like I said already, you make the decision to keep your family or you have your freedom to do as you please. Make that decision."

"What makes you think I'm still seeing Wilma, why do you keep saying that?"

"I'm a little smarter than you make out. You think I'm just here to satisfy you, have your children and when that isn't enough you find someone else." Tasha looked at him with determined eyes, "Dinner's made, and I'd appreciate it if you'd shut-up, be decent to the kids and me so the children don't dislike you even more. Is that agreed on? Remember, you don't have to come with us, it's your choice."

The kids were soon around the dinner table, chatting away about their afternoon and the stuff they did in the backyard. They, at least, were enjoying their evening meal together as a family not really aware of the disconcertedness of their parents. Except for Pete and possibly Tim, who knew their Dad had a decision to make.

"So, are we still going to move to west coast, Mother?" asked Pete.

Tim lit up like a Christmas tree. "I'm so excited about being able to go. Maybe the fresh air will be good for me? I know it will be for Jenna, the Lord only knows, she needs it."

Pete, as always in character, questioned, "Are you coming with us, Dad?"

"I'll ask my shop foreman and see if he can get me a transfer. They're always looking for people to work on the west coast. I talked to him about it a few weeks ago but didn't know if we should do it. Tomorrow I'm on the day shift so maybe I can find out after work."

Mother looked at him in disgust, "You could've told me you were with me in this move. I guess you made your final decision to come with us?"

By now boxes were everywhere because we had been packing for a couple of weeks. I hated the smell of the cardboard with musty dust flying everywhere. It always made me sneeze, not to say anything of all the papers all over the floor to wrap the china in. Mother was always such a neat person. How could she have such a big mess in the middle of the living room floor? Then, there was a knock at the door.

"Oh, come in Aunt Emily. What brings you here?"

"Aunt Emily," I gave her a big hug, "I haven't seen you in a long time." It felt so good to see her again. "I have a question for you."

"What is it, Jenna?"

"We call you Aunt Emily, but are you Dad's sister or Mother's? James says in order for you to be our Aunt you have to be one of our parent's sister."

Mother interrupted, "Jenna, you shouldn't be asking those kinds of questions. We call Aunt Emily Aunt because we love her. But if you have to know, she is Dad's half-sister."

Then Aunt Emily looked at Mother and asked, "Tasha, I can never get over how much Jenna looks like Josie. She looks exactly like Josie, your eldest daughter. Is that why you named her Jenna?"

"I didn't plan on it. I always felt that God replaced Josie with Jenna."

I just thought to myself, Tim was right, I'm just a replacement. Then I heard some more.

"Josie was too good for this earth so I only could have Josie for her first thirteen years of her life but God replaced her right away and gave me Jenna. We decided we needed to hide her because we didn't want that to happen again."

"How can you do that?"

"We didn't actually give her a name."

"Don't tell me, Tasha, you think the spirits are after your children? You're a God-fearing woman, how can you think that?"

That's all I needed to hear. So, I was supposed to be perfect. There isn't any way I can do that and now I had no name, at least officially.

"Only my girls, you knew both my miscarriages were girls? I didn't get to keep any of my daughters and I want to keep Jenna. We figured the spirit world couldn't call her if her name was never recorded."

"My dear Tasha, how can you be so deceived? God is greater than any so-called spirit—can't you trust Him to protect Jenna?"

"How could you understand my heartache? You have all your children."

That was all I could take and I wasn't about to listen to any more excuses about who I was supposed to be. Now I didn't even have a real name, nothing made sense anymore. I wanted to believe Tim and that he thought I was just like any other kid on the block. Now it sounded to me like Aunt Emily was the only one that made any sense. I wanted to believe that God was God. I wanted the faith of Aunt Emily but how could that ever happen? I didn't even know who God was.

My parents made it very plain that they didn't approve of lying, stealing or killing. They said the Bible had Ten Commandments that everyone must follow. Kind of like they were teaching us to be good, they just forgot to talk about God in our home. Oh, sure, sometimes Mother would read her Bible but then she said stuff like this. How can that make any sense?

Aunt Emily and Mother were still talking over tea. I busied myself with toys in between the empty boxes, trying to listen for what else I didn't know.

Then Mother went on to say, "It's going to be cold here soon and I want to get away from all of this."

"Fall is approaching quickly and soon the snow will fly again."

Mother was right about the cold weather. The hot weather had been bad enough but the cold was even worse. The leaves had already started falling from the trees all in shades of yellow, brown and red. It looked good and I'd always watch everyone grab them for fall decorations. It was a pretty sight, but after the hay and wheat season, I'd breathe a little easier until the mold on the leaves caused another problem. It went from one bad season to another. Not even the paper boxes were any good for me.

Trunks from the basement were now in our living room and there was Mother, packing everything we owned. I didn't even know we had so much stuff.

Before Aunt Emily could say, "Tasha you're moving again? For me, I couldn't move away, even if it's really bad here. I have never known anything but the Prairies, where else could you move to?"

"This time we're moving to the west coast where the kid's grandfather lives, so I have to get everything packed."

"You're moving where? What happened?"

Then I couldn't help myself, "Did Dad get his transfer, Mother?"

Mother turned facing both of us, "I don't know yet. We prayed to see what would happen at his work, but either way, I have to take all of the children with me."

If Dad wasn't coming, I knew it had to be because of what Pete told the rest of us kids about Dad's girlfriend. It must mean that Mother wasn't going to stay with Dad anymore. I knew it was too good to be true for anyone's love to be betrayed and then still want to stay married. Yet, I didn't know very many kids whose parents were divorced. Almost, like people didn't talk about the *bad stuff* parents did to each other, they just stayed together.

"Where will you be staying? I heard there is a severe housing shortage on the west coast," questioned Aunt Emily.

"Since the kid's Grandpa, lives there, we might be able to find a flat we can rent in the same building, he seems to think so. For now, I want to take Tim there because the doctor says it will be best for him and Jenna. It's Tim's last wishes and I want to give it to him."

"Mother, why are you saying, it's Tim's last wish?"

"The doctor says he isn't well. He doesn't' have much time."

"I didn't know that."

Aunt Emily stood up to leave, "Tasha, I wish I could go with you and help you, especially if Edgar doesn't go. You need to let me know if I can help in anyway. For now, I have to be going so I can get dinner together for my family. Remember, Tasha, if there is anything I can do, let me know."

"I will." Aunt Emily left while Mother continued to pack.

My mind was back remembering Tim going to the hospital because of his knee. It was so swollen and big that he couldn't get his pants over his knee anymore. Then he came home on crutches and one leg. It was all my mind could absorb and I didn't want to hear that he wasn't well again.

The last few days Dad had been coming home almost an hour later but excused it for a beer at the bar after a hard day at work. It surprised all of us when Dad walked in almost unnoticed because we weren't expecting him just yet. "You're home early, Dad. How come you are home so early?"

"Yeah, Jenna, I am. I have good news for Mother."

"What?"

"Let me tell your Mother first."

"Mother, Dad is home and he says he has good news for you."

"Oh, honey, you're home early."

"Have we gotten everything packed by now? What—it's been a couple of weeks since we started? The good news, I was able to get a transfer. We have only a week to get settled there and then I have to be back at work with the same company on the west coast."

"Good, I'm glad you've decided to ask for the transfer and that you're coming with us. Yes, to your question, I've already packed everything. Now we just have to get the stuff to the train station and whatever else we can't take with us we'll give to the Salvation Army. They've always been good to us. Maybe you can phone them to pick up the *other stuff*?"

"Good, I'll do that right now and get our things moved so that we can be ready to go. I got the tickets on the way home, so we are all set."

"What time does the train leave?"

"We were scheduled to leave in two days but if we want, we can leave on the 11 pm train, we just have to get there. There were a lot of available seats and sleepers, so if we can make it, we don't have to pay the higher fare. Do you think we have enough time?"

"We are ready right now so that should work for us. It's only four now, so you could contact the Salvation Army to have them come for the stuff we can't take and come back, I'll have dinner waiting."

––––––––––––––––––

Edgar wasn't done with his *old life*. He decided it couldn't hurt, to drop in to say goodbye to Wilma, it shouldn't take but a minute and he had a few hours to waste. Edgar knew very well, this was not the thing to do but, oh well, just one more time. Tasha would never know because he knew he could hide it.

"Wilma, glad to see you, well, this is it."

"What do you want from me? I'm never going to see you again."

"Who knows, I just may be back."

"I don't think so, Edgar. You haven't the guts to leave your wife and family. You'll just always find someone else to fool around with.

"We'll see about that."

"Come with me, you have a few minutes?"

"Not much time."

I have to go Wilma, our train leaves at 11 pm and I have to get the stuff to the train. Look I'll see you again."

"I bet we will. I have to go as well, so enjoy your stay in on the west coast."

They parted for the last time and as he arrived home again, Tasha had to say,   "And tell me, Edgar, what delayed you?"

Edgar didn't answer, he just joined the family for dinner and as the children chatted, the Salvation Army Van drove up. "Why don't you take care of the stuff for the Salvation Army while we clean up and pack the last of everything we need?"

Everything we had packed was already at the train station, awaiting the arrival of the train. Dad called for a taxi and packed it full of the remainder of belongings. We were off now, on our journey.

Mother was getting caught up in the excitement of leaving, "The train leaves in an hour, we need to get going."

If only the memories of the past could stay in the past and where they happened, then we wouldn't have to take them with us. We still had both our parents together, Dad wasn't about to be left behind. They had chosen their fate to stay a family and ignore their differences, at least I was hoping.

Finally, we were off to the train station and there it was, that all familiar Pacific Railway that would take us the entire journey. We finally boarded and soon Mother began making home out of the train. It would take a few days to reach our destination, but we settled in. Pete and James were looking around getting acquainted with their new surroundings while Cam and I stayed with Tim. Mother and Dad busied themselves sorting what we would use on the trip.

"Dad, we know where the bathrooms are and the café car. Are we going to eat there in the café?"

"We probably can't afford to eat in the café car but Mother brought a lot of food to get us through the couple of days of this trip. We should be okay and our food will be a lot better than what they have to offer on this train. At least you'll get full on what we have."

Tim joined in, "Good. You know we're always hungry."

"Yeah, I know, it's because you guys are growing, that makes you hungry all the time." Dad continued to say, I will never forget any of you. Please know that."

I knew what Dad was talking about. He was saying he would never leave us again but would my brothers believe him? I was trusting and I knew he meant it in his heart, at least. I hoped he did because there was no way under the sun I wanted to live in another foster home or orphanage. For me, I would do the same as Pete and James did the last time but I'd run away to Grandpa, he'd never turn me away. Grandpa was the one man that could be trusted all of the time and I was sure God just had to be like that too, even if no one would show us the way.

Somehow, I just knew Mother might not be well, but I prayed as best I could.

Chapter 15

Train Tragedy

"All aboard! All aboard!" The conductor repeated that until he seemed to figure everyone had boarded the train.

We sat looking out the windows in the twilight of night as the train finally pulled away from the station. That's when the conductor started his rounds to collect the tickets.

"Why does it seem so confusing to me, Dad? Some people move around before the Conductor sees their tickets."

Dad started to fill us in, "Only a few do that anymore, Cam. In the past, it was quite common for people to sneak on the trains without paying their fair."

James asked, "Wouldn't they get caught doing that?"

"You're right, the conductor will reach us soon to collect the tickets and if we don't have one, he'll make us get off at the next station."

Then Pete, thinking for a moment, "That means a person could sneak at least a *one-station-ride*."

Dad answered, "Exactly, station by station, people could get to where they wanted to go."

Cam asked, "Why didn't we do that and save the money?"

Dad chuckled, "First, we wouldn't because we aren't dishonest and even if we wanted to we have way too much stuff with us. You'd have to be willing to travel with just the clothes on your back. Would any of you want to do that?"

"I couldn't," Cam answered, "I want my cars."

"Yeah, Dad, talk about traveling light, eh? That couldn't work for us," was Pete's comment.

"Pete, you're right because we are actually moving to another place to live and until we get there, our whole life is on this train. Now for the Hobos, they usually jump on with the cattle in the container cars." Dad continued reminiscing, "Did you know that in the early days we didn't even have a train that crossed Canada, people would have to do the horse and buggy ride to cross the country."

Tim responded, "Then British Columbia insisted that having a railway to join the east to west was the only way they would consider joining the Confederation of Canada."

"I take it you learned that in school?"

"You know it, Dad, and I even know that it was Sir John A. Macdonald who promised a railway to link the eastern provinces within ten years."

"I think you are a smart brother!"

"I don't think so, James, you and Pete would've known that."

"Well, Tim, you said it for us."

We started enjoying the smooth ride as our train glided along the tracks. There was nothing for miles, just bare prairie and by now it was too dark to see anything. "Do you guys remember our cousins, Benny and Richard? Remember they used to jump on the train but they always rode in the passenger cars like us until they got caught."

"I remember that, Jenna. They said they would get miles away from home before they got caught just by moving through the train when the conductor would come to check tickets, just like Dad said."

"Like drifters or more like people with too much time and an anxious spirit."

"Maybe, Pete, no one cared what they did."

"Oh, I don't think our cousins had that excuse, Jenna, they just needed excitement in their lives. The rest of us are just plain chicken," Tim answered.

"Why don't we guess who the people are with no tickets?"

"Come on, Pete, how're we going to do that?"

"It's easy, Cam. Watch who the people are who move around every time the conductor comes near." Tim observed.

"Like the guys who roam the cars incessantly?"

"You got it James."

They counted while I watched. They probably were more right than wrong. "Where are the Hobos?"

"Like Dad said, those guys are the professionals, they don't hop on the passenger cars, they travel with the Cattle and sometimes you'll find people hiding in the baggage cars."

"Tim, couldn't they steal our stuff?"

"That's a little harder because that's where people keep their dogs. If the dogs make too much noise, the porters are going to investigate. The cattle cars wouldn't be checked so the Hobos get to go where they want. Yet, it's not like they have a place to go."

Then Dad said, "Since the war is on, a lot of Hobos have decided to join the Army in a chance to get an education after it's over. Now we see fewer Hobos roaming around."

Cam's curiosity was about to get the best of him, "Do robbers raid these trains anymore?"

"This train is primarily a passenger train. If we were carrying silk, a very expensive and rare commodity these days, then we would have guards everywhere. If word gets out that we would be carrying gold, for example, we could have a problem. As far as I know, we aren't carrying any of that on this trip."

Finally, Mother and Dad helped us make our beds for the night. Since the darkness was too intense and we couldn't see out the windows anymore, we bunked down. Being lulled to sleep by the sound of the trains wheels running across the tracks was the last thing I remembered until the sunrise woke me.

Two days had gone by now and we were counting everything next to the tracks, from poles to wild animals.

"Look, Tim. That's a bear."

"It is, Jenna, since this is fall and you can see the snow on the mountains, the animals want to feed. That means they have to come down to where it is still green. The bears need to eat a lot before they have to hibernate."

"They sleep the winter out, don't they?"

"They do, Cam. We are approaching the Alberta foothills now and then we go through the Rockies. I wish it would stay daylight longer so we could see more."

Dad was back in the conversation. "We'll get to see the beauty of the mountains everyday of our lives at the coast. It has to be one of the most awesome sights. You'll also get to see one of the most beautiful parks in the world, Stanley Park."

"Is it a park we can play in like the one we had?"

"Much larger than that, Jenna, it's a park in the middle of the city that stretches over one thousand acres. You'll see huge Douglas fir, Western Red cedar and Western Hemlock trees. They can be up to three hundred feet tall and over a hundred years old."

"I heard there is a tree that you can drive a car through in the park."

"You're absolutely right, Tim, people have their pictures taken there a lot."

"When can we go see it, Dad?"

"Just as soon as we get settled in to wherever it is we will be living, James."

"Is it possible to walk around the park, Dad?"

"I'm told that there is talk about putting a walkway all around it, a twelve-mile walk, how awesome that will be. But, yes, we can walk around it—just have to go through some obstacles at the moment."

As we started nearing the foothills the train's wheels began to squeal. It was finally nightfall again as the train jerked along the tracks into the mountains.

"Dad, is the train always so jerky?"

"When it goes through the mountains, it can't be as smooth as it was on the Prairies. Mountains are rugged and this is a long train that has to go around corners and through tunnels."

"I wish we could see where we are going."

"It's too dark Tim. There is nothing but darkness surrounding us now. Why don't we try to sleep for the night, kids?"

I was really tired, so I soon drifted off to sleep in spite of all the rocking along the tracks. In fact, I enjoyed being rocked to sleep but I couldn't remember how long I had slept when suddenly, Dad was running in all directions, yelling, "I need help! Someone please help me!"

Within seconds the porter came. "What happened? What's going on?"

"My wife is having a heart attack. She needs air…a fan, anything."

It seemed everyone was running down the aisles as best they could. I could see Mother's chest throbbing and I knew it had to be painful. Within minutes the emergency team was there with a tank pulled behind. Then I realized it was oxygen as the paramedics hooked the mask to her mouth. One of the men started talking, "We were just on our way to join a party going north at the next stop when we heard you needed help. Glad, we are here to help."

The porter replied, "We always have emergency equipment on board, but yeah, I'm glad that I didn't have to do this alone."

In minutes, they had Mother hooked up breathing from the oxygen tank. It wasn't long from then that Mother responded and was able to sit back and rest.

Mother started talking, "I'm so sorry."

"Keep your mask on for a little longer. Then you can talk and you don't have to be sorry for anything. We're just glad to be of help." After a pause for a moment, the paramedic checked Mother's heartbeat. "You're doing just fine. Just sit back and rest and everything will be alright, okay?"

"Thanks…I thought I would be alright. I don't know what happened there but I knew I needed air."

Dad answered, "Too much excitement, I'm sure. Stay with me Tasha, you know the kids and I need you." Dad meant that, I could hear the earnestness in his voice. There was no way he wanted to lose her now.

"I'll be just fine now."

I could see it again in Dad's eyes, he was terrified. This wasn't what he wanted. He knew that the future was grim for Tim who would eventually lose his life, according to the Doctor, but he didn't want Tasha to die. He had fought for her every inch of the way in spite of his own selfishness.

We just watched as Mother sat up in bed trying to rest. By now she was breathing without the mask over her mouth. It seemed she was recuperating rapidly once her heart settled down to a normal beat.

It was a very long night, but Mother was with us, so we tried resting again. All I could do was just watch and wait, praying that Mother would stay well. The praying part was confusing since no one could tell me what it meant—just that God would answer, like it was a promise that God always did.

Then we heard Dad pray, "Heal Tasha, please God. Make her well for her children's sake. Please God." Then it became silent again.

I heard the praying but in my heart, I knew that Dad wanted Mother well for us, like he prayed, not himself. He would do what he always did if he felt he had to for the sake of loneliness, should that be his lot again. He would never be able to submit himself to being alone with his children without Mother. He would make a way for himself while he'd find a place for us and probably an orphanage again only this time we'd be on the west coast. This was for certain.

Finally, Dad spoke to us, "Mother will be fine now. She just had too much excitement and she has never before been through these mountains. I don't think she realized it would be such a rough train ride with all the jerking the train does."

"Is this normal for the train to jerk so much, Dad?" asked Pete.

"It is. I've been on trains before. They can be very jerky."

James asked, "When were you on a train, Dad?"

"Way before I met your Mother. Actually, I went to Chicago to law school before I met your Mother and I took a train to go there. I actually went through Detroit, in the United States."

"Why aren't you a lawyer, then," Cam asked.

"It cost way too much even then, still I would've except for the Great Depression that hit us. Since I couldn't continue, I took over the running of a store that did okay until no one could pay their bills."

"I guess, if people can't pay for what they buy, you wouldn't have enough money to buy anything to sell," remarked Tim.

"You are exactly right. Then, when the banks started to fail because so many of their investments were in foreign deposits, the banks closed their doors and people lost their money."

"That's awful. Did you lose money that way, Dad?"

"I never had a lot to lose, but many people started hiding their cash in their mattresses. You know what can happen if you do that?"

James was engrossed in the conversation, "That's just stupid, what if your house burns down, or someone comes to rob you?"

"That happened a lot because on cold winter nights, people used stove ovens to heat their houses. Some people even would build an open fire in their house."

Tim couldn't resist, "Isn't that a little retarded, at the very least, dangerous?"

"You want to believe it was, Tim, people like that lost everything, even their lives."

"That must've been really awful, Dad."

"It was James. Anyhow, when I met your Mother, I think I already told you this part, all I had was in my pocket was enough for the marriage license, so I had to find a job that would at least pay something. I learned how to be a machinist. That's done well enough for us. You guys need food to eat and clothing to wear, so that's what I do."

"You never told us before, that's the reason you worked there. Do you like the work?" asked Cam.

"I do, but I'd rather build houses. Years ago, I worked construction. That was the most fun. Maybe, going west is a good thing and after we get settled, our dream is to find land so we can build our own dream house."

"That'd be fun Dad. If you ever do that, can I help?" begged Pete.

"You sure can. I'd love to have a son do what I like doing the most. All of you guys could help, even you, Tim. We'll make a way for all of us to build that dream house."

That was the first-time Dad had the time to stop and talk with us. We soon forgot that Mother had a heart attack but instead we were getting excited for what the future might hold. We could hardly wait for the train to arrive at our destination.

Mother was still asleep in her bed while Dad sat with us.

"Dad, I have a question." Then Cam came up with yet another question.

"What, Cam? What do you want to know?"

"Would you leave us again if something happened to Mother, would you go back to that lady?"

"That's not going to happen, we're all together now. We'll be fine."

Cameron seemed to be fine for now with that answer. I wasn't sure Dad even tried to answer it…more like he dismissed Cam's question. As long as he's okay, I'll be okay.

Sunrise was beginning to brighten the sky. "Just look at the sun coming up from the east. Don't you love that Tim?"

"Jenna, it's so beautiful. I've never seen anything like it. We are so lucky it looks so cheerful today."

By now we were all awake, hovering around Mother. "Mother, look out the window."

"That's the city. We must be nearing where we're going."

Tim was so excited, "I wanted to see this so bad. Thank you, thank you. There's the water! Is that the Straight, the Strait of Juan de Fuca?"

"I heard some of the passengers say that we follow the Fraser River into Vancouver," James replied.

Dad said, "Our train goes along side of it just before we get to the train station." He always sounded like a teacher. Just like he told us he had been to other cities, even Chicago. Sometimes he seemed so wise. He was a man with half a degree but maybe, someday he would do the delight of his heart and build us a home.

"Here we are, kids. Let's collect our stuff and help me unload this by the station."

James asked, "Where do we go from here, Dad?"

"Mother seems to know where your Grandpa lives, or at least has directions. We'll find him and see what he says."

"Edgar, he said in his last letter that there was a flat in his building that we could rent until we find a house."

"I don't know why you keep saying we are going to find a house, Tasha. There aren't any to be found. The flat will just have to be fine for now."

"I know there is a house waiting for us."

"You always do, Tasha, you always know everything."

I wasn't sure if that was sarcasm or that Dad actually agreed with Mother. Soon we were on our way and it seemed to be only a few blocks away when we saw a tall quaint looking building. They called it a *Rooming House.* From the outside, it was all red brick with windows every so many feet. Most of the curtains were closed, but there were a few with flower pots on the ledge. Mother said excitedly, "This is it, this is the address."

There were probably five or six cement stairs to the front entrance. No front yard for kids to play in but the stairs led into the hardwood floor foyer.

"Oh, look! Numbers and names are on the mail boxes," shouted Cam.

"Come, James, let's find Grandpa."

"Wait for me, Pete. I'm coming too."

Cam, James and Pete ran up the stairs into the hallway to find the room number. Tim stayed with us walking up the front stairs slowly.

I asked Tim, "Are you going to be able to climb these stairs?"

"I'm fine Jenna, I can do it. I just can't run like the others."

We rapped at grandpa's front door. "Not so loud, kids, he can hear us and we don't want to bother his neighbors." Mother was trying to keep us calm but it wasn't working too well.

"Come in, come in, the door is open. I've been expecting you."

Now we were inside Grandpa's tiny one room flat that had a potbelly stove situated next to his single bed. For his eating area, he had a small table with two chairs.   Except for the one light that hung down from the ceiling, the bulk of illumination came through the window. Soon we were hovering around Grandfather's potbelly stove warming our hands. It was so good to see him again.

"Grandpa, I've missed you so much." Cam said, "How did you know it was us?"

"Well, Cameron, I got a letter from your Mother and she told me what train you were on and when it was leaving Winnipeg. I check the arrival time from here," he motioned for Cam to come, "sit on my lap. I've missed all of my grandchildren. It's so good to see you." Then he turned to Dad, "Edgar, how are you? Were you able to get a job here?"

"I start on Monday morning."

"You don't have much time, do you? Why don't you look at these Newspapers? You might just find something there."

"Do you really think there might be a house around here? I heard there weren't any."

"You could possibly find something though, since we've been fighting with the Japanese, the Government has been gathering them up supposedly for their own safety. They are being taken to an undisclosed location, which is internment camps, just like they are doing in the United States. If these people can sell their homes, they can keep their money, but otherwise, they just have to leave. Could be you can find one of those houses for sale."

"Well, maybe, it's worth a try. Which one of you kids would like to help?"

Pete was right in. "I'd like to, let me look."

"Check the ads that say, "Houses for Sale."

"Okay, Dad. I'll mark the column for you."

"Go for it."

Within a few minutes, Pete had several marked out, "This one has six bedrooms and two bathrooms. It says that one bedroom is downstairs and it has a basement for a car. Want to see it, Mother?"

"Where is it?"

"Grandpa, do you know?"

"Yes, Pete. It's just two blocks down Richards Street, then turn right to Third Avenue and it should be on the corner. Those homes used to belong to some of the Actors from Hollywood—did you know that, kids?"

"No, what's an actor?" asked Cam.

"An actor is someone who pretends to be someone in a story and act out the story. Sometime, we'll have to go to the movies, then you'll understand," Grandpa was always full of answers for us kids. "Why don't you leave the kids with me and go check out the house, Tasha?"

"Let's do that. Edgar let's go, it's early enough—about two in the afternoon?"

"Yeah, but are you up to it?" Turning to Abram, "Your daughter had a heart attack on the train so I'm trying to keep her from too much excitement."

"I'm sorry to hear that, Tasha, are you feeling okay now?"

"I'll be fine and you know how it is for me when I have too much excitement."

Looking to Edgar, Grandpa said, "She'll be fine, you can't stop her from whatever she wants to do anyhow. She's very resilient."

"I guess I've figured that out by now."

"But she always makes it even when we think she can't."

"What're you saying, I'm spoiled, Abram?"

"Tasha, there is no good answer, but you and Edgar need to see the house so you can make a decision if you want to buy it."

Edgar and Tasha were off to see the house they had seen advertised. It wasn't a far walk, just a few blocks and as they turned the corner, there amid the spattering of businesses, they could see the large houses beginning to look as though they had been misplaced amid the businesses.

"The house in the ad was the one on the corner. What do you think of it from the outside, Tasha?"

"I love the gray wooden siding. If it was ours, would you paint it white?"

"We can do anything you want, Tasha. Just so it's what you like and we can afford to buy it."

"Let's find out."

Chapter 16

Time of War

Nathan settled to his comfortable chair from a hard day at work. In his job, he would always have to be prepared for the accusations of unsatisfied customers. Though, the hassles were few, still it made him feel as though the ungrateful were the norm instead of the few.

As he prepared for a hearty meal with his dog to woof up the scraps,
Nathan sat at his dinner table turning the dial of his radio to check for the news of the day. Sitting, gnawing at a drumstick, he looked through the sheer curtains of his kitchen window and couldn't help but notice that his neighbors living across from him were already in the process of moving. Thinking to himself, being a man of action, he decided to put dinner on hold and talk with them. He wondered what could be bad enough to result in sending someone packing so quickly.   Surely something must've drastically changed in a very short period of time. Nathan made his way down to meet them, hurrying to introduce himself.

"Hello, neighbors, my name is Nathan and I've been meaning to welcome you into our neighborhood but I wasn't expecting to say, hello and goodbye."

"Hello, hello. I'm Hiraku, Sam Hiraku." He proceeded to bow several times during the introduction. "We won't be your neighbors for long, though."

"Why would that be?"

"We have been told we will be moving to another location."

"But you only just moved here."

"Our Canadian Government says they have to protect us so they have prepared a camp location for us."

"No choice?"

"We have no choice. We told them we'd have to sell first but they gave us a time limit and that is now so we're putting everything we can into storage. If the War isn't over soon enough we'll lose all this stuff as well."

"I'm so sorry to hear that, it doesn't make any sense."

"They did say we could sell the house if we have a buyer before we leave. Otherwise, there goes that as well. Yet, our realtor says he thinks he might be able to find a buyer because of the housing shortage."

"My prayers go with you—not only to sell but that you'll be safe."

"Thank you."

"I'm sorry to see you go."

"All is not so sad. My wife Alice says she will be glad to move out of this house because she thinks it's haunted."

"Haunted?"

"We hear stuff but I keep telling her it's an old house so the noises are to be expected. Even the realtor says, not to worry, all the old houses have the very same noises in them."

"I suppose you're right about the noises but I'm still very sorry to see such nice people go."

"Thank you." Sam Hiraku bowed a few more times as he moved away to tend to the moving van.

No sooner did Nathan Return home and settle for the evening when he turned to look back at the house to see what the commotion was all about. Then he saw someone who appeared to be showing the house to a couple. 'That was quick. The others aren't even totally out and it looks as though it could sell already.'

It didn't take long for Dad and Mother to return with the story about the house.

"Grandpa, we looked at the house you suggested and I think we found our house. The people who own it are Japanese and they've been told they have to leave. They were hopeful to sell because of the extreme housing shortage but afraid it wasn't going to happen fast enough for them. They had the deed and bill of sale for the house ready just in case someone would come to buy it. A truck was already there in the process of loading their stuff for storage."

James started asking, "Why are these people being sent away? What have they done that's so bad?"

Then Pete spoke up, "They're Japanese and we're at war with them, how can we trust them?"

"Does that make them bad because those living in Japan want to kill us?"

"Think about it boys, "How can we tell if they are against us or not?"

"You mean, like they all look alike, Dad?"

"It's more that people around them might start fighting with them. At least that's why our government has decided to house them separately for their own protection."

"But aren't some of them Canadians just like us?"

"Sure, but how does anyone know the difference?"

"Well, I for one think it's cruel. Look, Mother, you're from Russia and no one sends you away. We are fighting with Russia all the time."

"Not so fast, kids. Remember the dog we used to have? Just because we called him Fritz, and because his name sounded German, kids would ride their bikes down the road and sneer at him, kicking him every chance they got. They kicked the dog so much that he died of his injuries."

Pete started, "Actually, he died from eating chicken bones. But, like you said, it's easier with the Japanese because they look different than us. You can't tell a European from any of us because we're all from there somewhere."

"You're talking prejudice and we aren't supposed to be like that, Pete," James jumped in.

Tim cut in, "It isn't us James—it's our government and not only ours because even the U.S. does that. They aren't any different."

"Come on, kids. We don't act like that in our family and that's a good reason for us to have bought this home. If we hadn't bought the house, that Japanese couple would've had to walk and lose the money. At least we did something good. We need to love people of other colors even if the whole world says it's wrong. God expects us to love our neighbor no matter their color or where they're from. Especially now, I'm really glad we were able to buy the house. We liked it and most of all it was affordable for us." This was Dad talking.

"The realtor is walking the papers to the title company as we speak so that it can close this afternoon which means we can move in tomorrow. It could've taken weeks but because of their situation, it's just going to be a day. We'll get the key as soon as the realtor comes back from the Title office."

"When will that be, Edgar?

"They said this evening or early tomorrow morning. So, either they'll come by here, Grandpa, or find us looking around at the house."

"That was fast Edgar. I'm glad for you and the kids."

"Oh, Grandpa, you'll have to come and see it. You'll like how large it is. Do you know there is room for all of us?"

"How would you know Jenna? You haven't even been in it yet?"

"She's right Cam. There are four bedrooms upstairs and an extra room downstairs we can make into a bedroom, as well.

"Your daughter already has work for me to do and we haven't even moved in."

"Edgar, she'll find a lot more you can do for her. Remember, she's Tasha."

That part I didn't understand. It almost sounded like there was something very special about Mother but no one was talking. It's like when I asked her if she'd ever go back to visit Russia. It doesn't make sense that other people can visit there, yet, Mother insists for her it's different. I'd like to know why.

"Enough of the excitement for one day, tomorrow the house will be ours. Come on kids, help me make dinner."

The enthusiasm had stirred so the willingness to work together seemed obvious. Everyone wanted tomorrow to come more quickly than it could. Dinner was soon over and with the lateness of the hour, we all bedded down on the floor wherever space permitted. Though restless, tiredness soon took over and no sooner, it seemed, morning came with the sun creeping through the windows in the early hours of the day.

"Do we have to be up already?"

"It will be okay, Pete. We need to do this one by one, so you can be the last if you like."

"Thanks, Mother."

It wasn't long before we were ready to examine our house, though the realtor had promised to show up at least by morning and that time had already come. It was a cool fall morning as we all walked down to see the house from the outside. I couldn't help but think that the lake in Winnipeg would start to freeze over already only to have snow while we were enjoying what everyone called our Indian summer. Cool, yet not cold, just very nice.

As anxious as we were, we would have to wait to go in until the realtor would come with the key. We just stood gazing at the house trying to comprehend the size.

"It doesn't have a fence around it, Mother."

"Just give us some time and I'll build that white picket fence Mother likes so much."

"See the bay window in front with a balcony above it? That's where the master bedroom is. Look at the porch on the side of the house, its door goes into the dining room," Dad was giving us the full tour of the house from the outside.

"Is that the back door, then?" Grandpa asked.

"No, there is a back door that leads to the yard and a shed. But we figure the side door must have been the utility entrance or maybe for the kids coming in instead of through the front door. This house is almost like the one we had on Ross Avenue, isn't it?

"It seems large like that one but maybe that's why I liked it, only now we own it. If I'm not mistaken, a grandparent to one of the Movie Stars lives two doors down from here, at least that's what the realtor said. We'll find out soon enough. I must admit, Tasha, you were right again."

"Edgar, God does that for us."

I said, "It's too bad we have that one business between these houses."

"Jenna, that's industrialization. I've always said, they should have codes for different areas and keep businesses out of neighborhoods."

"Actually, Edgar, the city probably rezoned this, thinking it would all go into businesses since a lot of people are trying to move out into the country now." Grandpa thoughtfully answered.

"Kids, there's even a back yard where you'll be able to play. Knowing your Mother, we'll probably have a garden, chickens in the shed and anything else the city doesn't object to."

"You may be in luck on stuff like that because I don't think the city has faced the fact that people who live in these homes would want to raise chickens and other farm animals. Check it out at City Hall, Edgar."

"You bet I will, Abram."

Jenna asked, "How do you like it, Tim?"

"It's wonderful. I wish I could go inside and see it."

"It's taking a little longer. I had hoped we could get the key this morning but it seems it might take another day, Jenna. Then we'll get our stuff from the train station and bring it over here. James and Pete can help Dad bring it over and Tim can stay with Jenna so she doesn't get herself hurt. Anyhow that's the plan for now."

"As soon as we get our stuff in the house, we need to see a local Doctor for Tim," Edgar insisted. "We can't hesitate on that. Our doctor in Winnipeg gave us the name of a doctor here we need to see and said it was all set up as soon as we make contact."

"I'll be okay Dad."

"How's your other leg feeling?"

"It hurts but not as bad as my left one did."

We were back at Grandpa's house for lunch with the groceries Mother and Dad bought on the way back from looking at our house. The seating was sparse so we ate our sandwiches wherever it was comfortable enough and that included the floor. Dad just stood at the counter and ate. Cozy and comfortable but the best part was that Grandpa's home was very close to ours. I just knew we would see him a lot.

We spent the second night in Grandpa's flat with pillows on the floor, sleeping as best we could. The excitement kept me from a sound sleep and I was pleased when I saw the sun peek through the shades of Grandpa's window.

Breakfast didn't take long and cleaning up was a pleasure since we all wanted to be on our way to snoop around our new house once again. We were almost out the door when Mother said, "We're just going to go over to the house and see it again. If the realtor comes by tell him where we are. Once the house is in order, Grandpa, you will have to come and inspect it, how's that?"

"I'll be delighted to, Tasha, but it won't need inspecting, though I want to see it, of course."

We were in the front yard, looking around, when someone approached us, "Hi, I'm your neighbor, just across the street from here. You are the lucky owners of this house? By the way, my name is Nathan."

"We just bought the house. Just as soon as the deed is recorded, we should get the keys. My name is Edgar Nedder and this is my wife, Tasha."

"I don't know where all the kids went, but we have five."

"I'm pleased to see you will have room here. You deserve to be able to have a large house like this one. Did your Realtor tell you that your neighbor is Yvonne De Carlo's grandmother?"

"Yes, he did and I think it's awesome. Oh, here comes the realtor now."

"I'll leave so you can take care of your business—see you around."

The realtor approached Dad, "I knew you would be here looking around. Well, folks, here's the key, Congratulations! Enjoy your new home. You've already signed everything and the Deed is recorded. It will be mailed to you in about ten days."

"Thank you, Mr. Wilbur, we will enjoy the house, I'm sure. I know the kids are excited."

"Well, good, I hope you enjoy it. If you have any further questions, give me a call."

"I'm sure we'll be just fine."

We headed back to Grandpa's to pick up what little we had left at his place. It didn't seem more than a few minutes that we headed to our new home with all that we could carry in our arms. Pete and James didn't stop to talk a lot, just excused themselves and by the time we noticed they were well ahead of everyone with the house key in hand, nothing could stop them. The rest of us were just minutes behind ready to get to work and make this house our home.

It didn't take us more than a day to clutter the house with our stuff. For the first night, we slept on the floor and this time it was fun, more like camping out. Not so easy on Mother and Tim. Dad had to rest because for him it was back to work the very next day which meant it would be up to Mother and my brothers to put the house in order.

Soon, Cam and Pete were running through the hallways and through the kitchen chasing each other. "Stop that playing and come help us set your rooms up! If you want to have your own rooms, you're going to have to work for it. I can't do it alone, you know."

We knew Mother meant business but who could complain with all the room we were enjoying.

"I don't like that," complained Pete. "I need the book case on the other side of the room."

"Then you move it yourself."

"Oh, come on James, I need your help. If you help me set up my room, I'll help you fix yours, but do mine first."

It was nice that the previous owners left their book shelves and a few tables and chairs in the bedrooms. At least we had some furniture. They even left their living room furniture for us to have. The dark blue velvety couch and chair was really cool and I knew that Mother would match curtains to it somehow, she did everything just right.

"Mother, can I have a cat, please?"

"We'll see, Jenna."

"I want a dog. Please, can we have a dog, Mother?"

"Cam, we'll have to wait and see. I'm not sure you'd take care of your animals."

"I promise I would."

"I don't know, Cam."

With chaos on the one hand and contentment on the other, soon no one knew who was in what room. Momentarily we were standing together listening to Mother tell us what she was going to do while Dad would be at work. Then we heard a load *clunk* as if someone had dropped a tool.

"What was that noise?"

"We are all here together so maybe something just fell to the floor upstairs. Maybe one of our books fell off a shelf, Jenna?"

"That sound could be anything. Maybe Dad left a hammer on the edge of a chair?"

"I saw all his tools in his tool box, Mother. He said to keep them together so when we needed them they would all be there."

"I wouldn't worry about it Pete. This is an old house, almost one hundred years? There will always be noises to hear from time to time."

"You're too wise Tim. Thanks for the comfort from my own son."

Chapter 3

God's Delicate Touch

Bit by bit everyone's room was arranged and then rearranged, that is accept Tim's room. He was very accepting of anything his brothers would do for him. I could tell he wasn't feeling very well anymore. Finally, even his room was all set up but within a week, Tim was back in the hospital. Every moment was spent back and forth for both Mother and Dad.

Then one day, Mother came home and said, "James, Tim wants you to come to the hospital tomorrow."

"Tim? He doesn't like me, he hates me. Remember he tried giving all my Christmas toys away on the street last year? Toys you had just given me, I would have lost everything if you hadn't stopped him."

"I remember that, but I don't think he hates you.   You'll see when you and I visit him tomorrow."

"Why should I?" James was being stubborn.

"Tim wants to see you and I'm insisting you will be there."

Nothing more was said. Morning came and immediately after breakfast we all left for the hospital. The rest of us were too young to see Tim, so we sat in the waiting room while James and Mother went to visit him.

––––––––––––––

"Hey, Tim, what's up?"

"Hi James, Mother can you leave us alone for a minute?"

"Sure."

After the door closed, Tim, said, "James, I want to apologize to you for all the things I did to you. Can you forgive me?"

"Me forgive you?"

"I want you to forgive me, let me explain. With this illness, I have, sometimes my brain can get a little scrambled. I forget what I'm doing and then I'd do dumb stuff. It isn't an excuse but I'm sorry I hurt you when I tried to give away your toys. In my mind, I was giving away my old toys, not yours. Then Mother came and stopped me. She told me what I was doing. You never forgave me, but I'm sorry, please forgive me."

"Who am I to forgive you, I'm not God."

"The Bible says that for God to forgive us, we have to forgive others. I want you to be forgiven just as I have been. I want you to come to know Jesus, just as I have," Tim hesitated for a moment as if to catch his breath, "you see, I saw an Angel last night who came to me and told me that I will be going home to Heaven. I told the Angel I wanted to talk to you first because I want you to come to Jesus."

"Mother says we're too young to know that stuff. When we get to be eighteen or so, then we have to make choices when we understand."

"James, you know that Jesus died for your sins, and then rose again the third day. That's why we celebrate Easter. He died for our sins. The Bible says, *'For God so loved the world that He gave His Only Son, that whosoever believes in Him should not perish but have everlasting life.'* That's John 3:16."

"I guess I heard that in Sunday school, but I didn't know I had to do anything about it."

"It's a lot like getting a gift at Christmas. You know it has your name on the package but you aren't interested so you leave it there. It isn't yours until you take it and make it yours. You have to open it, to make it yours. You have to accept it. Jesus is God's gift to you for forgiveness of your sins. You have to ask him to forgive you, come into your life and believe in your heart so that He can give you eternal life. It's eternal James. You and I will one day be together again. You didn't much like it when we were separated when Dad left us, did you? God doesn't ever leave us. In the end, like me, we go to be with Jesus. We have a home in Heaven, James. I want you to be there."

"What did you do, Tim?"

"I asked Jesus to forgive me and come into my life. I want you to ask Jesus to forgive you, to come into your life, believe it in your heart and then Jesus will do that. James, *'we've all sinned and come short of the glory of God. There is none righteous, no not one.'* That's God's word and that's why He invites us to come to Him. I want you to do that today. That's my last wish and I can help you if you need me to."

Both boys bowed their heads, and together they prayed for forgiveness while James asked Jesus to come into his life.

"One last thing, James, I'm going home to Heaven. Please, James, don't look sad, but I want you to tell your brothers and sister so that they can come to Jesus, especially Pete? Please do that for me. You will be the oldest in just a short time. That's my last wish."

James rose to open the door after he wiped away the tears as the nurse and Mother came back in to make Tim as comfortable as possible.

James pondered what he had just done. He knew that Jesus had saved him and life would never be the same. Thank you, Lord, but do I have to be the oldest son in our family? God, I don't like that at all, I just don't like that, God.

Soon, we all left the hospital with plans for Mother and Dad to return in the evening when that fateful phone call came. Mother put the phone down turning to us and said, "He's gone to be with Jesus and Jose, finally."

Once again, another Limousine would usher us to the graveside. There would be a service, a man would say words like, *ashes to ashes and dust to dust.* Then we had to watch as they lowered the coffin into the ground. I always hated that the most, I only wanted to remember Tim as he was. Seeing him now was almost too hard, it hurt to know Tim was gone forever. I could never again talk with him and he would never again be there for me. I felt lonely. Yes, I had three other brothers but none of them would ever take the place of Tim. He understood things that no one else ever could. He always encouraged us not to panic, just be still and listen to God. He wasn't afraid to talk about God even though according to Mother, anyone under the age of eighteen was too young to understand. It was over now and the four of us were told by Mother and Dad to spend some time with Grandpa while, Dad and Mother would try to regain their composure.

In the months to come we would put our attention on Grandpa who would gladly take us for walks up town. My favorite pass time was to window shop with him, looking at the window decorations, especially the toys placed as though they were ready to tell a story. I would dream that I was a part of that story until Grandpa would pull me away and we would look at yet another window.

One day, Grandpa was walking a little slower so we would make more stops on the way home. "Grandpa, are you okay?"

"I'm okay, Jenna. I'm just very tired. I think I need to go home and rest."

Mother perked up, "Take the kids with you. I'm going to be with Dad for a bit and then he'll go to work. Then I'll be over to get the kids. You could stay with us, you know."

"No, Edgar gets out of sorts if I do. I don't need him to be jealous over me."

"Oh, he should be over that by now. He's funny that way, always afraid of losing my attention. There was probably a lot of truth in that. Instead of going to him for advice I'd go to you making things worse and then the kids always came before him. I'm the one that should smarten up but I'm not sure I can. It seems that someone is always ill and needs my attention. If not them, then it was me."

"I'll be fine on my own, I'm just going to go and rest."

We went with him and sat with him awhile until Mother came for us. At home, Mother would just sit and meditate. We figured she was remembering the days with Tim.

Then one day after a visit, Grandpa left for his own apartment, just to rest, as he would say. It was the last time I ever saw him alive. He was tired and like Mother said, God called him home. "The strangest thing happened, just as soon as he died, his hair went jet black, the same color it was when he was younger and I was a little kid."

"Mother, how come no one in our family has black hair? You always have told us that if there are people who think they might be related and they have black hair—there is no way they would be."

"Oh, don't worry about that, your Grandfather was different."

Everything is always different for us when people don't want to give an answer. One thing was for sure, it did mean another funeral in one more limo with an additional missing person from our family.

Mother again gave us her philosophy, "Kids, this just means we have one foot in Heaven and one here on earth. My heart wants to be with everyone that has gone before us but we need to stay here and take care of everything. Please, guys don't worry, God does have a plan and

I'm sure you all have a lot of living to do. You are young and God will keep you."

I knew I wanted to live because I had so much I needed to know, like things about God. There just wasn't anybody that could tell me.

The mysteries of life remained untold.

We were all sitting at breakfast when unexpectedly, the earth seemed to stand still. I looked at the cat standing in the middle of the floor, bracing with all four paws, as though she was holding on. It looked strange. Had life suddenly stopped? There was no movement anywhere. All my senses were telling me that it was very dry, and yet damp and humid, like two opposing forces fighting in the atmosphere. The earth felt void of any breeze causing a thickness all around us, so now it wasn't just hot anymore. I looked through the window, not even the all familiar Seagulls could be seen flying. Had God summoned His creation, *"Don't move, just stay where you are."* The day had already been slightly different with Dad trying to earn extra money, he had volunteered for the weekend graveyard shift making him absent from our family on this Sunday morning in June, 1946. The war was already over so not even the radio gave us any exciting news. Just quietness, not a stir from anyone, it appeared to be a peaceful morning in an eerie sort of way. No, something was wrong.

"Mother, why is it so warm today?"

"I don't know, just one of those hot, quirky days, Jenna."

"But the air isn't even moving."

"Sit by the fan and you'll feel better. It's a good job we have fans, it must be in the upper 80s, and humid. When there isn't a breeze, it gets hot."

The cat started turning her head from side to side. Suddenly she stopped and just began staring, "What's wrong with the cat, Mother?"

"What is she doing, Pete?"

"She just stands there. She's looking at the door and then she turns and looks at us. Will she be okay?"

Before any of us could mutter another word, I heard the rumble, like the earth was beginning to roll around. The lights over the breakfast nook shook intensely. I hung on to the edge of the table afraid to move for fear I would stumble and fall. I was sure the earth was about to open up. "What is that?"

Mother shouted, "Stand in the doorway, it's an earthquake! Pete, where are you going?"

"I'm going outside—this house is going to fall down! It's old, it has to fall."

"No, it isn't, Pete, if you run down the stairs you'll fall and hurt yourself. Just stay put. Stand in the doorway! Everyone stand in the doorways—it'll be over in a second."

Pete insisted, "I'm out of here. The house is coming down. I know it is!"

Mother shouted, "Stop Pete, James grab him, now!"

James reached over from his safety zone in the doorway and grabbed Pete's arm.

"Let me go! You guys are crazy!"

Cam started yelling, "Get under the table. Our teacher at school says to get under the table, it will be safer."

The rumble stopped just as quickly as it had started. It was like nothing we had ever experienced before. We had only heard about the San Francisco earthquake and had seen pictures of the devastation of it but that was like, *those things happen to other people, not us."* This was the shaking of the earth.

"I think it quit, Mother, can we go out now?" Pete wanted to.

"Okay, kids, let's go out and see what happened but be very careful of the stairs, they may not be solid with all that shaking."

Gingerly we walked down to the ground level from the back-porch stairs, looking everywhere. We walked over to the laundry adjacent to our house, "Look, the earth caved in here, Mother, see?"

"In the middle of the road."

"So, it did. There is an indentation in the ground and it looks like it sunk about a foot." We looked back at our house, "But the house is still standing. It must have been a well-built even if it was built in the 1840s, making it just over a hundred years old. "They certainly knew how to build houses then," Mother commented. We walked around the house to see if we could find anymore holes in the ground.

"Mother, shouldn't we check on Yvonne's grandmother?" We had been friends with Yvonne De Carlo's grandmother ever since we had moved to this house. Yvonne had just been named *The Most Beautiful Girl* in the World, in 1945, just a year ago. Mother loved to listen to the many stories Yvonne's grandmother told about her granddaughter and how she had changed her name from Margaret Yvonne Middleton to Yvonne De Carlo. She used her mother's maiden name but in her family, she was always referred to as Peggy.

"Thanks for reminding me, Jenna, let's go check. She's given you so much from Yvonne, it's the least we can do."

"Yvonne even gave me a picture of herself, autographed. I will keep that forever, Mother. She even gave me that shell bracelet."

"Your desk is from her too, you remember?"

"I enjoy the desk because I can put my stuff in it. It's very nice."

We found Mrs. De Carlo well in spite of the awful scare. She assured us she would be okay.

"Thank you so much for coming. Here let me make you a cup of tea, dear."

"This time we can't stay, my children are outside but I wanted to make sure you would be fine since I know how much it scared us."

"Thank you again for coming but you must come again."

"We will."

The fear we had just experienced showed on each of our faces and Mother realized it.

When Dad finally arrived home, he joined our interrupted breakfast, we were all over him with questions. Pete asked, "Dad, did you feel the earthquake at work?"

"I was standing at the bus stop when I felt it. We don't usually get earthquakes here, at least not very often. We'll be able to see how bad it was when the paper comes out in the morning."

We weren't too comfortable in playing for the rest of the day. Most of the day was spent in silence, with nothing to say. Everything had been too much out of our control. Was God talking, was he trying to get someone's attention? Mother realized we had unanswerable questions and as soon as Dad left again for his graveyard shift, Mother decided to gather us all around the table opening her Bible turning to a passage that seemed to be familiar to her. Then she turned, looking at each of us and asked if anyone would like to read the words in her Bible, "Now, remember, kids, you can't tell Dad that we are reading the Bible."

"Why, Mother, why can't we read the Bible? What's wrong with reading the Bible?"

"Jenna, Dad has forbidden it."

"But why, what did God do to him?"

"When we first moved here, Tim and then Grandpa died so we thought maybe we should do something good like inviting the kids from the neighborhood to our house and start a Bible study class with them. We didn't know how to do that so we contacted our church."

"I didn't know we had a church," piped up Cam.

"Well, we did. We asked them if they would start a church in our home and they just said no. They said the church wasn't into doing home churches because they have a building they use on Mitchell Island for a Sunday school. They considered it to be enough of an outreach. Then, they just had to say because we didn't contribute enough money or dues for their records, we weren't in good standing. That's when Dad said, 'okay, I don't ever want to hear about God or see you read the Bible in our home.' That's why I never do it when he sees me. I still believe God and love Him but I don't want Dad to get mad. It made me very angry too, but like you say, that isn't God's fault. I know we've been too poor to pay dues so I guess we have to go it alone. That's why it has to be just God and us," Then Mother took a deep breath, "but let's read what God says about the last days. My English isn't so good, so who would like to read?"

There was an awkward hesitation, expecting James to answer but when he didn't Pete answered, "I would, I'm not afraid to read the Bible."

Pete read from Matthew 24. Mother told him to read almost all of it and when he came to, *"but the one who stands firm to the end will be saved."* It scared me, what were we supposed to do in these last days, *"Nation will go to war against nation, and kingdom against kingdom. There will be famines and earthquakes in many parts of the world.* "What are we supposed to do, Mother?" asked Cam.

"You have to just love Jesus with all your heart. He will keep you, Jesus will help you. You will be okay. When you are old enough you will understand."

James was quiet. He wasn't the kind of brother that would knowingly do anything that had been forbidden by a parent. I wasn't comforted, there surely had to be something more to life. Just loving God couldn't be enough. I knew I loved Him, after all He was my Creator but how would that alone bring me comfort in these days of uncertainty. Something had to be missing—there had to be more to that message, but what? Nobody was talking so how would I ever know? Can't anyone tell us? I just said, Oh God show me the answers I need, show me the way.

The morning after the earthquake we were still restless. Dad had just come off the graveyard shift, had breakfast with all of us and then was off to bed. Mother wanted to give him a quiet house so we left for the park and to town for the day.

"Read all about it, read all about it!" The newspaper boy was shouting at the top of his lungs, "Earthquake devastated Courtney. It measured 7.3, and the epicenter was on Central Vancouver Island. *Read all about it! Read all about it!*"

"Did you hear that Mother? I heard the paperboy say that a man died because his boat capsized."

"I heard that too, it was a really strong earthquake."

Pete continued on his theme, "Mother you know if the house had fallen down we would all have been killed, you know that."

"But it didn't Pete. God was looking after us and he will always look after each one of us."

"I still think we were just very lucky. Farther north from us, a whole school collapsed."

"Actually, the roof fell in. But it wasn't a school day so no one got hurt."

"Mother, you're saying that God looked after us and that's why we were safe."

"That's what I've been trying to say."

Pete couldn't stop himself, "Then why did that man die when his boat capsized?"

"His time was up, Pete. God only allows that when He wants to take us home."

"So then, it isn't luck that nothing happened to us. God was protecting us because He wants us to live a little longer."

"That's right kids, it's what I believe. Maybe He has more for us to do on this earth."

Was it luck or just very fortunate? It was soon after that, our parents began to make new plans. Maybe it was because we had too many memories in this house already. They wanted a new life in another town.

Chapter 18

I Don't Believe It

It was shortly after the earthquake I heard Dad say to Mother, "Did you know our government is making available homesteads for anyone who can qualify? That means they give you acreage to farm and build your home on but it's up around Prince George or even farther north."

"Why don't we see if we can qualify? Then you could do what you've always wanted, build our dream house."

"Does that mean we will be moving again, Mother?"

"If we can, it would."

Dad and Mother were serious about this idea and soon they completed the questionnaire to see if our family could get the free land.

After reading the forms, Dad said, "I'm not sure we can qualify. If any of our family has allergies or a heart condition, they just very well may not allow us to go. We have to have clearance from a Doctor."

"Let's fill it out anyway. Maybe they'll see our other good qualities."

"Okay, Tasha, let's give it a try."

They sent the letter but within days the answer came back. As Dad frantically opened the letter addressed to him, he hesitated. He then showed it to Mother. I knew instantly that Dad was not pleased. "It's a no go, Tasha. The answer came back negative."

Yet, I could tell, they hadn't given up on the idea of moving out of the city. It was a dream that would not be easily extinguished. "This is just a detour in our lives. If that isn't the answer, there'll be another place that's even better for us, you'll see, Edgar."

"Do you really think so, Tasha?"

"I do."

"Not to change the subject, but the telephone company is coming to install our phone. We have finally been approved for a phone."

"I never could understand why we couldn't have a phone when we had one on the Prairies. We might've been on a party-line but at least we had a phone."

"It was because of the War. It caused a shortage in production of materials for everywhere. When we moved here, there was no phone in the house so we had to go on a waiting list."

"Tasha, it appears we were one of the few families chosen to get one so soon because of the size of our family mattered, also the fact that we've had a lot of medical emergencies in our home. Anyhow, the phone company said they would be here first thing tomorrow morning."

Dad went to work and shortly afterward there was a knock at the door, just as Dad had promised.

"I'm here to install your phone."

"Come in, we've been waiting for you. I recognize you, aren't you Nathan, our neighbor?"

"Yeah, I live in the red brick house. Okay, so where would you like me to put the phone?"

"Over here, the living room wall side, across from the stairs. We usually sit in the living room, so that's a good place."

"Okay, Mrs. Nedder. I can put the wire through the attic and then work it down the wall. That should work."

"Good, we'll let you get to work."

It wasn't long before our telephone was installed, the technician said, "I'm sure you know how to use a dial telephone, right? A lot of the smaller cities still have an operator to get your number for you. Even with a dial phone you still have a party-line. You can get a private line but that's a bit more expensive."

"Like you said, on the Prairies we just picked up the phone and asked the operator for a number, sometimes if we forgot the number we could ask for the person."

"Shall I show you how to use it?"

"Oh, I think we can figure it out. My sons are good at that kind of stuff. We should be okay. Thank you for all your work."

The telephone technician left and Mother was anxious to have us help her figure out how to use it. Mother said, "Who's going to test it out, kids?"

"Why don't you Mother?"

"Sorry, Pete, I don't talk on those things. I'm not touching it."

"Who used the phone when we were on the Prairies?"

"Dad did, but there it was different, like the technician said, we had operators that called the number for us. If I used it, I would just say get me the corner store, and they would. I know nothing about dial telephones."

"Let me try, I'm not afraid." Pete was never afraid but always the first for everything, "What do I dial? Here's a number, let me try that…that's not working."

"Let me look at what you're dialing, Pete."

James looked at the phone book, "That's an address! You have to call the phone number. See the seven-digit number at the end? That's the phone number."

"Why don't you try phoning?"

"Not me, you're doing okay."

"Okay, let's try the number you suggested, James. It's for a business…hey, it's ringing! They answered … "Hello, no I just wanted to see if our phone actually worked. Thank you, I'll hang up." Pete put the phone down, "It works and now we know that for certain."

If Dad had been home, he would've known how to use it. He used the phones on the street corners if our home didn't have one when Mother got sick but now we had a phone in the house again. My brothers and I were new at this game and Mother wasn't about to get involved.

Dad came home and inquired of our day and saw the phone. "How is it working, Tasha? Have you tried it?"

"No, but Pete did. He's never afraid of anything but his shadow."

"Well good. What's for dinner?"

"I made a stew for tonight, Jenna's favorite."

"Yeah, Mother makes the best stews."

Dinner time was when we all told our stories and made a few jokes of what happened to us. It was always a really good time. After dinner, we did the usual hovering around the radio to listen to some of our favorite programs. We were listening to *The Shadow* when suddenly we heard noises.

"The bathtub water is running. Who turned that on?"

"We've all been here, Dad, with you," James answered.

"I better go check upstairs, maybe a pipe burst. After all, this is an old house."

Curiosity made us all follow Dad to the upstairs bathroom. Dad looked around, testing the water faucets, but no leak. "No leak here and I can't hear it anymore."

"Just a ghost, that's all it is."

"Oh, Mother, none of us believe that stuff, there isn't any such thing," that was my summation of the situation.

"Well, let me tell you why I said that. Last night, Edgar, when you went to work and after I put the kids to bed, I tried to sleep. Then something woke me, like I felt someone staring at me. I opened my eyes and saw this little woman sitting at the foot of my bed. It was strange, like a ghost."

"How would you know she was a ghost?" Pete asked with curiosity.

"You can tell it's a ghost when you can see through them. I could see through this ghost, almost like a shadow on the wall only she sat at the foot of my bed. I asked her, 'What do you want from me?' She said, 'I don't want anything. It's just nice being with you.' Then she disappeared and I couldn't see her anymore. I wondered what that Ghost was trying to say."

Cam and James just sat there quietly. Pete was now getting fidgety but I still didn't believe this stuff. It's like, show me and besides, if I can't see the ghosts, they can't be real. Dad wasn't saying anything either. Dad was a smart man, as far as I could tell. Finally, James made a comment, "Mother, if you mess with that stuff, you open the door to more serious stuff. God wants us to trust Him not the spirit world. You know that, Mother."

"But James you can learn so much just by having an open mind, besides, it's fun and I like to hear what other people think. It won't change what I believe anyhow."

It wasn't but a few days after that, I heard Mother say to Dad, "Edgar, I met a lady at the grocery store. She seemed to be having trouble with her son while she was trying to buy groceries. I asked her if I could help. But she only said that her son wasn't well, that she had to be careful because he would get seizures every now and again. Her husband was working so she couldn't leave him home alone. She told me how lonely she would get because she was so tied to her son's care.

We talked for a while and then she said as a result of being house bound she got interested in the spirit world and she learned to talk with the dead. Then I told her about the Ghost that comes to visit me. Anyhow, I thought I would go over and visit with her tonight. I won't go alone, I'll take Jenna."

Dad just asked, "Are you sure you want to get mixed up in that stuff? You heard what James told you—he may be just a kid, but I think he might be right."

"I know what I'm doing, no one can fool me, and I'll be in control. I like to see what they do and how they do it."

Within the hour, we were walking over to Second Avenue for that visit. Was this now a plight of mercy or self-indulgent? Mother always had more up her sleeve than that simple easy explanation and I just knew I would prove to be right.

Mother was always a little mysterious and somehow, she had changed just a little since we had been reunited after her hospital stay. She always told us that God had sent her a messenger to tell her she must be strong and hang in because of her family. Somehow, even though that was good advice, I believed that messenger had to be a real person. With all that Dad, had done to her, how could she act the same as before? It was soon after that suddenly everything changed and we were moving to Vancouver. I remembered hearing her say, "Uncle Abram, can you watch the children for me while I go to town and get a few things?" I had never heard Grandpa called that before. Did that mean he was her Uncle and not her Dad? I was always too afraid to ask but instead I hoped we would just stay together as a family no matter who we were.

Then Grandpa said, "Of course, Tasha, I'd love to."

Whether he was really Grandpa or her Uncle Abram, it didn't really matter; he was a wonderful substitute anyway. He loved us and there wasn't one of us kids that would've misbehaved with him around, all we wanted was to please him. He was gone now, home with God just like Tim.

We were now sitting and visiting for the first few minutes, talking about nothing like adults always do. It wasn't long before I knew that tonight Mother had questions about Aunt Tina. Mother wanted to know about her sister or was it her cousin, in Russia.

"Myrtle, when I was in Russia, my parents used to visit a soothsayer who would tell fortunes and even sometimes the future.

People used to laugh about it but my own mother used to say it was a good idea to go see Wanda because of the many people that came her way. She would hear all the recent news sometimes before everyone else. Wanda even told me who I would marry and in the end, she was right. Can you do that kind of stuff? Do you talk to the dead?"

"I can do that Tasha, because I do a lot of talking to the dead. What did you want me to find out for you? Which one of your relatives do you want me to talk to? Tell me about them, it always helps to know something."

I thought that was an easy guess. If Mother would give her the answers, then Myrtle could put it together. Couldn't anyone do that kind of investigating and be more like a counselor? Mother continued on, "Since you are a spiritualist, and you commune with the dead, I do have a question for you. I had a letter from a friend of my cousin," she turned to look at me, "I mean my sister Tina who hasn't been very well. In fact, she isn't expected to live."

"What is your question, Tasha?"

"I want to know if Tina died or did she get through her illness? If she did, is she coming to Canada?"

I thought to myself, Mother told the lady everything she needed to know. If Myrtle played her cards right, she would have a friend for life. Even I could make a smart guess as to whether Tina was alive or dead.

Then Myrtle went on to explain, "I can see her as you described her to me." She waited a moment as she bowed her head to meditate. Then she looked up to the ceiling and said, "She has died. I'm sorry, but I can see her as plain as day."

Mother asked, "Can I see her? Can I talk to her?"

"No, Tasha, you have to be lifted in the spirit. That takes special training. Almost like you're lifted up into the clouds and then the wind blows parting the clouds. I saw her but only for a moment…just a mere moment and then she was gone. If she hadn't died, I wouldn't have seen her at all but she couldn't talk to me, almost like she was with God and He wouldn't let her come to me."

"You are right about that, she is with God, He won't let her go. That much I know for sure. The part that she is with God makes me feel at peace because she will never have to suffer anymore. But I really wanted her to come live with us—I have missed her so much."

In my mind, from what Mother told her, it was an easy guess to say Aunt Tina had died, after all, isn't that what Mother already predicted would happen with the news she had received earlier? As far as Myrtle was concerned, she was at least fifty percent correct and chances are she was exactly right.

The very next day, a letter arrived in the morning mail, Aunt Tina had died. Now it was confirmed that her struggles were finally over. Mother was sad especially since she had just lost the last of her closest family in Russia that she knew about.

––––––––––––––––––

Edgar had already gone to work when Tasha settled into a light sleep. Suddenly she awoke and saw the little woman at the foot of her bed again.

"You're here again. Who are you and what do you want?"

"My name is Rosie. I don't want anything and like I said the other time to you, I just like being with you. I feel alive when I'm here."

"Rosie, I really want you to leave me alone. You've lived your life already and now I have to live mine. If you came to tell me Tina has died, I already know that and now I haven't anyone other than this family here in this house. Just let me live my life."

"No, no, Tasha. I couldn't know that Tina died. I'm not God. I can't know any of that stuff. I only roam around here because I like you."

"But I need you to leave me alone, Rosie. Please let me live my own life." With that Rosie was gone just as suddenly as she came.

––––––––––––––––––

At breakfast, before Edgar was ready to leave for work, Tasha said, "Rosie came again last night and I told her again to let me live my own life and then she left."

"Oh, now she has a name? Did she really leave, Tasha? You guys were complaining this morning about more noises. If she left, what are all the noises about?"

"Some other Ghost, Edgar?"

Then Jenna spoke up, "I'm still not with you on that stuff, Mother. You guys seem to belong to another world and it certainly isn't mine."

"Oh, Edgar, another thing, the phone dial keeps turning itself. Would that be Rosie doing it?"

"Tasha, call the phone repair man and have him check for a short in the wires. That's all it can be."

Not even Dad was getting into this Ghost stuff. I couldn't blame him, though.

The next day the telephone repair man came, surprised, Mother said, "Nathan, I see you're our repair man as well—come in."

"Your husband said you have a short in the wiring, is that correct?"

"Either that or a ghost keeps dialing the phone?"

A bit startled, Nathan said, "A ghost? How do you figure?"

"A woman who calls herself Rosie sometimes comes to me during the night when I'm sleeping. I know she's a ghost because I can see through her and she always disappears into thin air when she's done talking to me."

"Actually, I heard from the people you bought the house that it was haunted but for me, I just don't buy into that stuff, it's just not for me. Why you see them, I have no idea." Then Nathan proceeded checking the wires. He turned to Mother, "I don't see a short. It all appears to be in good working condition. I just have this screw to put in and then I don't know what to say."

Nathan put the phone together and back on the wall, and as he was still looking at it, even I could see the dial turn again. Okay, so I was wrong! It did turn itself, but that's all I ever saw in the Ghost realm.

It didn't take seconds for our repairman to be out of the door and in his truck. I turned to follow his exit but all I could see was the dust behind the truck as it roared down the road. I looked at Mother, "Can a heavy truck even drive that fast? Was that man scared?"

"I guess he was. But you saw that, didn't you? Now do you believe me?"

Chapter 19

The Fire

I was getting tired of playing board games, "I think if we have to play Chinese checkers one more time, I'm going to die!"

"How about playing a game of Snakes and Ladders, Jenna?"

"Hey, I like that idea, Cam, let's do it."

The winter nights in Vancouver were long. It would get dark early in the afternoon meaning we would be stuck in the house often with nothing we wanted to do. This particular Saturday evening Dad was home and since he liked playing board games, that's what we had to do. I could tell that everyone was feeling the doom of another game and if our parents wouldn't pick up on our mood, we'd soon be at one another in some type of argument. We certainly were ripe and ready to get into mischief when Mother said, "Come on, kids, let's sit around the radio. One of your favorite shows is on in about five minutes."

Cam asked, "What's on, is it Superman?"

"How about listening to Country Western music?"

"You and your music, Jenna, why don't you just let it go. Maybe we could listen to a boxing match, I'd like that." James said.

"I can't believe you like that stuff. All we ever hear is Pop, Pop, for every punch they take and then the one, two, three until they reach ten when they tell us the guy is knocked out. How can that be fun?"

"You always just like the nice stuff. Everything isn't always so nice, you know."

"You have a sour attitude, Cam. Life is what you make it to be if you ask me."

"And you're always talking as though things will turn out good in the end when we all know that's impossible."

"Let's stop that nonsense and see what comedy shows are on," Mother was always trying to simmer the pot to keep it from boiling.

"It looks like the Red Skeleton show is about to start."

"Clem Kadiddlehopper is my favorite," Pete said, laughingly.

"I like Willy Lump, Lump, the drunk," added Cam.

I looked at James who had a frown that looked like scorn when Cam made that remark, like the drunk was really a bad guy instead of just a funny guy. "Come on James, Willy Lump, Lump is just a funny drunk…you need to laugh."

"Being drunk isn't a good thing," James answered in a solemn tone.

"We know that, James, but this program is meant to be funny. It shows how foolish drunks act." When Mother said that, he settled down to enjoy the program with the rest of us.

By now we were all ears, concentrating on the comedian when James and I together, just happened to look over and notice that the night sky was a brilliant red, shining through our kitchen curtains. He spoke up and said, "How come it's red behind the curtains?"

"Red?" Without another word, we ran into the kitchen and flung open the curtains. The entire sky was a raging fire coming from about a half block behind our house.

"Is this war time? Are we being bombed?" I asked.

"No, the war is over, Jenna, that's a dangerous fire. It's coming from the Lumberyard…Edgar, the Lumberyard is on fire!"

"I can see that, Tasha. I wonder how that got started. I know according to the papers the Lumberyard wasn't very profitable lately."

"What's that got to do with the fire, Edgar?"

"I don't know, maybe one of the workers got careless."

"Would anyone be working on a Saturday night?"

"They used to but that was when they had two shifts going in their more profitable times. I don't think they've been on more than one shift for months."

"Someone could have been smoking and let a match fall into the sawdust."

"They aren't allowed to smoke in that building for that reason."

"How could it happen then if they're not even open for work?"

"Like you said, a worker probably did that…got careless. I'm sure of it, Tasha.

"But you just said, it's Saturday, so no one would be working, right? Look, look! Two men are running up the alleyway past our house to the street!"

"Who are those guys, Dad?" asked Pete.

"I don't know, doesn't look right, does it?"

"Edgar, you saw them?"

"I think we all did."

James was becoming vocal now, "The fire's coming this way! I can even feel the heat penetrating the windows."

"You can hear the fire trucks coming down the road toward us—hopefully they'll get it out shortly."

"But shouldn't we get out of the house, Dad?"

"I can hear more fire trucks coming, James. They'll let us know if we need to do anything but they're right on it, so I think they'll handle it."

James wouldn't quit with his comments, "That was a huge lumberyard, it'll burn for a long time, anything could happen."

I could tell Pete was starting to show the terror in his eyes. Sometimes he was the only one with any common sense. He insisted, "We need to get out of here or we are going to be nothing but ashes."

Cam started sorting things out in his mind, "Those guys we saw running had no reason to be there at this time of night. If it wasn't them, they would've seen who did it but instead, they were running like they thought no one would see them. Well, I saw the one man clear enough."

Mother asked, "You did?"

"Well, I saw his gray suit. Why would anyone be dressed up except if he was the boss watching over what was about to happen? Even then the guy is just plain stupid."

"Cam, you're making good sense, how did you figure that?"

"Dad, you hear so much these days on the news that you just have to think about things that happen. Everybody isn't honest."

Then James answered, "I've been saying that all along, those guys have to be crooks."

Pete asked, "Do you think someone paid them off to do that? Otherwise, why were they running from that fire?

"I did see them, Tasha. Do you think they set the fire?"

"Why else would they run away?"

"I'm scared Mother. Is our house going to burn down? Are we going to burn to death?"

"Jenna! We'll be okay."

I wasn't so sure…then we heard a loud rapping at our door. The Fire Marshal was screaming at the top of his lungs, "Get out of your house, the fire is getting too close to the power lines and your house is the next to burn. Get out now!"

"Dad, see the sparks? Most of them are missing but won't they hit the wires soon?"

"Pete, James, and Cam, get out!" I just stood there frozen to the floor, I couldn't move. With one good shove, Mother pushed me out into the snow. I fell and stumbled then sat in the snow for a moment. "Get into the street, kids get away from the house! It's going to burn!"

I pushed myself up as we all ran to the street. Then I looked back and saw Dad heading back into the house. "Edgar don't go back in there, you'll die!" Mother was screaming at the top of her lungs.

The fireman hollered, "Sir, get out of there now, I'm ordering you to get out!"

Dad ignored the shouts and ran back in.

"It's too late for you to find the breaker box. It's on the top floor—you won't make it, Edgar, don't do it!" No matter what advice Mother was yelling at him, there was no stopping Dad, he would do what he needed to do.

With the door, ajar, I could see Dad jumping two steps at a time. Meanwhile the fire had reached the power pole and began licking its way up to the live wires. The people in the street just stared, horror-struck for fear that Dad would burn alive. The police stood in silence as the firemen were preparing with the hose aimed to water down our house.

Dad was puffing when I could see his body reappear in the doorway, "I made it! I made it! Tasha, you will never believe it—what I think happened just now. When I reached the top of the floor," he was still puffing, "I felt something like a wind blowing out of nowhere. I know I was pushed toward the wall and when I looked up, I saw the breaker box. I reached for the leaver and pulled with all my might.   It was like an Angel helping me. When I ran down, I'm sure I skipped most of the stairs." I could see he was breathing hard and was finding it difficult to talk anymore.

The Fire Marshall was now standing at Edgar's side, "Well, sir, you saved your house. Congratulations! It was a stupid thing to do but you saved the neighborhood from burning as well. Thanks."

It took most of the evening for the fire fighters to put out such a gigantic blaze. It was hours later that Dad and the Firemen checked around our house for stray sparks but found everything to be safe, so we were allowed to go back in. The fire was surely out but the memories of it lingered fresh in our minds. I knew we could have died, but Dad saved the day.

———————————

Nathan restlessly moved about his kitchen. He couldn't stop thinking about what he had just seen. It was too obvious to have witnessed such a devastating fire that could have destroyed the entire neighborhood and then, who was to say that the same two men he had seen running wouldn't do it again. He couldn't help but think of what interest they might have in the burning of the Lumberyard. He remembered the last report in the Vancouver Sun that said that the Lumberyard was having financial problems after the workers had gone out on strike for higher wages and more benefits. Since then, competition in the lumber production had become extreme making it hard to stay in business, all according to the latest news report. Now, after the fire, Nathan felt compelled to make a report of what he saw and so he called the police station.

Police in uniform soon arrived at Nathan's home to take his report of what he had witnessed. "Tell us what you witnessed the night of the fire."

Nathan proceeded, "I clearly saw two men run up the alleyway of the house on the corner, you know, the haunted house, next to the Laundry."

"Haunted, huh? So, we've heard," changing back to the subject of the fire, "did you get a description of the men?"

"One wore a gray suit and the other was just dressed in black. I still can't understand why the one guy wore a suit—it just doesn't make any sense."

"Gray could blend well into the surroundings making him more invisible. Black, of course because it was night, he would've thought he would be more unrecognizable."

"Still doesn't make sense. They came into clear vision because the fire was so brilliant and with the snow on the ground, I couldn't help but notice, yet I was too far away to see their faces clearly."

"Did you happen to see the direction they ran in and was there a car waiting for them?"

"I saw that as well…they ran toward town but only a block away, they jumped into a black limo and sped away. I guess that's why I'm reporting this, just too obvious to let go and besides, I'm afraid they want to burn down the whole neighborhood. There has been talk of changing this neighborhood to an industrial area, only. I think this area was recently rezoned for that."

"We are very interested in everything you saw. Anything more you can remember, please let us know."

Anthony felt satisfied that he had made the call, perhaps now the burning could be stopped.

———————————

"You know, Edgar, I still can't get over seeing those men run from that enormous fire. I know it was a few days ago since this all happened," Mother continued to talk, "do you think we ought to report what we saw to the police?"

"Oh, those guys we saw running down our alleyway? Do you think anything would come of it?"

"Isn't that the right thing to do, though?"

"I suppose. They could strike again and burn homes the next time. There are people that do exactly that, it's like an illness," Dad thought for a moment, "maybe that would get them to stop setting buildings on fire. Well, okay, let me call them and see what they say."

The decision was made to make the call to the police station. Edgar called, "I want to make a report about the Lumberyard fire that happened a few days ago. We did see a couple of guys running from the fire." Dad hesitated to listen, "You'll be over shortly to take the report?" Then I heard him repeat our address, "We live right directly in front of that Lumberyard. Okay, we'll see you when you get here."

Dad hung up the phone, "They're coming but it could be about an hour by time they get here to take our report."

"Good, I do think it's what we should do as good citizens."

"I suppose."

Within the hour our doorbell rang but instead of seeing men in police uniforms, the men identified themselves as police officers but were dressed in plain clothes. Dad said, "I expected to see you in uniform."

"We don't usually come in our uniforms on an investigation call. But tell us what you know or observed about the fire."

The men sat and listened but even I sensed an apprehension before they heard the story that Dad and Mother were about to relate. Then, without hesitation, the man who had introduced himself as George, said, "While we appreciate your reporting this, is there any kind of a description you can give us of those guys other than 'two guys' running down the alley? Type of clothes, how they ran? Is there anything?"

"Well, no. I was too much in shock to comprehend any of that." Turning to Mother, "Did you see the color of their clothes, Tasha?"

"No, Edgar. It was evening, although the snow on the ground did brighten it a bit. But I just didn't think about anything except what had just happened."

"I thought it looked like the one guy wore a gray suit," everyone turned to look at Pete as he continued, "almost looked like the color of the brick on the building next door. Come to think of it, sir, the color of your suite. I have to tell you they were good runners—they were fast." Pete answered.

"Did any of you kids see any more than that?"

"Pete probably saw the most of what the men looked like. We were looking down on them so they pretty much matched their surroundings," added James, "and we were more concerned with the heat of the fire…we could even feel the heat inside our house."

"You see, that's our dilemma. If we had a better description, it would help us. Let us know if you can remember more. For now, there isn't anything we can do."

The cops left leaving our parents to ponder the situation.

The next day was Sunday so after breakfast, Mother spoke up and said, "Let's go look at the Lumberyard and see what the damage looks like."

"I'd love that," Pete jumped up from where he was seated, in excitement.

"You guys can go, but I'm staying home." James was determined he wouldn't get involved in what was now in the past.

"I want to go," Cam piped up.

"I'm going. If you guys are going, I go."

"Okay Jenna, let's go, if James wants to stay home, he can. But we want to see the damage from the fire." Dad was determined to see what had really happened.

We carefully made our way over to the remains of the Lumberyard. Most everything was badly charred, more ashes than wood lay burned on the ground. Some of the lumber had been chopped to pieces by the firemen with a scattering of good lumber everywhere.

"Look, perfectly good boards," Pete said.

"Why don't we take some of these, Edgar? They'll just plow this stuff up and take it to the dump."

"Okay, Tasha, if you think we should, Pete can take what he wants."

"There isn't anyone around, probably too early in the morning. Pete, would you want to take a few smaller boards and maybe Cam can help?"

"I'll do it, Mother, I don't mind, beside they're too heavy for Cam."

I wondered why Dad didn't lift a board or was it because he didn't want to get caught? He could always say, Pete's just a kid and doesn't know any better.

"Dad can help you guys make things you might like to build."

"Now, you're talking, Tasha."

Together we came home with lumber. Pete wasn't satisfied with the first load. "James, why don't you come with me and get some more lumber?"

"It isn't ours to take, Pete. I'm not doing it, that's why I didn't go with you in the first place because I knew you would take that lumber if no one was looking."

"James, it is okay if you don't want to but let Pete get what he wants. All of that stuff is just going to be destroyed. You guys might just as well get some pleasure out of it."

"Okay, Mother, can Cam come with me?" Pete asked.

"If he wants to come with us he can."

"I think I'll just pass on that."

Off went Pete to see what he could find. James and Cam went off to play in their rooms, minding their own business. James wasn't about to be involved in the lumberyard heist, taking wood that didn't belong to him—in his mind it was nothing but a heist.

I sat in the living room within hearing range of Mother and Dad's conversation while at the same time thumbing through magazines and dreaming about toys that I couldn't have. It was fun to dream, though.

Dad turned to Mother while they were sitting in the kitchen over a cup of tea, "I'll bet they were bought off. Otherwise, the police would try to do something and would've been more receptive about getting the two men that ran from the fire."

"Surely, they get to collect a part of the insurance money because they've probably made a deal, so they're happy. We could have lost our lives and our home but that didn't matter to them. They made the money and here we sit poor as desert rats." Edgar said in total discuss.

"Just like the Communists in Russia, they do as they please. Oh, sure they say they are for the people, the poor people who have nothing. Their big ploy was to take from the rich and give to the poor. My family was the rich and they took everything but the poor didn't get anything but starvation. It was all words so they could pad their own pockets. They're doing the same thing here—take and put it into their own pockets. Total corruption, you can see that by how they weren't interested in the guys running from the fire. They call that justice?"

"I'm sorry, Tasha, but there is no justice in this world, you and I both know that."

Now was I beginning to observe a scheme for a ploy?

"If that's how they're playing the game, how about this, Edgar?

"What are you talking about?"

"We live in a haunted house and everyone believes it is, so let's use it to our advantage."

"Tasha, I don't believe you. I thought we were supposed to trust God in all of this, I don't get it. You're always the good person, trying to do the right thing. What happened?"

"Life isn't fair for us, is it?"

"I've always said that, but you down play it."

"Not this time, just give me a chance and I'll show you what I mean. It's that gray suit that gets me every time."

Chapter 20

Burst of Hot Rubber

Most of my days were spent convalescing at home trying to overcome Chicken Pox, Measles or a cold bug that would torment me until I couldn't breathe. The doctor said it was my bad set of lungs I just needed to live with. It was because of this that I was home schooled by my Mother who only spoke broken English. This made for arduous learning.

Mother and Dad had decided it was time that things just had to change. This time it was with extreme determination. Somehow, they were going to find a way. They had always seen the glistening of the rocks and wondered why no one would mine them. Maybe it was just missed. This particular day, Mother said, "Let's go to the sea shore and maybe you can play in the sand."

"What about my studies?"

"You've been doing very well, you'll be okay."

Doing very well was just a way of saying we needed to put the studies off and get doing more important things. Dad was home from his night shift and I could tell they had a plan they wanted to expedite. So off to the beach we went, it wasn't far from our home, only about a thirty-minute walk.

Usually, I would be watched closely but this time Mother had another plan, "Jenna, why don't you go play in the sand nearby, just over there? She motioned me to go to the designated spot, "Make sand castles and when you are finished, show them to us."

"Okay Mother, but it's no fun to play in the sand alone."

"Do it anyhow."

Off I went, struggling to walk through the sand. As I sat digging the sand with my bare hands until the water came to the surface, I looked over and saw what was happening. Dad and Mother were chiseling into the rocky surface, chipping away.

I came back, "What are you doing, Mother?"

"We're trying to dig the gold out of the rocks."

"I didn't know there was gold here."

"It looks like it to us. We are going to dig it out and then take it to the assayer's office to have it analyzed for gold content."

They worked hard while I sat there and watched. My energy level was fairly low but sitting outside at the seashore was nice. I'd often watch the tide g in and out. "Mother, I want to walk on that sand out to the water."

"We'd have to be careful, because when the tide comes in it comes fast. If we were out as far as you can see, we'd never make it back on time. Neither of us can swim so it wouldn't be a very wise thing to do."

"Dad, can you swim?"

"Oh, I could if I wanted to."

"Why don't you?"

"I'm always, working"

"Working too hard, right?"

"I have to. Have to keep food on the table. If this gold pans out to be real, maybe things will change."

"Jenna, I'm hoping you'll never have to worry about working for a living. That's why we are trying to see what we can get here."

Mother and Dad sent their findings to the assayer's office and within weeks the answer came back. Dad ripped open his letter and began reading, then turning to Mother, he said, "Looks as though what we found is called *fool's gold.* They're saying we haven't been the first to come across this shiny mineral in the rocks."

Since the gold didn't pan out to be anything, Mother said, "Let's go out to discover if we can buy land. There are some cheaper lots in the town next to ours. I understand the streets aren't paved and the sidewalks are wooden."

Saturday afternoon came and our entire family made the trolley ride to that next town.

"Cam, look the wooden sidewalks, aren't they cool?"

"Yeah. You can see through the slats right down to the mud."

James noticed, "It looks like they just graveled the streets, though."

Then Dad spoke up, "They do that to keep the dust down but you'll find that on the dirt roads they put oil down. That's also done to keep the dust down in the summer. The gravel keeps the roads from getting too muddy in the winter. You can see how the mud is under the sidewalks."

"Look at the shops. Are we going into Woolworths, Mother?"

"I think we could, Jenna."

"Can we buy something?"

"Yeah, can we buy a toy?"

"Okay, Cam, if I can find one that's cheap enough. Keep your hands in your pockets kids because I don't want to pay for anything you break."

"Okay, Mother," Cam and Jenna spoke in unison.

"But before we buy anything, let's sit at the counter and have an ice-cream cone. How would you like that?"

"Yeah, we sure would." All of us were excited to have such a treat, since it wasn't an everyday occurrence. After we finished our treats, we walked up and down the wooden sidewalks looking on both sides of the blocks. We walked toward the hills into the bushes but Mother wasn't settled on anything too rough. Hill climbing would limit her but she said nothing. Dad's eyes told us that he understood and then led us down to the flatter land.

"Look at this, here's a *For Sale* sign. It looks like it can be bought from the Municipality meaning it will be affordable so why don't we check this out, Tasha, it appears to be a large piece of land. The lots at each of the corners have already been sold and then past this piece of land it looks like houses are being built farther up the street. Mostly everything across the street is sold as well."

"Edgar, I think I like this. Which lot would you build our house on? Why not right in the middle. That way our neighbors won't be too close."

"Or, Tasha, we could build right next to the neighbor on our left where it's a little flatter, might be easier to put our house there. Then when we want to sell any of the lots off, we could do that."

"You're thinking, Edgar. That sounds wonderful. Let's check it out to see if we can buy it."

Mother and Dad found the land office, they were serious about the move. Within the next few days they the down payment to secure the land.

"Edgar, I wonder if we could move our house on this land?"

"Let's see if we can get permission."

Cam sputtered, "Mother, you're going to move all the ghosts with you then."

"Maybe they'll stay where they are. They wouldn't know what to do with themselves out in the country. Besides, I haven't seen my friend, Rosie since I told her to let me live my life."

A week went by before they heard anything but the day came when Dad opened a letter once again, he had anxiously been waiting for. "I'm sorry, Tasha. It seems as though every time we write a letter, it comes back negative. I give up."

"What's wrong, Edgar?"

"Our house is too tall to get under the power lines. They're saying it can't be done, so that means we have to sell it."

"Can we sell a haunted house?"

"Do you have to tell everyone?"

"No, I guess I wouldn't have to tell anyone. You have to admit it is fun to watch the surprised expression on people's faces and then when they hear the noises.

"More scared than surprised but you have to stop that, Tasha. We want to move out to our new place, don't we?"

"Okay, I promise."

I knew it would be nearly impossible for Mother to keep from telling people about our haunted house. She somehow loved it and that's why she wanted to keep it even though she knew it had to be sold. For some weird reason, she enjoyed the company of Ghosts. It seemed to allow her imagination to stretch beyond her difficult surroundings.

Soon Dad was at our property every night after work, building our new home. It was exciting to see the cornerstones laid and then the walls going up. Dad enjoyed himself to be able to finally build his dream house, or that's what it started out to be. One day a couple came strolling by and stopped to talk with Dad. "Sir, we see you are in the process of building your home."

"I am. I want to get it completed before winter sets in."

"We were wondering if you could build for us a one room house. Later, we will want to build a larger house on the property but for now that would get us moved here."

"You're willing to pay me for the job?"

"Yes, of course. We'll get all the lumber, just tell us how much and what we need—we just want you to build it. Would you do that for us?" He knew it would slow down the building of ours but the money was good.

"I suppose I could. Doesn't sound too complicated and I think I could complete that fast enough to still have time to finish ours. Like I said, I do charge for my work."

"We realized that. Come with us and we'll show you what we want. Then you tell us what to do."

Soon they were making plans on the size and type of wood. I watched Dad intently, how he drew up the plans for the land office to secure permits and inspections.

"Jenny, you've watched me draw up the plans for our house, how would you like to do that for this house?"

"You know, Dad, I would love that!" It was the most fun thing I had ever done. Now I was the *architect.* It wasn't long before Dad conscripted me to do his drawings for him on other projects and that excited me to no end.

Mother was busily cooking chili on an open fire. "Chili for lunch kids—how does that sound?"

"Wonderful, it could be my favorite."

"Hey, James, isn't this fun?"

"Yeah, just like we're camping out in our own backyard."

"You must admit, kids, it is large enough and do you see all our trees? It really is camping out. Only thing different we do is go home for the night, more like a *day camp.*"

Cam inquired, "I've never heard of a *day camp.* Why do you call it that, Dad?"

"It's because we go home at night to sleep in our real beds instead of sleeping in a tent."

Pete chimed in, "Why don't we pitch a tent and just stay here overnight? Look the work we would get done."

Mother answered, "Maybe we could make a makeshift tent. It gets too chilly, so I'd take Jenna home with me but the rest of you could if you wanted to."

James insisted, "I'll go home with Mother, but you guys, Pete and Cam, why don't you do that?"

————————————

The decision was made for them to pitch a makeshift tent. Blankets and thick branches cut from our trees made a nice warm tent.

"This is fun, Dad. How do you like it?"

"The ground is hard but we do have plenty of blankets to keep us warm."

"Cam and I'll make breakfast, Dad, so that you can just do the carpenter stuff, how's that?"

"I like that Pete. You kids will be my helpers."

Everyone was set to sleep with not a sound to be heard but a few crickets to break the silence. "What was that, Dad?"

Edgar awoke from his sound sleep. "It's just some wild animal howling, we'll be fine, just go back to sleep."

They weren't back to sleep more than thirty minutes when Pete woke to hearing voices. "Dad..."

"Please not now...we need to sleep, just go to sleep!"

"But don't you hear men's voices?"

Startled, Edgar sat up, now listening intently. "Shush. Don't make a sound, just listen."

Cam was scared, he couldn't say a word but Pete looked like he was about to defend all of them. "What're they saying Dad, can you understand them?"

"There going away...when I turned on this powerful flashlight, they left. Those guys were probably drinking up a storm, too drunk to know where they were. We should be okay now. Let's just go back to sleep."

Morning arrived none too soon. It wasn't long after breakfast that Tasha, Jenna and James arrived back with lunch ready to heat on the open fire.

————————————

"We are so glad you guys are here. We had all kinds of excitement last night."

"What happened, Pete?"

Pete told his story but it was more like an army converged on their camp. In his excitement and fear, life always became larger than life. Somehow, Mother and Dad understood and soon we were back to enjoying lunch.

Dad had already finished the neighbor's house a week earlier, now concentrating on building ours. "Tasha, I'm going to the lumberyard to order the rest of what we need to complete our house, should be back shortly."

When Dad came back, "Tasha, we are at a standstill. The Lumberyard just went out on strike. They're delivering everything I could get, but they're out of the lumber I needed for the windows and the floors of our house. That will slow us down now for sure."

"We needed the money when you built that couples' house and now we'll be spending the extra cash on the increased cost of lumber. We never can win, Edgar. Somehow we'll get through it all and maybe we can get rid of the huge stump in the back yard while we have to wait."

"How're we going to do that? Burn it? It must be five feet in diameter and it's so old nothing even grows on it anymore. It'll cost a fortune to have a backhoe pull it out. Maybe burning it would be the best thing to do."

"We should at least try burning."

"Okay, Tasha let me find tires and anything else that will burn. I'll throw kerosene on it."

Dad and Pete scoured the neighborhood to find all the rubber tires they could find. They told us they knocked at one door that had a police car parked in front.

––––––––––––

Pete asked, "Should we knock at this guys' door, Dad, it must be the home of a police officer?"

"He has a car, so for sure he'll have old tires around."

The door opened, and Dad couldn't believe his eyes, "You're the man that came to our house and…"

"I am. Do you live here now?"

"We do, just on the next block from here. Did you guys ever catch those people for burning the Lumberyard down?"

"No, but whatever happened to your house, did you sell it?"

"Are you kidding? It's haunted, remember? We're still trying to sell but my wife has to tell everyone it's haunted."

"Yeah, I remember. Actually, I was surprised your house didn't burn when the Lumberyard did, it was supposed to."

Pete spoke up, "Our house didn't burn because Dad pulled the breaker even though everyone yelled at him not to go back in the house. But, the Fire Marshall said he saved the entire neighborhood from burning down."

"So that's what happened. I wondered how it could've stayed standing with such a raging fire." Then George turned to Pete, "Here, why don't you take this tire and wait outside for us, I have something to show your Dad."

George looked at Edgar, "You know I could help you with your house?"

"Just how do you figure that?"

––––––––––––––––––

It didn't take too long before they had gathered enough tires for the fire to be set.

"Okay, everyone, get as far away from the fire as possible. Pete, James, Cam? Are you out of the way? I'm pouring on the kerosene and then I'll throw on the match."

Somehow, Cam couldn't move. He was too fascinated by the scene so he just stood there watching.

"Cam, move away, you are too close." By the time he heard me, it was too late. We heard the sound of a loud blast as it spewed out its venom of black rubber. All I could see was a splattering of hot rubber from the tires burst into the air, spitting bits of it onto Cam's face. "Mother, Dad…Cam is hit! He's blinded!"

Everyone came running, "Cam, are you all right? Can you see?"

"It hurts, it's sore but I can see."

"Thank God! You weren't supposed to be that close."

For hours Mother sat there soothing and washing the rubber off Cam's face. Bit by bit, Mother tried to erase the spots. Finally, it looked like Cam had a case of the chickenpox so Mother kept him home from school for the week so that she wouldn't have to explain to his teacher.

So much for remembering the stump that couldn't be removed, after a few weeks of hard work by Dad and a few more tires, Mother said, "I think we've been stumped! Let's put good planting soil around it and build a garden to enjoy the sight."

––––––––––––––––––

"Talk about being stumped, Tasha, when Pete and I were trying to get all the tires for the stump fire, you'll never guess who I ran into over at our Burnaby property?"

"Don't try to make me guess, Edgar."

"Remember the cop that came to take our report when we called about the Lumberyard fire? He lives just down the road from where we're building, actually a block west of us."

"Well, I'll be. Did they ever find those guys that started it?"

"No, but he told me something interesting, he said they wrote it out as being faulty wiring and said that our description was much too vague to include in the report."

"What was he thinking—I've got to go see that man! If he's not reporting that correctly, I'm going to give him a piece of my mind!"

"I don't think that's smart, Tasha, there's more to that story."

"Edgar, what are you talking about?"

Chapter 21

Smoke Screen

"Okay boys, you need to be quick or you'll never make it to school on time. You have a long walk ahead of you." This particular morning everything seemed to be hurried and more driven out of necessity.

"Don't worry Mother, if we run, we can make it in fifteen minutes."

"I don't want you to have to run all the way, just leave on time."

James remarked, "We're okay, we're all good at it, we always do it."

Somehow, Mother seemed preoccupied after the house was empty of everyone but her and me. Suddenly, she stood up, looking at me, and then insistent that I should wear my best dress. I was the little girl of the family, so I would always be dressed in a pretty red dress. "I thought we were going on a picnic, why would I dress up?"

"You look good in that dress and besides, I made it for you."

"Aren't we going to take sandwiches with us and have lunch in the park? Maybe we could feed the ducks in the pond or even the birds, Mother?"

"We're just going to go and walk around in the Park. At noon, we'll come home and have lunch."

Mother had planned the morning's excitement alright, her way of having a good time, was just to be sitting in the park to watch the birds, dogs and people. Mother hurriedly whisked me toward the front door, "Jenna, go out into the front yard and wait for me there--it's much too nice to wait in the house. I have the laundry to hang on the line in the back and then I'll be right out."

There wasn't a lawn in our front yard because Dad wasn't about to get involved in mowing grass but you couldn't say the yard was bare either. In fact, you couldn't find a weed even if you tried. There was a winding path through a beautiful flower garden that attracted butterflies, often bees and maybe even the odd humming bird.   It was warm but cool with a definite breeze this morning so I looked up into the sky knowing I could watch the fluffy white clouds flutter around. There were no rain clouds to be seen, but it wouldn't be uncommon for them to blow in as though on a sudden request from God. I reached toward the sky to catch a butterfly, knowing full well it could never happen without a net.

Ordinarily, on a bright and sunny day like this, I'd be glad for the break from studying yet instead, my thoughts were distracting me. Nothing made any sense. There was an odd strange feeling I couldn't dismiss. Why was my mind questioning this morning's outing? Maybe I felt conflicted because I wished I could be like every other child and be in school. No, that just wasn't it, I knew that for certain. Shouldn't I be writing my lessons instead of the planned park event with my Mother? It was a no brainer for me, by evening I'd have that same old problem with my breathing and then I couldn't do anything. By all implications, I should be reading and writing like I did every other day, not planning a trip to the park. Something just wasn't right.

Amid the spring air, the flowers were blossoming with all the colors of the rainbow and between sneezes, it was still very beautiful. The bright red poppy flowers, the pansies, even the tulips stood straight up and I just knew they could feel the soft breeze and warm sun just like I could. Even the spring roses, my favorite, were in full bloom. It was simply a pleasant spring morning. So why do I have this feeling?

The front door opened but instead of seeing Mother, I saw a stranger come out. I froze in my steps, trembling as he walked toward me. He was a man in a grey suit, holding about three volumes of books under his right arm against his body. Now there was no question, he was coming my way. All I could think was that Mother was supposed to be alone in our house so who was this man? He approached me mumbling sounds that I supposed were words, yet unidentifiable as a language…it just wasn't making any sense. For a moment, I thought, is he foreign? I was just a wee bit familiar with English, Dutch and German but what this man spoke resembled absolutely nothing.

Suddenly the man turned, stepping to my left making his way through our front gate toward the road. I gave a deep sigh of relief as my eyes followed him walking toward town. Again, I noticed that ugly gray suit. Now I could see plainly the color of the books, red, yellow and gray. I wanted to say I had just looked at the yellow one with Pete, last evening. Surely, I recognized it from Pete's collection. My mind reasoned that logically the man must have come in the back door. Mother must have allowed him to come through the house and out the front for whatever reason she had.   Now I stood motionless, my body refused to move for the moment. When I came to my senses, I ran the few steps to the house facing the door as it opened again but now Mother stood there.

"Are you ready to go, Jenna?"

"Who was that man, Mother?" Mother had to have seen the fear in my eyes for she made every effort to distract me. "What man?"

"A man came out of our front door just before you came."

"What did he look like, Jenna?"

"He wore a gray suit and had a stack of books under his arm. What was he saying to me? Did he come in from the back door and you let him out the front?"

"I don't know what you are talking about. There was no one with me in the house and all I did was to hang the laundry on the line." She made no hesitation to say, "It must have been a ghost."

"The man didn't look to me as though he wasn't real. I even watched him walk away toward town and if it was a ghost he would've disappeared into thin air."

"Jenna, there wasn't anyone in the house with me and you know this house is haunted."

I knew I needed to be submissive to my mother so I conceded, "If you say so, but I never see any of the stuff you guys always talk about."

"You saw the telephone dial turn itself, didn't you?"

"I guess I did see that. But that's all I ever saw."

Changing the subject Mother said, "Let's go to the park while it is still nice. We never know when it will rain and then we'll be stuck inside."

Walking slowly toward the park, mother kept looking back as though she saw something I couldn't see. I guessed I would have to *chalk-it-up* to another very odd day. To me everything was too weird— the odd seeming normal and the normal looking odd. Who could know the truth anymore?

Hard times were everywhere for us. It wasn't really that long ago since Tim died and then Grandpa. Mother said Grandpa died of old age.

Then for refuge, my thoughts started reminiscing as I remembered a few days ago a hobo dropped by and my parents invited him in to join us at dinner.

"Someone's knocking at the back door, Mother. Can I answer it?"

"No, Jenna, let me check. No one ever comes to the back door. I wonder who it is?"

Mother opened the door, I saw a man dressed in tattered clothing from head to foot and then heard him say, "Ma'am, do you have any food to spare?"

"Yes, of course. Wait here, I'll get my husband."

Mother closed the door, and went into the living room, "Edgar, there's a Hobo at the back door, hungry. Do you mind if he joins us for dinner?"

"Do we have enough food for all of us, Tasha?"

"We can make do. The Hobo will be hungry and we always have food. May not be plenty, but we do get to eat."

"Surely, let's do that, then."

Money and food were always short for us, yet, we would gladly feed just one more person even if we barely had enough for our own family. My parents never refused to give food to anyone who was hungry. "God will take care of us," always quietly said. It wasn't at all unusual to see hungry people, probably because the trains ran down the rails just a few yards behind our house, between our house and the burned down Lumberyard. The hobos were always honestly hungry, yet, they never lingered or even made a nuisance of themselves—they just joined us for food and then went on their way like they had some other place to go.

Here I was in the reality zone, as we were walking toward the park and Mother was still totally absorbed in looking behind us but by now with intensity. Again, she turned toward the direction of our house yet neither of us could see anything. Finally, we sat on the park bench when Mother asked me, "Jenna, can you see anything coming from our house?"

"No, Mother, I don't. What am I supposed to see?"

"I just keep thinking something is wrong."

"What could be wrong, Mother?"

"I don't want you to worry, just play a little more before we have to go home."

I thought to myself, play with what? I just sat there beside Mother realizing she was too absorbed with what she seemed to be worrying about. If I was to play, I'd have to go to the other end of the field where the swings and slides were. Without the energy to suggest going there and knowing full well, under normal circumstances, Mother would have suggested it herself, I resigned myself to just sit and watch people with their dogs come and go.

A half hour had gone by when Mother said, "Let's go home. I'll make lunch and then we can get back to your lessons." Nearing the house, "I really smell smoke, don't you, Jenna?"

"No, and I can't see anything either."

We were at the gate when Mother said it again, "I smell smoke, you stay outside while I go in and check to see if everything is okay."

I still couldn't see any smoke. "You can't do that! I'm coming in with you." All I could think was if there really was a fire, no way should Mother go in there—we should be calling the firemen instead!

"No, I'll only be a minute, you have to stay outside."

I couldn't be stopped, I had to follow. I couldn't be without my mother if something should happen to her so I ran into the kitchen after her. Following my mother's gaze to the floor by the coal and wood stove, I was horrified as I looked down to see a small patch of ashes. It looked to have been a smoldering fire that couldn't gather enough fuel to start for real. When Mother realized, I was staring at the spot, she said, "Jenna, you can't say anything about this to anyone! Do you hear me? No one can know about this." Then as if she thought I might have figured something out, she said, "I'll never do that again." Then one more time, "Jenna, you can tell no one what happened here!"

Oh, God, please help me to forget what I'm supposed to forget. I'm just a kid and I'm supposed to forget this. Please erase this, Dear God, from my mind.

"Jenna, that man you saw this morning? You have to believe that he was a ghost. So, when we talk about it tonight, you will say you saw a ghost. You believe he was a ghost, don't you? We hear and see things all the time in this house because it's haunted."

I was getting the picture from Mother's insistence, "Okay, he was a ghost but where did he get those books? Were they ours from upstairs? You know how Pete likes his old books—I'll bet they were valuable."

Mother ignored me and soon we were back to my lessons making every effort to concentrate. Since Mother couldn't read English very well, teaching me was almost impossible so somehow, I had to teach myself most of the time.

"Mother do I have to copy these lessons? Can't you just read them to me?"

"You know I can't read well enough but if you keep copying you'll eventually get it. You are doing better than you think. You've already written a couple of letters to the school. You do very well and even the school thinks so."

"It takes me hours to write one letter."

"Keep it up Jenna, that's how you'll learn."

This time it was especially hard since there was no amount of concentrating possible. I just had to keep my thoughts in check and do and say as Mother had asked me to. Indeed, if this was an endurance test, I was learning at least that.

It wasn't long before my brothers were all home from school. Mother was busying herself in the kitchen with Pete helping with supper preparations.   When we finally were at the table together, I could see Mother's gaze as she made sure the conversation was turned to me.

"Tell everyone, Jenna, what you saw today," Mother turned looking at Dad, "she saw another ghost, would you believe? Tell them what he looked like, Jenna, and what he said."

My whole being went cold for a moment as I tried to give the answer as instructed, "I don't know," Mother's face was beginning to turn white, so I continued to relate the story as instructed, "I told Mother that a man came out of the front door wearing a grey suit packing a couple of books under his arms. He said some words to me that I couldn't even begin to recognize."

Pete asked, "Did it sound like Dutch or German?"

"Nothing like what Mother and Dad speak. I guess he was a ghost. Like all of you say, this is a haunted house we live in."

"You said he was carrying books, why would a ghost need to carry anything?" piped up James, "We had some old books upstairs, aren't they yours, Pete? I'll bet he stole them!"

"How could a ghost steal?" asked Cam. "Isn't this a haunted house?"

"But he took them with him," James insisted, "I'll bet we could figure out if he stole them, all we would have to do is check to see if any of ours are missing." It almost was like James didn't believe anything about ghosts, either.

Then Pete said, "Wasn't one of the guys that ran from the fire in a grey suit? Remember, I said, why would he dress up anyhow?"

Both, Dad and Mother kept silent, so I asked, "When Tim was alive, did he ever see any ghosts here?"

"Don't remember, I'm sure he did," Mother insisted, "I told him about the vision I get every so often at night," Mother began relating the tale one more time but it was no longer the *dream* she had, now she called it a *vision*. "You remember the lady that comes to my bedside at night and just stands there until I tell her to go away?"

Cam wrinkled his nose, "Why does she come to visit you Mother, what does she want from you?"

"She says she likes being with me. Then I tell her to go away and let me live my life."

Pete asked, "Dad, does that lady ever come see you?"

"No. I'm probably not interested enough in that Spiritualism stuff. It doesn't make a lot of sense. I've only heard noises like the rest of you but I'm not into Ghosts much."

Pete had a quizzical look on his face, "Are you saying if we don't entertain them, they don't come to us?"

"Ask your Mother."

Mother responded, "I don't ask them to come to me but I am interested. I want to know all I can and if there are ghosts I want to know about them. I want to know why they are here. But they can't deceive me, I know what I believe. I believe in God but I know the spirit world is for real also."

Then Edgar answered, "Let's not go there, Mother. It may be easy for you to tell right spirits from wrong ones, but unless you really know what you're doing..."

"I think I know what I'm doing but you kids don't need to go there, Dad's right. Let me work this stuff out for myself."

"Okay, boys, you know who washes the dishes tonight, so let's do it."

"How come Jenna never has to do anything, Mother?" asked James.

"She's too young and if you want her to do it, you have to pay her from your allowance."

"Oh, let me do it, I like doing dishes," begged Jenna.

"I'm not giving her my hard-earned money," complained James.

"Then do your job. You get an allowance, she doesn't."

We seemed to squabble from time to time, who should do this and who should do that. Probably normal for siblings but these ghost sightings still didn't make any sense, even though I needed to do what I was told.

Chapter 22

Hope is on the Way

It had been days since I was up and around to work on my lessons. I worried that I would get too far behind since it took me hours just to compose one letter, one word at a time. There had to be an easier way to do the learning. Mother couldn't read to me since she had a language barrier. Yet, seeing the words I was working on day after day made them familiar to me.   I wished over and over again, if only I had a real teacher. Dad could've done it for me but he was always too busy trying to build our house and work a full-time job, all at the same time.

In between the learning, it was very common for me to wake up, unable to breathe. Here I go again, trying desperately to rest. Mother tried to offer me food but breathing seemed more important.

"Jenna, you have to eat, try something."

"Do you have any fruit?"

"I have bananas."

"Peaches, pears, even raisins would be good, Mother."

"We haven't been able to get raisins for a long time. Maybe I can get canned peaches, would you like that?"

"Fresh would be better, but at least, I'd like some fruit."

"Here try these."

Mother handed me a bowl of peaches. Slowly, but mouthful by mouthful I would eat. It helped but I was still very weak. Sometimes it was too hard to lift my head off my pillow.

"Sit up for a bit, Jenna."

"I get dizzy when I sit up."

"That's because you've been lying in bed too long. Try to sit up, here I'll prop you with the pillows, how's that feel?"

"Easier, I like it but I'm so tired."

"Of course, you are, just rest."

It seemed like Mother and Dad were beginning to make plans for my soon departure from life. Instead of lying in bed, I was moved to the sofa where I could more easily be propped up and tended to.

––––––––––––––––––

"Edgar, I don't think Jenna will be with us much longer, but I'm going to run over to Safeway and see what kind of fresh fruit I can buy. That seems to be her last wish, so I need to try very hard. Sometimes, getting what you really want can make the difference between life and death."

"I can go for you if you like. It's almost a mile just one way."

"I need the break and maybe being alone for just a bit will help me."

So off on the trek to buy fruit, Tasha kept thinking about how hard she had been trying all these years to keep her daughter alive and now she had to give her back to God.

"God, what do you want from me? You know my children mean everything to me. I've promised I would raise them as Christians but somehow that isn't enough, what do you want?"

It seemed God would be quiet for a time. Tasha made her way into the grocery store, looking and touching fruit, trying to remember what Jenna had last requested.

"Ma'am, can I help you?"

"What kind of fresh fruit is in season today?"

"You can buy California grapes. The ones grown locally can be a bit sour to the taste. Then there's always bananas..."

"No bananas. My daughter is tired of bananas. I've been giving those to her in place of ice cream and she just doesn't want that anymore."

"Don't think I blame her, Ma'am, but how about peaches? They seem to be good and juicy."

"Give me a couple of pounds of the green grapes and peaches. I'll see if that will work."

Then Tasha headed for home when she noticed a church building with the front door ajar. 'Well, maybe I'll go in there for a moment. Maybe pray, I'll keep my thoughts together and maybe God will tell me what to do.' Tasha entered through the large doors, seeing that there were others praying. She made her way to the front and knelt at the cross, hesitating and then praying aloud, she said, "Please, God, talk to me." It was at least five minutes, when finally, Tasha felt a hand on her shoulder. She turned to look up but there was no one there. "Is that you, Lord?"

Then a still small voice whispered to her heart, *"…the very hairs of your head are all numbered. Fear not, therefore; ye are of more value than many sparrows …. Come unto me, all ye that labor and are heavy laden, and I will give you rest. Take my yoke upon you, and learn of me; …ye shall find rest unto your souls. For my yoke is easy, and my burden is light."* Then He said, "Trust me, Tasha, I care, I will take care of you and Jenna. Go in peace."

Tasha stood up and made her way out of the church feeling rested inside; knowing Jesus was in control, whether He was taking Jenna home or making her well.

Edgar met Tasha at the door. "What's wrong, Edgar?"

"Jenna seems more out of it than in it, if you know what I mean. She doesn't stir much and I can't hear the raspy breathing anymore."

"Let me try, hi Jenna, I brought you some fruit. You wanted peaches and I was able to find some, so let's sit up and I'll get a bowl so you can eat."

I opened my eyes only to hear Mother continue, "Let me help you sit up. I'll prop you up so you can eat this fruit. I even found some sweet grapes, what do you think?"

I whispered, "I'd like that."

I smiled weakly, but piece by piece I swallowed the fruit, attempting to sit in an upright position. Soon I would be lying down again though it was tiring to lie there day after day, but sitting up made me dizzy. Soon, I felt a peaceful sleep come upon me.

Tasha was surprised by the doorbell, making her way to answer it. "Oh, come in, I didn't expect anyone."

They stood at the entrance of Jenna's room and lamented with Tasha showing her empathy for all the suffering she had been enduring.

"We've come to see how Jenna is, Tasha. Is she any better? Can we talk with her?"

"She's resting now, I think she's asleep. You can see her from here."

"What does your doctor say, can't he do anything?"

"No, I've called him but he wanted to give me more of the same and all that just makes her worse."

Suddenly I awakened but froze as I realized Mother assumed I was asleep or at least not conscience, and then I heard her say to her friends, "I decided to release her to God. There is nothing anyone can do for her and God only knows I can't do anything anymore. I've been praying that God would let her die so that she wouldn't have to suffer anymore."

"Tasha, I'm surprise to hear you say that. You've clung on to her all this time and now you're giving her back to God?"

"I've tried everything I was convinced would make her well. None of that is enough so I can't do anything anymore. She just suffers day after day. I want God to take her out of this miserable suffering, she doesn't need this world anyhow, and it isn't always the nicest place to be."

"You must be exhausted or you wouldn't be talking like that. We'll pray for you Tasha, so you can accept whatever God wishes to give you. You know God has a plan for her and you."

"Thanks, and I guess I need you to pray, I don't know how we will get through what God's will is for us. We try to prepare ourselves just as we tried with the other two children but it isn't really possible. It just doesn't get any easier. Why don't you come into the kitchen and I'll make a cup of tea for us?"

"We can't stay and I don't think you need the extra work, Tasha. Rest if you can because God has your answer and it's coming for you soon."

"Thank you, Mary. Actually, thank you both for coming to visit. I appreciate it very much."

The ladies left and I prayed silently hoping God could hear me, "Oh, God, please don't let me die, that can't be what you want for me. At least don't let me die until I can come to know you. You have to let me live and if you do, I promise when I get better and can learn to know who you are, I will. I've got to have that chance. I'm not a perfect person.

How can I be good enough for you? I just want the privilege to live, God."

Everyone had left the house when Mother decided to wake me. "Come, Jenna. I'm going to get you dressed in your best dress."

"But, Mother, I'm so tired. Why do I have to get up?"

"It'll be good for you and I want to take some pictures. You've always been so sick that I don't have many pictures. I never took many pictures of your sister before she died and not even Tim. I need some pictures of you. Here let me help you get dressed."

I had just heard that Mother had decided I would die. She didn't have many pictures of me but she wanted a few before she gave me back to God to take home. Mother struggled to dress me and I did feel pretty in the black dress with white dots. It was one of my favorite. Mother sat me on the sofa chair and started snapping pictures.

I hung on to the arms of the chair trying to sit up. "I'm tired, Mother and I'm dizzy, just a bit dizzy." Mother was still taking more pictures but soon Mother realized I was too tired to stay sitting. She laid me back on the bed so that I could rest. Then she tried again, "Just a few more, Jenna. Okay, smile. Good, that'll be a good one for my album."

"There, I'll put pillows behind you so you can sit in bed. It'll be better to sit. Laying all the time makes it hard for you to breath and it makes you dizzy. I think you breathe better sitting up, don't you?"

"It does feel a lot better and it feels good to be dressed up, Mother. It did help me."

Before long, Mother put me back into bed seeing I was exhausted from the picture taking feat she had attempted. I dozed off only to be awakened by hearing Mother on the phone to the doctor. I heard her say, "Something new? But every time I try to give her the pills, she throws them up. That can't be good. Well, I don't know what to do. You say you can give her a shot instead of the pills? I just don't know what to do. I'll let you know if I think I should try that again." And then she hung up the phone and just looked at me.

The night was hard as Mother continued to rock me on her lap. The next morning, I was half dozing again when there was a knock at the door. Mother answered it to find our familiar Fuller Brush man selling his wares. He looked over into the living room to where I was laying and asked, "I see you have a sick child?"

"I do. She has Asthma and the doctors don't know what to do to make her well."

"You say she has Asthma? In my going from door to door, I have seen many families with sick children and even adults who have problems breathing. In choosing products to sell, one day I came across a medicine that doctors recommend. It's being advertised as a guarantee for people with Asthma. I've sold it now, probably to ten different families and each of them has reported enormous improvement. Every time I go back to those homes, they tell me the good news. The adults have been able to return to work and the children were able to go back to school."

"What is it?" Mother asked.

"It's a solution that is put into a pump." The salesman opened his suite case on our staircase in the hallway, to show Mother what it was he was about. He pulled out a small bottle with medicine. "You have to pour just a drop into this pump and then the patient just breaths the mist it gives, see?" he pumped it once or twice so that she could see the mist. "The patient has to inhale the mist. Like I said, I now sell it and guarantee that if you let her breathe this stuff, she'll be up and around in a day. I can even sell this pump you have to use with it."

"Guaranteed? Are you sure?"

"I am sure. It has worked well for a lot of people who have used it. When you need more, you can even buy it at the local drugstore. You don't even have to wait for me to come to your house."

"It sounds like what the doctor was saying to me but I didn't believe him. The doctor has told me so many things I should and shouldn't do that I didn't think it was possible to have something new that could work. It's worth a try; let me buy it from you."

"You'll see—it will work."

Mother bought the medicine and closed the door behind her.

"Okay Jenna, I want you to sit up for a minute. Okay, here, the guy said you just have to breathe this stuff. Let's try it."

I did as the Fuller brush man had instructed and just like he said, within minutes, I was beginning to breathe well.

"I'm hungry Mother."

Mother was so happy to hear those words, "Of course, let's have lunch."

This was only the beginning for me. Instead of keeping food from me that might not be good, it had become open season for whatever I could eat. If it was there and I was hungry, Mother wanted me to eat. She was anxious for me to become strong and healthy.

Now I was interested in the events for the future. I wanted to go back to our new property and watch Dad continue to build our new house. I enjoyed seeing the foundation blocks being set into the ground. The framed walls going up and the boards being nailed to the two-by-fours and after that the tar paper that was to be nailed down before the siding would go over that.

Dad said, "We have to wait until the strike is over before we can buy the siding for the house."

"I really hope it will be over soon, Edgar."

"I think I've got all the windows to go in the house, Tasha. That'll help a lot."

Saturday rolled around again, so as a family we headed out together to work on our new house. It amazed me, how Dad could figure out how to put it all together. We'd sit at lunch together, waiting for the milk man to come by with his horse pulling the carriage to bring everyone fresh milk. Home delivery every day was a way of life even though we were a little way from the big city.

It didn't take very long before I was up and around. "Thank you, God, but who can show me the way?"

Chapter 23

The Rooster Sacrifice

I could feel it in the air that we were planning for the inevitable move as soon as Dad and Mother had their preparations completed. This morning sitting around the table, Mother started talking, "Before we move all our stuff from this old house we have to get everything ready to go. We don't yet have a barn for the chickens so we'll be canning the chickens we have."

James jumped in, "You can't kill my pet rooster!"

Pete said, "I have a pet rooster, too. You can't kill mine for food!"

"Okay, okay," Mother tried to calm the two boys, "you can each keep your favorite chicken. But the rest we need to can for the winter. We don't know if we'll have enough food for all of us unless we do that."

"I for one am glad you're going to cook them. They're always trying to bite me when you send me to the shed for eggs."

"Stop it Cam," James argued, "It's because you don't talk to them. You first have to call them by name and then go about collecting eggs."

Mother ignored the personal chicken conversation, "It's settled then, Dad will kill the other chickens and you guys can help me pluck them while I start to do the canning."

Mother brought out the big vats and began pouring in the scalding water. "The water's hot, we could burn ourselves."

"Just be very careful and grab the legs, Pete, then start plucking the feathers. Put the soft feathers in the paper bag on the right and rough big ones in that paper box because we will keep emptying that one into the garbage."

"What are you keeping the soft feathers for, Mother?"

"That's the stuffing for your pillows."

I counted ten chickens before Mother said, "Okay, we need to burn the fuzz off these and then we can clean them up for canning."

"How're you going to do that?"

"Watch me, Pete. I roll up a bit of paper then light a match and scorch each of the chickens."

"Can I do that for you?"

"I think it might be best I do it, Pete. I don't want to burn the house down. I always do it over the sink so that I can douse the flame with water if I have to." After the tenth chicken, Mother invited us to help her in cutting the chickens open and cleaning the insides.

"Mother, let me do that."

"You have to be really careful not to pull too hard Pete, don't let anything burst open."

Pete loved pulling the insides out keeping only the heart, gizzard and liver from each of the chickens. "That's the stuff we use for flavoring when I roast these chickens."

"I hate the liver."

"Come on, Cam, that's good for you!"

"I like the heart and the gizzards."

"You would, Jenna, that's the best part of a chicken but there's just never enough to go around."

"I'm not eating any of these chickens."

"James, don't say that. When you get hungry, you'll want to eat them. We didn't kill your pet roosters, so you can eat these."

"The idea sickens me"

"James, get a grip. I wouldn't eat our pet roosters but after all, chickens are for us to eat. That's why God gave us these birds, isn't it Mother?"

"You're right, Pete, that's why God gave us animals, they're food for our families."

"I can't stand the smell of wet feathers, and the guts…ugh!"

"That wasn't all you smell, Jenna, you can smell the …" But Cam wasn't going to be allowed to finish his sentence when James said, "Stop that! We all know what everything smells like, so just stop it!"

Mother ignored the comments and just simply said, "Thanks, kids for helping with the canning. I think we canned plenty for the winter, so we should be just fine."

"Ten at a time, and we've finished already?"

"See how time flies, Pete? Did you enjoy that?"

"Yeah, kind of, and now we know how it all fits together."

It had been the norm for us to bus our way to our Burnaby property where Dad and my brothers would continue to work on our house almost every evening and on weekends. Summer would soon come to a close and our house needed to be complete before the school year started in the fall and it wasn't that many weeks away. However, today Dad said he was a little tired but promised to resume building the coming Monday evening. We were about to settle in for another boring evening when, Dad announced, "Since we're not going over to the property tonight we're all going to go for a walk. I'm going to check the shed and make sure the roosters can't get out for the night and then I'll be back. If everyone could be ready, we'll head out and be on our way."

"But Dad, I don't want to go."

Dad stood his ground, insisting, "Cam, we need to do it one more time before our big move. We've been walking together for years, so tonight's the night to do it again."

"Oh, come on Cam, stop the grumbling, I like walking, it should be fun."

"Jenna, you think everything is fun. I wanted to play with my cars, do we have to go?"

Before the other boys could say anything, Dad answered, "We haven't done it for a while because we've been trying to build our new home but Mother wants to walk tonight."

"Why don't you let me stay home? I'm old enough."

Then Mother spoke up, "No James, we always do this as a family and the doctor told me I needed to do all the walking now because the day will come when I won't be able to walk anymore. Today, I feel I'd like to do that and want our whole family together."

"On the way back, can stop for ice cream?" pleaded Cam.

"Dad, do I get to have ice cream too?" Ice cream would be a break from a banana in a cone as a substitute. Sometimes anything *cold* would make it difficult for me to breathe.

"It's warm enough, what do you say, Tasha?"

"Sure, why not. Jenna's been doing well so once shouldn't hurt."

Without any further discussion, Dad left for the backyard and within about ten minutes he was back.

"Let's go, guys." As I looked at him, I could see he wanted us to move out fast. He started pushing us toward the door. "Come on kids, let's go."

"But I want to work on building something with all that lumber we have, Dad."

"Pete, you can do that later, I'll even help you with it when we get back."

"Can't I stay at home and listen to the boxing match on the radio? I don't need to come walking with all of you. I'm older so can't I stay at home?"

"No James, I already told you we're going together, we just discussed all that and I said we want to walk as a family. Like I said before, the doctor says that I need to walk now since I have so much trouble with my knees. He really doesn't think I'll be able to do this much longer."

I thought to myself, Mother is almost talking like this is her last wish. Does that mean she's dying or she just won't be able to walk? I think I better just let the family problems take care of themselves. Mother will do whatever, no matter what.

"Come on kids, we're going to do this as a family. Mother likes walking and it's good for the rest of us. I want all of you to come with us and we need to leave right now." There was that urgency again, becoming even more definite in Dad's voice but it puzzled me in spite of the thought of the ice cream I would get to enjoy for the first time in years.

"I was working on something in the backyard, let me just put it aside and then I'll join you."

"No, Pete, it can wait. I promise I'll help you with whatever you're doing later."

We proceeded as Dad started pushing us out the front door. At first the walk was quick and brisk. I couldn't believe how well Mother did considering we probably walked a good five blocks in just a short time. "Aren't you tired, Mother? We're walking fast even for me."

Then Dad spoke up, "Okay, we're going too fast for Mother and Jenna. Let's slow down a bit."

James asked, "How far are we walking today anyhow?"

It was an incredibly nice *Indian summer* evening, cool and pleasantly warm.

"Are we buying our ice cream at our corner store or away out here so we can eat it on the way home?"

"Pete, why don't we wait until we get to our store next to our house, on the way back, then we'll really be able to enjoy it."

Walking for our family wasn't unusual but the hurry I sensed had me wondering, still, if I could have ice cream, I wasn't going to look *a gift horse in the mouth*, since the privilege had been handed to me, nothing else mattered.

Nathan was about to settle into his arm chair, sitting next to his radio, thinking he would have a nice relaxing evening, soon to succumb to his much-needed sleep. Turning his head to take one last look out of his living room window, he jumped to his feet, realizing there was a burst of smoke followed by flames. He turned from his easy chair, grabbing his phone to dial the fire department. "I need to report a fire just across the street from me…yes, on Third Avenue, south of where the Lumberyard was before it burned to the ground." He hung up the phone and ran out of his house, as the neighbors began to converge around the area, "Does anyone know if the Nedders are at home?" Nathan ran to the front door rapping as loud as possible but there was no answer.

Another nearby neighbor responded, "I think they might've walked up the street. I often see them walking as a family, and if my memory serves me right, they were together."

"Oh, thank God! That's the last thing they need to have something happen to any of them. The Lord only knows that they've had plenty of other problems, with the health of their children."

Moments later, the Fire Trucks arrived and began hosing down the shed as the flames continued to grow ever brighter.

"Hey, Tom, you saw the kids with their parents, right?" Nathan asked one of the neighborhood kids.

"Yeah, they were all together and I think Pete told me they were on their usual walk for the evening."

"Go run after them and let them know what just happened. They need to be here."

Tom was a good runner, the star athlete of his school track team and it wasn't long before he reached the family who were now looking into store windows enjoying the pleasant evening air.

We turned to look from where the shouting was coming from, "Your shed is on fire—your shed is on fire! The flames are burning high and it might even be at your house by now."

"Mother, that's Tom, he's shouting at us! That has to be our shed he's talking about."

I could tell Tom was totally exhausted by the time he had reached us with the news. Pete was about to run on ahead with Tom when Mother said, "It's okay. The firemen will be there and will take care of it. I don't want you near it, so just stay with us. We'll get there soon enough."

"But our roosters are in there, they'll die—my pet rooster will die!"

"James, it's okay. If any of the roosters can be saved the firemen will do it. You can't do anything about it. Just stay with us, we'll get there soon enough!"

"You have to let James and me run over there, maybe we can save something. I know you can't hurry, but let us run," begged Pete. "I have those boards in the backyard I was going to work on."

"No, you need to do what Mother says. We can't risk you guys getting hurt," and when Dad had spoken, that was the end of the subject.

I just knew we were now walking even slower, something wasn't right. When I anxiously looked at Mother, she said, "I can't walk any faster, my knees hurt now."

As we got closer to our house, all we could see was the smoke rising up into the atmosphere. Just when it looked up came one last vicious flame that was immediately doused.   Finally, we stood in the alleyway beside our shed, staring at the ashes on the ground. Pete ran to the back of the house anxiously checking to see if any of his lumber was still intact. Dad stood there speaking with the firemen as they checked for live embers. "Sorry, we lost your chickens."

James asked, "Sir, how did the fire even get started—who set the fire?"

"We can't tell how the fire got started though maybe it was a short in the wiring, since I can see the shed had been wired for electricity." The fireman continued to talk, "With these old sheds, you never can tell but at least it didn't spread to your house. Your neighbor called us when he saw the smoke, that's what saved the day." Looking to Dad, he continued, "I would've felt bad if your house had burned because then you'd be homeless with all your kids. You know it's not easy to find another home for the size of your family and it can take months for the insurance to pay."

I looked at my parents, thinking, oh God, they are disappointed! I dared not say a word—I knew something must have gone wrong according to them. If the fire had burned the house down, they would only have the land to sell and how could land alone be more valuable than the house on the land? Nothing made sense anymore, so I said, God, help me forget, I'm just a kid and I don't need to understand.

The firemen were now gone but it all felt too strange. I just couldn't remember that we had electric lights in the shed for the chickens, although it was a splendid idea for the winter when darkness came early. That had to be why Dad had wired it, how thoughtful of him. I hadn't remembered anyone talking about electricity. I just had to ask, "Mother, I didn't know we had electricity in the shed."

"Jenna's right, we didn't have electricity in the shed. I always had to use a flashlight."

"Pete, let's not get into that now."

Pete was never in the habit of letting anything go until he understood. "But the fireman said he saw it was wired for electricity and that's why the shed burned down."

Mother pulled Pete away and out of ear shot.

"Pete, I need you to promise not to talk about the electricity in the shed. Just don't make anything out of this situation, leave it alone."

"But, Mother, we lost our pet Roosters—James and I, lost our pet Roosters!"

"But Pete, that's all we lost. We already took care of the other chickens before—you remember we canned the meat."

"So that's what you did and because James and I begged you not to kill our pet roosters, you didn't but then…"

"Pete, you must hear me out. You must never talk to anyone about this!"

Soon they were back with the rest of the family, but I could see the tears in his eyes and then I looked at Mother as I heard him say to her, "Okay, Mother, I promise."

The incident was soon out of my mind as we were too busy now to reminisce. We needed to get our packing done knowing that our move to our new property in Burnaby was eminent. I was in reasonably good health, looking forward to attending a real school with other kids in our neighborhood.

"Okay, kids, today is the day when we pack everything we own. We've hired a moving van that will be here shortly. I think Mother has all the good stuff packed already so it shouldn't take long to put everything in the van. When we're done, we'll go on ahead and the van should be there a few hours after us. That way we don't have any down time.

"But, Dad, the new house isn't ready," Pete pleaded.

"We need to move so that we can relocate you kids in the new school district because I know how hard it will be if we don't."

"That means I get to finally go to school!"

"It sure does."

"That also means you have to buy me new shoes just like the other kids."

"You're right. Now that you aren't sick anymore, you'll want to play with everyone else."

"But, Dad, what're we going to do for walls? All we have is two-by-fours and shiplap on the outside walls."

"Pete, I told you, everything will be okay. I'm going to tar paper the walls, put the *gyp-rock* up for our room and we should be okay. You'll all have your privacy at night. I can build around us when we are there. Actually, it will be easier because I won't have to go from work to the new house then back home for rest. It will save us a lot of time and my work location is also closer to our new home."

Too busy to worry about all the details, we packed everything we could. "Just throw your garbage in the rooms and we'll clean up later," Dad summoned.

Throwing our garbage in the rooms to clean up later, made no sense to me at all because Mother was the cleanest person on earth. In the past, not even we would get away with that. Come to think of it, when we moved from the Prairies to Vancouver, we not only kept things neat but we scrubbed the house from top to bottom. I suppose things just don't always have to make sense anymore.

Chapter 24

The Strangers

"Hey, Mother, it's snowing!"

"I know and we're hoping it will stop soon. To me it doesn't look like it can last, it's just not cold enough out. You can see the clouds beginning to clear up so it might even be sunny soon, Jenna."

"Oh, Mother, I like snow and I want it to last."

Snow had come early this year with the promise of a cold, hard winter bearing down on us and here we were in an unfinished house. Night time temperatures were beginning to reach into the lower 30 degrees Fahrenheit. Dad had nailed the shiplap over the heavy tar paper with insulation stuffed between the two-by-fours. The inside floors were made of plywood covered with a scattering of throw rugs. Mother had already completed curtains for each of the windows to keep the house warmer. The stove in the kitchen was stoked up, burning day and night. While we were in the living room, Dad had placed two three foot kerosene heaters, figuring it would keep us warm and snug over the winter. Often we hovered around the open oven door to keep ourselves as comfortable as possible. Our kitchen table was an antique trunk with a few old chairs around it. We enjoyed our sofa, beds and radio that we had kept from the old house. As the heat seeped through the walls of the house, huge ice-sickles formed, hanging from the eaves on the outside of the house.

Mother decided to keep me out of school until she felt we would be settled in our new home. "I don't want you to start school in the winter, Jenna. We can't afford to have you catch cold."

"Oh, Mother, how will I ever catch up?"

"I'll let you start after Easter. You don't have to worry about catching up—we'll study at home until then."

"That just isn't fair. I wanted to start with the other kids."

"Jenna, I have to keep you well."

Nothing more was said but I knew she would keep me busy with stuff, whether I learned or not, I would find plenty to do. That wasn't exactly the way I had planned my life. But she promised I could try school in the spring yet I knew she was reluctant to let me leave her even though it was only for a few hours a day. I wasn't very thrilled about the idea of waiting when I saw my brothers come home with their quarterly report cards that showed evidence of the hard struggle they had. My heart ached with the desire to learn yet terrified that Mother would find more excuses to keep me home with her. I hated that desperate feeling of not having my own freedom to dictate my own fate. I begged Dad to show me how to print, so he showed me how to write. That excited me for a time, but I wanted more, I wanted to just be with other kids my age now even more than anything. Yet, I had that uncanny ability to add and subtract. It was more the common sense logic aspect of life. Watching Dad make the numbers work for building purposes didn't hurt. I'd think to myself, if only Tim was here, he'd help me.

It was Friday morning when I realized Dad hadn't gone to work. He seemed to work 24/7, so I thought this to be very strange and then I heard him say, "Tasha, two men from the other block should be over shortly. I think that's what they said."

"Is it today? What time will they be here?"

"Around ten, I think that's what George said."

"Oh, okay, today's as good a day as any and the sooner the better."

I didn't say anything, but I remembered the cop that lived not far from us, was in that general direction. Dad had been visiting him frequently lately and he'd always say to us it was so nice to have the police living closely for safety purposes.

Mother straightened the house as much as she could and soon I heard a knock at the door. She answered it before I could volunteer, so I just continued to play with the few toys I had in the kitchen on the old trunk. Sensing that invisibility for me might be the best thing, I buried my head amidst my toys. Glancing up I immediately realized one of the men looked familiar but then I quickly turned back to my toys, playing quietly.

"George, I think you know my wife, Tasha. Your friend's name is?"

"We don't use his name and he's not a friend. He does what I ask of him and he gets his cut from whatever you get."

No name, but I took a quick glance realizing I could never forget the scar that ran down the right side of his face. I wondered if using no name meant he had been in a serious fight. He had a distinguished black mustache graying at the tips. I had never seen him before but I knew if I ever saw him again, I would recognize him. It was George, I knew that man but didn't dare to look at him directly for fear he would know who I was.   Then I remembered again how I hated gray, how drab and dirty the color appeared to me. Why anyone would wear a gray suit was more than I cared to understand or was it the guy wearing the clothes that bothered me?

They sat for a moment and then Dad asked, "What's the plan?"

"The plan starts with you. First, did you prepare the house as we suggested?"

"We did, George. There is plenty of paper on the floors in the house and the backyard has a lot of scrap wood lying around so it should be ready."

Then Mother added, "The house is all ready for you to do what you do."

"Okay, we should be able to do that tonight sometime. Now, remember the cut we get."

Then Dad spoke up, "If your luck is like ours, it won't work and there'll be no insurance money, remember that was the deal, if we don't get any money, then neither do you."

"We guarantee our work. Our agreement includes that if something goes wrong or not, you don't talk."

Suddenly George turned to look straight at me, and said, "What's that kid doing listening to us?"

Mother said, "Oh, don't worry about her. She doesn't know anything and she won't understand what's going on."

"Get her out of here. I don't want her to know or hear anything!"

Did he recognize me? Could he be the man that I met coming out of the front door of our old house? Without *further ado* I was shoved outside into the snow. I had a boot on one foot and the other foot in a sock. It was cold but I sat there thinking, so now I'm an idiot. I'll bet she told him the first time we met, that I was learning challenged. So she obviously didn't tell him I wasn't in school because of my health. Funny how I figured that out! Now my mind was wound up like a knot. Mother doesn't think I can learn and that's why she wants to hold me back from attending school. Strange how she doesn't know how to teach but it's still my fault. This hadn't been the worst day of my life, after all. That was still to come, I was sure. The men visiting my parents didn't know, I could still hear the conversation, though faintly, through the unfinished walls.

They only said one more thing, "Remember, you talk and you never see your family again. You also need to remember, we are your neighbors. Need I say anymore?"

Mother answered, "No, we understand. You will get it done, is that right? As my husband said, when we tried, we couldn't do it, even with your advise the day you came to our house to look it over. Or, did you know it wouldn't work that way?"

It was the voice of the unnamed man, I was sure, "You don't happen to be professionals but we are. I strongly recommend you not find fault with us. The Lumberyard went off without a *hitch* so you remember we've done this before? The word on the *street* is that you were the eye witnesses not to mention the report you tried to give George. This time I don't want any eye-witnesses. You got that?"

"Don't worry about us. We got that and besides, George should remember the report we gave and somehow, it didn't get reported. I'm sure you needn't worry about that, right George? As you said, we didn't have enough of a description, correct?"

That was Dad's sarcasm, I was sure.

"Now you're remembering too much. Just do as we say and nobody gets hurt and if you don't..." I couldn't hear the end of that sentence. The last comment I heard, "Is that clear?"

The men left and soon Mother came to bring me back into the house where I could warm up. Dad made himself busy in the backyard for the rest of the day while Mother prepared the meals for. None were too *chatty*, they just kept doing things like cleaning and yard work.

Finally, it was time for my brothers to be home from school.

"James, Pete and Cam, you know what chores you need to do. I don't want to hear that you haven't done them. Do them and then it will be dinner time. After that I want you all to clean up and then you will be going straight to bed. Also understand there will be no cutting-up at dinner tonight. Do you hear me?"

I could hear Pete whisper to James, "What's with Dad? What happened, have you heard anything?"

"Nothing at all, maybe it's been a very hard day for him."

"But I don't think he went to work, didn't he say he was staying home?"

"Are you sure, Pete? Maybe he's just sick."

"That could be."

No one dared ask me for fear they would be heard. Cam just stared at James and Pete but didn't dare say anything. Again, when Dad spoke that was the end of subject, there was nothing more to be said or done. I looked at both Mother and Dad but I could see they were running on nervous energy. They were both jittery at every sound. Pete still tried to lighten up the evening at the table, by saying, "Isn't it going to snow tonight or are we going to get rain?"

Then we heard, "Pete knock off the talking at the table." We quit the small talk, ate our dinner and then helped with the cleaning.

Without any more *to-dos*, we hit the sack but I lay there wide awake, unable to sleep. The evening was still young but Mother and Dad weren't saying much, they just sat in the kitchen drinking tea—clearly, they wanted to be left alone. From my bed in the living room, I could hear the muffled whispers but I was unable to make sense of anything they said.

Saturday morning came none too soon when the boys and Dad started again working on the completion of our home while Mother and I walked to town. We heard, loudly and clearly from the newspaper boy on the street corner, "Read all about it! Read all about it! Attempt to burn haunted house foiled! Read all about it! Read all about it! Two men were seen running from scene!" Mother walked over to buy the paper.

"Ma'am, those are the headlines but if you read the paper, it says that a neighbor had seen the same two men that ran from the Lumberyard fire, run from the Nedder's home." He handed the paper to Mother.

Now Mother was totally quiet as we made our way to the corner store for the few groceries she said she needed. When we got home, Mother handed Dad the papers as she motioned for him to read, but not a word passed between them. Dad retreated to their bedroom for a lengthy amount of time.

The silence was finally broken by the ringing of the phone. Mother answered, "Hello. Yes, I read that in the newspaper. No, I heard what you said, just so you realize that since you couldn't do the job, there will be no money and the agreement was, if we don't get any money, neither do you." Mother was silent for a moment, "I heard that—it's what you said before." She was again silent until I heard, "At the old house, when? Okay, I will tell him." More silence, "I'll have to check with him, it will be up to him. Yes, I heard that the first time." Then she hung up the phone.

Dad came from out of their bedroom as he must've heard what I just heard, the one sided conversation. Without a word, I saw them both just stare at one another for a brief moment and then they both left for the backyard.

Pete nervously sat trying to relax as he spoke, "Did you hear about the guys that went fishing, but couldn't find any fish?"

"That's enough, Pete. I don't want to hear it." The silence began.

We could almost hear the sound of food being swallowed as we ate in silence looking at one another we realized Mother and Dad looked stone cold, not even a wrinkle around the mouth to show that there might be a smile coming. Something was very wrong, but no one except for Mother and I, then later Dad had seen the Newspaper. They weren't about to volunteer any information. After dinner, both Mother and Dad busied themselves outside in the back yard again. I could tell when they came back, a plan had been conceived. I only hoped it would be a good one.

Chapter 25

Ghost Chasing

Appearing in court was no easy task for Edgar and Tasha. Making their way, first on the bus, then the trolley to downtown where they were to meet with the court appointed attorney.

"I just don't know what this attorney will be able to do for me, Tasha. I just wanted this to be over with. You know our dilemma and I can't risk anything to happen to you and the kids."

"Edgar, I don't want you to go to jail. You didn't set the fire, you know that. Why can't you just be honest and say that to the attorney? Let him figure out how to help us." Soon they were in the lobby, seated and waiting. Tasha worried that Edgar just wouldn't cooperate with the attorney.

Finally, the Attorney's secretary, announced, "Mr. and Mrs. Nedder, the Attorney will see you now. Why don't you come with me?"

Dad couldn't help but think about the guilt of having to sit in Attorney David Swain's office. It was almost too much—what had they been thinking? If they had only used their heads and stayed out of such a corrupt situation. Even if they thought the whole world could do such a thing and walk away from it blameless, who were they to think they could? The answer to that, they now knew only too well.

"Okay, Edgar. I've gone over the details of this case and I think I can get you off if you're willing to cooperate."

"How can you do a thing like that?"

"We have on record and have been following, for quite some time now, the two men that we believe to be the people you know about. You are the only two who can give us the break we are looking for. Here's the catch, we will give you a break if you work with us."

Tasha couldn't help but say, "I thought when we originally reported these men, no one was interested. No one was willing to find them or at least say they would look into the matter."

"Here's how it works. The man called, George Knight, is one of the men that came to your house when you made the report. I have that report here and he really didn't report it falsely, more incomplete. He just said that you didn't give enough of a description. So, if I'm reading the report correctly, you couldn't give a description other than *two men running* away from the scene."

"It would've been impossible to see their faces from one story up in our house. We were actually looking down on them."

"I have a question I'm not sure you want to answer. If not, you need to think about it at least, how did George re-connect with you?"

Tasha eagerly responded, "That's easy. He's our neighbor in Burnaby—he lives a block up the street. Edgar was looking for old tires so we could burn an old stump in our backyard since the cost to have it moved was prohibitive. He and our son Pete went door to door collecting old tires.

Edgar added, "He recognized me and reintroduced himself. He immediately invited me into his home. While my son was waiting outside I asked if the people who had started the Lumberyard fire had ever been caught. He said, 'Not if I can help it.' I didn't understand that so I asked what he meant. He just told me to come by when I would be alone if I was interested because he could help us with our haunted house."

Tasha continued, "I didn't understand what he meant either so I thought maybe he had a buyer for it. That's when I suggested, Edgar and I go back to visit with him and find out what he really meant."

David Swain asked, "I can guess, you were tempted to go with his advice, correct? Besides, who's going to buy your haunted house?"

"You have that right," responded Edgar. "I told him how corrupt I thought the whole situation with the Lumberyard was since he had said to us that they couldn't do anything. Now I'm guessing, and for him not to get caught because of what he just said to us, he gave us the offer to help. Actually, it was worse than that, once he realized he revealed too much, he wasn't about to just let me walk out of his house. To appease him, I said we'd give it serious consideration."

Then Tasha said, "I knew we were in trouble. He had our number so the only way to play the game was go with his plan and so we did." Tasha reluctantly related the story from the beginning. "We just couldn't do anything right according to George's advice. Sometimes, I have a feeling he knew that"

"You might want to know, a neighbor of yours also reported those guys seen at the Lumberyard. His description wasn't much better. However, George wasn't on that call. That's why we've been looking for them for quite some time. We were suspicious and decided to find out if it was an inside job. They would only do such a thing if they were being paid off by possibly the CEO or someone like that from the Lumberyard. I can say, we've had our eyes on a few possibilities but we can't go there without your assistance."

"What do you want from us?"

"Edgar, I need to know the description of the guys you worked with but also your willingness to tell the court."

"But if we do that, they will kill my family, they already said as much."

"We'll provide protection for you. Either way, we will be watching out for your family because if these guys are who we figure, they may prove to be big time gangsters."

"What do you want from me?"

"I need you to tell the court that you didn't actually burn down your house but that the two guys suggested the idea."

"I know from the three years of law school that I had, if these guys are gangsters like you say, his attorney will attack me until I can't stand it and finally say I did it. Then, I've not only identified them but they kill my family and I'm still going to jail."

"I know it's a tough call. If you could hold your own, we would say that this was a good tactic to catch these guys. Think of it this way, they didn't burn the house down and they didn't get any insurance money. That means we could pull you out of the implication. Why would you want to spend time in jail for them?"

"So, they don't kill my family?"

"I said we can protect you. Besides, they would be in jail for a few years."

"They'll get out and they know where I live."

"We'll move you and your family. Remember, these guys have cost a lot of money. A lot of fraud has occurred because of them and we want nothing more than to get them but we need your cooperation."

"Tasha and I will have to talk."

"Your court date has already been set but I'd like to know your answer in just one week. Here's my card, please call me at your earliest convenience."

With that, both Edgar and Tasha made their way home. "Edgar, can you do what they ask?"

"I just don't know how. I can't risk losing you and I know I can't live without you. I've already proved that to you."

"Let's not go there, but I'd really like you to do as the attorney advised. We can easily pack up and leave again. Maybe even move south where it's warmer. Wouldn't that be nice?"

"Gangsters always get their guy. You know that."

───────────────

My mind went back to the phone call that Mother and Dad weren't talking about. It sounded serious and I hoped that their visit to the attorney's office had solved all of that.

However, when Dad and Mother came back from the visit with the Attorney, it wasn't over yet and I knew Mother wasn't done with our old haunted house in Vancouver either. Mother insisted, "It's still our house and we need to get it ready to sell again." Finally, Mother brought it up again, "Edgar, do you think you'd like to come with me to check on our old haunted house, see what burned and to see if Rosie still lives there? You probably need to come with me."

"You know I can't go. I'll stay home with the kids. I'd be happier if you didn't go either. There isn't anything we can do anyway and if something happens to you, I'll never be able to live with that."

"Either way, I need to go there to check on it to see what's left of it, what actually burned and to see what we have to do to clean it up for resale again. We don't even know what it looks like anymore."

"I'll go with you, Mother," Pete was anxious to be included; "I want to check if some of our old books are still there. I keep thinking that the books have to be there and maybe I can bring them back with me."

"Don't leave me at home, Mother, if you're going I'm coming with you."

Dad said, "You don't have to go, Tasha. We discussed that and you know what my plan is."

"I'm going. Maybe with Rosie's help, I can fix your plan." There was never anything anyone could say, as always, if Mother was going somewhere to do something, she was going. All I could think, what plan did Mother want to fix this time and if there was such a thing as a ghost, how could they possibly help?

The sun had gone down and it was a very dark night but we could see the stars so we knew it had to be cold and when I felt my nose, it proved to be true. My hands had mitts on, so I was warm enough. We did the bus ride, finally transferred to the trolleys that would take us the rest of the way. It was just a block from the trolley stop from where we would be able to see what was left of our haunted house. My throat began to tighten, feeling like darkness was about to swallow me up in one big gulp. We hadn't even brought a flash light to see where we were going. The only light available was a mere street light. Finally, we stood there in the dark, looking at our house.

Mother said, "I would like to see if Rosie is still here."

"Rosie?"

"You know the ghost."

"I know you keep saying that but she isn't real, Mother." Then I looked up and to my amazement I saw a light shining inside the house. "There's a light in the house!"

"Yeah, Jenna, it's in that back bedroom," she hesitated. I could hear her take a deep breath when she spoke, "it has to be."

"I see that, I don't understand it, there was a fire here."

"Doesn't look burned from the outside, does it Pete?"

"Yeah, it doesn't look burned. I can't see the house too well because it's so dark out here."

Mother wasn't saying anything now.

———————————

Nathan was sitting in his easy chair, as his mind was reminiscing about all the scenes he had witnessed just so very recently. First it was introducing himself to the new neighbors across from him. How the Howaski's had to leave so quickly because of the War with Japan. Then the Nedders came on the scene, buying the so called Haunted house that the Japanese people left behind.

Nathan's mind continued to remember once more how the Nedders bought that very same house and soon he had been summoned to check the electrical wiring for the phone where he witnessed for the first time in his life, the dial on the phone turning itself without any human intervention. It didn't take Anthony but a minute to be gone.

He also remembered the Lumberyard fire but it didn't end there. Instead, there soon was a shed fire in the backyard of the haunted house. Suddenly, he saw another fire inside the house. Just because of Anthony's vigilant watch, the last two fires were spotted on time to prevent any catastrophic event from happening and immediately extinguished by the quick response of the local fire department. Yet, somehow, nothing fit together anymore.

<hr>

By now we were at the front door of our house. I just knew Mother wanted to go in to see whatever it was she needed to see. I was terrified and my stomach was churning everything into sour milk. I knew I needed to be cool about all this or I'd throw-up and that wouldn't be good. At least Pete was here with me and Mother. Mother made it sound like she was still *ghost chasing* but I knew everything was very twisted. I hadn't forgotten that one sided phone conversation I heard before she and Dad went to see the Attorney.

I thought for a moment and realized that just maybe it had something to do with the man in the gray suit and the bearded man who insisted on going *nameless*. I remembered my mind telling me they were planning something that was very wrong. I shook my head, realizing I was still standing at the front door.

Anyhow, Mother nudged the door and it finally creaked open— this just can't be good. We all knew there had been a fire so how could it be safe? The darkness was so intense that I couldn't even see in front of my face because my eyes hadn't adjusted yet.

Not even Pete was saying anything. That was so unlike him, he was always the first to volunteer and the first to say something. Come to think of it, that's why we were both here because he was the first to say he wanted to go with Mother. I came because I worried something would happen. Even in the darkness, I could see the fear in Pete's eyes. He knew I was right, we were not looking for ghosts—we were now looking for people. Come to think of it, Dad was too afraid to come with us, so why did he permit Mother to do this? But who can tell Mother anything?

I was now scanning the entrance way inside the house at the foot of the stairs like a hawk searching for his prey. Finally, I could see a glimmer of light that filtered through the window from the street light. My shaking hands were on the wall trying to find the switch.

"There is no electricity, you can't turn the light on, Jenna," Mother whispered. "If we are quiet and careful, we will find them first so we can know what to do."

I whispered back, "So now we aren't *ghost chasing* but looking for *them?* Who are these people?"

"You were right, Jenna. Mother, you need to tell us what we are doing here."

"Pete, you and Jenna have to keep your eyes on whomever shows, watch what they do and say. Here, take these bus tokens—if you have to leave without me, please run."

Pete said the most sensible thing in his life, "I know the power is off but I can't figure out the light we just saw in the back bedroom. It means these guys have the only lights in the house. Did we even think to bring a flashlight?"

"Who are these people you're meeting here?" I asked.

"You've seen them before, Jenna and I'm here to make a deal for your Dad. I'm hoping he won't have to go to jail for something that was kind of my idea in the first place. I have to do what I have to do. I've done worse things than this just coming to this country—surely we will get through this as well."

"We aren't leaving you here, Mother. Either you come back with us or whatever happens to you happens to us. Dad can't make it without you. None of us want to be sent to an orphanage again."

I just wanted to scream but there was a frog in my throat that left me speechless. Maybe, that was God stopping me. Then I whispered as if to force my whole being so that I could be heard, "Let's not go there now, Pete. Mother, we are kids, do you understand? How will we know what to do?" I wasn't sure anymore if I could even be heard.

"Just do the listening. These guys don't like kids but I'm hoping they'll go easy on me and Dad. They never know what to do when they see you kids just standing there. So, stand there and watch. If you have to run, do it. Remember everything you see but don't say anything."

"Like you said, we need to keep our eyes open. Can you do that Pete? I have no idea what this all means, but for Mother's sake, let's give it a try."

"We can do it, Jenna. Mother needs us now so let's just remember that."

Chapter 26

Sighting Fires

____

"Hey, Nathan, have you seen anymore fires, lately?"

"None, Charlie, hopefully it's stopped for good." It was not uncommon for Nathan to chat with his neighbors for a moment just before he made his way to work.

"I'm going to miss the Nedders. The neighborhood is just too quiet without them here." Charlie had a distant look about him.

"Did you know them well," inquired Nathan?

"No, just that they lived in that haunted house is all. I can't believe that ghosts actually roam around."

"Oh, you knew about that, too?" Nathan was surprised.

"Yeah, the whole neighborhood knew about that even before they moved here."

"I knew these things because they called me to look to see if there was a short in the telephone wiring because as they said, the dial would turn on its own sometimes."

"That can't be possible."

"I didn't think so until I was called to fix it."

Then Nathan told the story of what happened. "I've often wondered if they were ever told about the house being haunted when they bought it. I didn't even believe any of it until then." Nathan went on to explain, "Then it became my job to look into the matter. This wasn't the kind of job I wanted but working for the Telephone Company all these years, it was my job to do it."

"What was wrong with it?"

"I don't know to this day. I went over there, like I said and Mrs. Nedder explained that her husband thought it was just an electrical short. Lo and behold, when I checked it out the wiring was perfect but when I put the phone back together again and was finished with the last screw, the phone dialed turned itself. Let me tell you Charlie, I grabbed what I had and I was out of there. I almost tripped over the front stairs, I was so scared."

"You saw that happen? So, the house really is haunted. Do you suppose the fires are set by Ghosts?"

"No, Charlie, because I saw a couple of guys running from the Lumberyard fire and I even reported that."

"But Nathan, what about the other fire, like the shed in the back of their house?"

"The firemen said that was an electrical short."

"We owe you a lot for reporting what you saw. I was beginning to think our whole neighborhood was going to go up in flames. After the first fire, I finally put insurance on my house. Before that I always thought it would never happen to us. Now, hearing you say the Lumberyard was deliberately set doesn't make me feel any better."

"Well, it seems like it might have stopped at least for now. Sorry, Charlie, but gotta go or I'll be late to work. Hey, Charlie, it's been good to talk to you. Take care."

"You, too, Nathan, see you around."

They parted ways and all was soon forgotten. Or was it? Not more than a few days later, Nathan was again trying to listen to the radio when yet another fire and this time it was the haunted house and the smoke was coming from inside. He had talked to the Nedders when they moved everything out so he knew they couldn't be in the house. Immediately Nathan called the Fire Department again, but to his horrifying amazement he saw the same two men running down the road as he had seen when the Lumberyard burned down.

Without hesitation, Nathan reported it to the police but this time they seemed much more interested but didn't say much.

It probably was about a week after that, when Nathan looked over and saw the brightness of a light burning up on the second floor and assuming he had missed whoever had gone in, he carefully continued to watch. He knew it couldn't be safe for anyone to go in that house with all the fire damage. Then, to his amazement, he saw Mrs. Nedder and two of her children about to enter through the front door. To himself out loud,

"Don't do that, you guys," Nathan was shocked when he heard himself. "I'm going to have to go after them because someone else is in there already. I don't know how they got a light turned on in a burned-out house, anyhow."

Chapter 27

Maggie & Rosie

—————————————

"I just don't know, Maggie, what's with these people? They keep starting fires, then an angel comes by, blowing like the wind and pouf, the fire is out. That was the first fire the lady of the house started."

"Rosie, I think they call her Tasha. She didn't start that one alone. I don't know what that guy was thinking but he knew very well it wasn't going to work. He just wanted her to hire him so he could cash in on the deal."

"Sometimes, I just wish we could do good stuff for people."

"Don't let the boss hear you say that. How could that be possible anyway, we had our chance to be good when we were alive."

"Well, Maggie, I like the fact that we have Tasha convinced that we do good things for people. She believes in us, don't you think?"

"I think you're making a big assumption. There's no way she can believe in us and in God. She entertains us because she wants to know beyond what God allows."

"Linda says we should let them do what they want and stay out of their business."

"That's okay for her to say. She lives in Yvonne's old house and Yvonne's grandmother can't hear very well anymore so if she makes noises or wants to be seen, the old lady will never even know. Her eyes are not what they used to be, either. I heard someone say she's well into her 90s."

"Rosie, how do you and the lady of this house actually talk to one another? Every time I try that the people get freaked out."

"Well, Maggie, you have to be really careful. They can dismiss us if they're Christians and plead the blood of Jesus on us but the lady of this house kind of likes it when I show myself to her. I think she likes the company."

"But Rosie, if they know how to dismiss us we go back into the pit until God calls us to judgment. If we stay away from doing evil stuff, we might at least have some freedom to just float around until then."

"I hate to tell you this, but God isn't our boss anymore. However, with Tasha's desire to entertain us, our boss thinks he might gain a stronghold. That's why he has us in this house to begin with."

"I knew the lady of this house might be okay because she's always visiting that old lady on Second Avenue who believes in spiritualism. That's our realm, you know. She worships our boss. Can you believe that? Why would a person with a choice worship Satan?"

"Not smart but then we have nothing to brag about ourselves. Sometimes people in their ignorance like to play with us just for the fun of it, thinking they can gain insight into things they don't understand and then we deceive them into thinking they're right. Little do they know we pick up all our information from them by listening carefully? Yet because they get so anxious to know stuff that's none of their business, they tell us enough for us to deceive them. Ironic, isn't it?"

"That's how Myrtle does it. Did you hear her talking to Tasha? Before Tasha was done talking, Myrtle could make all the guesses she needed to and tell her whatever it was she wanted to know. Myrtle had no clue that Tasha's cousin was dying until she heard her say so."

"She's such a fake, Rosie. No one can call back the dead and ask questions of them. If the dead are Christians, for sure they can't because those people are already with Jesus. Wasn't it Jesus who said on the cross to one of the guys hanging there along with him, *"I tell you the truth, today you will be with me in paradise."* Paradise has to be Heaven. There's no way that Myrtle…"

"We even found out Myrtle's name just by being on our toes."

"I listened to Tasha—she's a good one to listen to. Sometimes I even think her attachment to us is that we might know something from God so she can get lucky and then pretend to be the *all-knowing* one."

"I'll bet you're right, Maggie. She craves the attention you get when you're smarter than anyone else, especially if it's about the Spirit World. We aren't God so we can't know stuff, past or future, but I'm not sure she believes we can't. She is a good person and I'm sure she loves God. She'd be the one to have mercy on us even now if she could."

"Get a grip Rosie—she isn't God even if she likes to talk with us."

"I still like visiting with Tasha but I wished I had listened when I was alive and heard God call me. You know he calls everybody?"

"I know and I didn't listen either. It's funny how we don't have anyone to blame but ourselves. Excuses aren't going to do us any good now."

"Yeah, Maggie, I remember one time when a really good friend of mine wanted me to come to church and I gave her some lame duck excuse like I thought Christians were hypocrites. I said they all fight with each other just like everyone else and how come they couldn't obey God's Word and love one another? My friend said it wasn't God's fault that Christians fight and sometimes don't do the right thing when they know they should but God still loves them. She said that God wanted me just as I was with all my idiosyncrasies and faults. It didn't matter to God what I had done wrong. He would forgive me. I knew she was right, but I just laughed at her. After a while she left me alone. I couldn't even blame her because I wasn't listening to anybody and you know what, I wouldn't have listened and God knew that. Yet, God never gave up. He kept sending people to tell me that I needed Jesus. I just kept saying no until the plane crash…it crashed in seconds. I was knocked out and next thing I knew I was here, with nowhere to go but to wait on God for judgment."

"Almost the same thing happened to me, Rosie. Only I got really sick and I kept daring God that he should make me better but I wasn't about to promise anything. He would just have to take his chances on me. I was having a good time and I wanted to get back to that. My boyfriend, Mike, was a gambler and he'd just throw money at me all the time. I spent it anyway I wanted. I steered clear of Christians because I knew I'd have to give up my life style and I wasn't about to. Like I said, I got sick and while I was in the hospital a police chaplain came to visit me and told me that Mike had been shot dead. Even then God pleaded with me to come to Him, but I said no. I just wanted my life style back. Well, here's where that all got me."

"I'm just hoping our boss will go easy on us if we try to convince people to follow him instead of God."

"You have to admit it is fun leading people away from God."

"How evil that is of us! Do you think we'll ever convince Tasha to give God up, Maggie?"

"Our boss says we have to keep trying or he'll have someone else take care of us. We gotta obey him now, we have no more choices."

"His time is coming too. God gets the last say, no matter what."

"What's bad, the angels are always doing good things for these people. If it was me I'd say, *enough already*, handle it yourselves if you want to make wrong choices but the angels never give up either, they keep trying to take care of the Nedders."

"That's because God never gives up on anyone and he assigns his angles to each of His children."

"I desperately tried Rosie, to do what our boss wanted when Edgar ran up the stairs to pull the switch on the breaker box but before I could get near, his angel just pushed his hands toward the switch. I couldn't believe it but God wanted that man to live."

"I heard the owners of this house made a report about those guys that set the fire. Little did they know those were *our guys* that came to take the report, or like our boss said, it was only half a report."

"Yeah, but Maggie, the last fire that those two men set in this house would've burned everything around here but the guys were confused and scared when they heard us. That one backfired on our boss, that's not what he wanted."

"Oh, you mean the business next door to here? That fire didn't even get reported. It would've been bad, that would have taken care of a lot more and probably killed a few people in the process but it backfired all right. Yeah, that would've been bad. I think those guys wanted to burn the whole block down if they could make some money."

"How would you know that, Maggie? Who told you that?"

"I heard them. They were sneaking around that business building. I wanted to get in on the action so I made sure they saw me. They looked like scared rats and ran."

"They didn't get to set the fire, as I recall. You heard what they do, didn't you? Well, let me tell you, they try to force the businesses to buy special hazard fire insurance from them and if they don't the business or home burns down. Clever, don't you think?"

"Did they do the shed in the backyard of this house?"

"I'm pretty sure that was Edgar's own doing. The Nedders don't have money to pay anyone to do such a thing."

"I guess their good angel was too busy to do anything to stop it, what do you think, Rosie?"

"Yeah, that one I didn't even expect. I'm sure it caught everyone by surprise. They lucked out because the neighbor called the fire station."

"Besides Rosie, I don't want them to sell their house. Someone else could get rid of us."

"I don't want to change the subject but take a look out there—do you see what I see? We could have fun tonight. It's those men again. Why would they come to a burned-out house?"

"Look, here comes the lady of this house with two of her kids, now. We should be in for some more excitement tonight. We had better stay on our toes, it seems like a fight might be brewing, a battle with their angels and us.

"Yeah, Maggie, the one is scared of us and the girl doesn't believe us…she isn't at all like her mother."

"Let's see if we can get involved here."

"You mean like…"

"Yeah…scare tactics, Rosie. We have to create chaos somehow."

"But with God's angels here, it's going to get a bit sticky."

"I know, but we'll use our scare tactics."

"And scaring any of them is lots of fun, Rosie."

"We can't stop the bullets, if our guys start shooting. Do you think they will? I'd enjoy fireworks, wouldn't you?"

"We're in for a riot! What am I saying, it's those people and little do they know they are in for the party of their lives. Put the pot on low to brew, it's going to be a good night. We'll turn up the heat in a minute, let's give it our all."

Chapter 28

Going In

I just didn't know what to think any more as we stood inside our burned-out house. We were now standing in the entrance way to the living room. It seemed to be the place with the most light coming from the one working street light seeping through the front bay window.   It was close enough to our house to make a difference between totally black to a mere trickle of light.

I looked up toward the second floor in the murkiness of that light, barely being able to see the amount of fire damage. As hard as it was to see, the fire had only licked the railing at the top of the stairs, barely charring the banister. It appeared the fire only had enough time to blacken some of its surroundings.

Here we were waiting. It felt like we waited ten minutes when Mother whispered, "I wonder what they are waiting for? Surely they heard the door open."

All I could think, we're just kids and God, you have to believe me, we're scared stiff! Lord, our Mothers' life is at stake, can you please help us God? If you don't, I know what comes next—its orphanage, here we come if we survive.

"Maybe we're supposed to announce ourselves—that we're here?" whispered Pete.

Slowly, we started up the stairs. I whispered, "Why aren't they going to meet us downstairs? Is it smart to go up and get trapped?"

"Now you're talking, Jenna. Come, Pete. They already know we're here. Let's go into the living room until they come down. Then we'll talk and I mean we'll talk. We can't allow them to corner us. Pete, go open the back door, so if we need to we can escape from there."

"I don't get it. Let's just go ask them what they want—what's wrong with doing that?"

"Don't be dumb, Pete, they're the ones that want something from Mother."

"They do…they are? What do they want? Who are we talking about Jenna?"

"Ask, Mother. She heard the whole conversation. I only heard her talking on the phone."

"Jenna. You weren't supposed to hear that!"

"But I did. First I believed that you really wanted to see what our house looked like after the fire but now that we saw the light upstairs, I remember that phone call you had."

"Mother," Pete was very anxious now. "Tell us what these guys want. By the way, who are these guys? I figured out about the shed, but I didn't know anything else." He insisted again, "Who are these guys?"

"Pete, what do you mean, 'you knew about the shed fire'? What happened there?"

"You need to stop talking and just listen, kids."

I couldn't be stopped now, "I think I know who these guys are. I can put that part of the puzzle together. My question is, Mother, what do they want from you?"

"Quiet, kids, you'll know soon enough. Remember, just watch and run if you have to, they don't want you. I shouldn't have brought you in the first place and you need to know that I'm very sorry. I love you guys, but run if you have to and Pete you have the tokens…here they come, I think I can hear them."

In the shadows, I could still barely see but I knew it had to be those men again. Nervousness ran through my being as I realized they might recognize me. I moved slightly into the shadows, pulling Pete with me. We didn't need to be seen right away, if at all.

"Mrs. Nedder, is that you? Are you with your husband?"

"It is me, and no, Edgar is not with me. I just have my children with me. Edgar was afraid to come. I assured him you would be fair but he wouldn't come anyhow."

Both men swore in unison. I didn't know that was possible, but they did.

"Why did you do that? I told you we could make a deal if you and he came by yourselves."

"There aren't any police here. So, go for it. Talk to me."

I was hoping Pete could see what I saw as I looked at the man with the beard—he had that same stare but his right hand was in his bulging pocket. "Pete," I whispered, "Do you see the bearded man's pocket?"

"I do, Jenna."

We would have to be extremely careful because we now knew they were armed and dangerous.

"Tell, me," Mother started talking. "How will you keep my husband out of jail if he doesn't talk?"

"We wanted you and your husband here!"

"You didn't get what you asked for because you couldn't do the job as promised, now what are you going to do?"

"We don't make deals with women."

"Oh, don't you?"

I couldn't believe my eyes or maybe I was losing my sight…no my senses. I saw it as clearly as life itself, someone just walked between us and our assailants. "Mother, did you see that?"

"I did Jenna. Just be quiet."

"What are you talking about? What was that?"

"Nothing, it's just Rosie dropping by."

"I've never seen Rosie and I don't think it was her. That was an Angel that just came by me, I know that for sure."

"I don't see anyone."

"If you want to, you can see Rosie." Mother started to insist.

"I don't see anyone but you and your kids, now stop the nonsense."

"If we are going to made a deal, you need to do it right here and with me."

"You heard the man. George said he isn't making deals with women."

"You're the man with no name and a scar, right?"

"So?"

"Afraid that someone might tag you with something you've done before?"

"Stop that. Here's the deal."

"George, you said…"

"You're right Bud. We're going with our original plan."

Mother asked, "Which is?"

"Mother, there she is again. Who is she?"

"That one I don't know, maybe God has sent your Angel, but they're all over here. Can't you feel them, Jenna and Pete?"

"Stop that! I felt that and it's just the wind."

"Sorry, George, that wasn't wind. Maybe Rosie's trying to talk to you."

Finally, Pete couldn't help himself, "Don't you guys get it? It's a ghost. That's what you feel and that's what you're hearing. We can see them, don't tell us you can't."

Mother insisted, "You were talking about a deal, what's the deal?"

Bud, stomped his foot, "It's a bullet to the head."

"Mother, he has a wooden leg, did you hear that?

"Quiet, Pete."

"That's no deal! You know you can't get away with such a cowardly act!"

"Call it what you like…"

"How do you plan to get away with shooting us?"

"No lady! Not all of you, just you. The kids come with us."

"No way, my kids are mine and they have nothing to do with this deal."

"You should've thought about that before you…"

Suddenly the living room door swung open with a force so strong the top hinge gave way.

"Who is that?" demanded Bud. The other seemed to be frozen from the breeze, Rosie, or was it the Angel, moving around him.

Another shadow appeared in the open doorway, "I called the cops, Mrs. Nedder. I didn't think you should be in here alone…"

"You did what? I told you no cops!" George screamed at the top of his lungs.

"Sorry, guys, I didn't do that, this is my neighbor, Nathan…" Before Mother could complete her conversation, the men ran for the rear of the house.

Pete perked up, "Uh, those guys are in so much of a hurry and can't wait for introductions. Too bad Mother, I'm now sorry I listened to you and opened the back door."

Just as they stood there, they heard glass shatter and then running down the back stairs.

"Wow, I heard the glass smash. I'm going to check it out, Mother."

Pete shouted back, "Look what I see, blood." By now everyone was standing around to see the results. "They went through the glass…ugh, that must've hurt, you think? They figured the door was locked, didn't even try it first."

Mother added, "I certainly hope they hurt themselves plenty good, those murderers."

"As I remember, Mother, those outside back stairs weren't that sturdy to begin with. Do you think they made it?"

"I guess they did, there they go.   Want to try and catch them?"

Nathan responded, "I got a good description of those guys this time. Oh, here are the cops."

The cops heard the commotion, and quickly made their way to the back door but too late—all that could be seen in the shadows of darkness was a speeding car with no headlights. They turned to face Mother, "If you can give us a description of those men, maybe this time we'll be able to crack the case. We've been after them for a long time. If you remember after the Lumberyard burned down and you filed a report, Nathan? Your neighbor here, the Neddar's also reported the same incident. At the time, we didn't have enough evidence but now with both your help, we should be able to get somewhere." Turning to Mother, he continued, "We just need your husband's help."

"He's too afraid to say anything."

"We can only cut him a deal if he'll talk. Come, we'll drive you home or you'll never get there. They probably know you ride the buses so that's where they'll be watching for you."

Pete asked, "Are you going to chase them down?"

"We have alerted our beat cop in the city but I doubt these crooks will show themselves. We'd be able to catch them if you guys were the bait, but we're not going there."

Mother said, "Let me be the bait, then you'll have your men."

"Sometimes we actually use civilians for bait but we need someone who is more agile, someone who could run. Besides, you guys have been through enough for one night."

There were no more words. Everyone knew, the plan was for both Mother and Dad to come and then they would have killed to destroy the two people that had a definite description and the motives needed for a conviction.

"Mother, do we have Angels?"

"I'm sure we do. You saw what happened tonight. I just know Rosie was there before the cops came."

"Who is Rosie?" asked the officer, I didn't see anyone except you, your two kids and your neighbor."

"Mother seems to think a ghost comes around to help her when she's in trouble. I know different because I saw my Angel here tonight."

Pete was answering again beyond his years, "Mother's gotten to know a ghost she calls Rosie. But you heard Jenna and I'm more inclined to believe our Angels are the real help. Still, Mother likes to have Rosie around."

"We heard the house was haunted but I didn't know you could see them."

"Ask our neighbor. He's experienced them as well." Mother turned to face Nathan, "You remember the telephone you tried to repair?"

"I guess I do. But I'm with your daughter. She knows what she's talking about."

I could tell Pete was in seventh heaven to be riding in a police car. He was busily chatting about catching crooks and how were they going to catch these guys, anyhow. I was just too tired to care anymore and just wanted to be home with my own thoughts.

Finally, we drove up to the front yard of our Burnaby house. I said, "Thank you for saving our lives." If no one else was going to say anything, at least I could. I knew God was taking care of us and I knew his hand was on me. I just needed to find out how I could really get to know God. *Please, let me know you*," I whispered under my breath.

Mother was still too shaken to say anything. I said nothing more but I just knew the cops would want to talk to Dad as he stood on the porch waiting for us to come home.

"Mr. Nedder, your wife will tell you what happened. I wouldn't much go to that house without a police escort anymore. Just to tell you, we really do need your cooperation in catching these two guys. Talk to your wife and the authorities will be in touch with you shortly."

This had been a heavy night and we knew there was more to come.

Chapter 29

A New Beginning

We were on that infamous walk again on a Saturday evening. The air was crisp and dry. The snow was all but gone again for a while though it had been the beginning of an early winter for us. Usually we wouldn't have snow until January. This year was different in many ways. We were once again walking as a family though Mother had tremendous problems with her knees. We walked west following Hastings Street along our wooden sidewalk looking into each store window as we passed by. Mother called it window shopping, when we didn't spend money, but instead we just looked. Much like looking in department store catalogues, always dreaming if only we had this or that, how much fun that would be. Special decorations were already up for Christmas, nonetheless it was only nearing the end of October.   Every desirable toy was displayed in the store windows as we anxiously stared knowing not many were for us. At least we could look and enjoy the sights.

In the distance, we could hear the sounds of a band playing music. This time it wasn't the sounds of minstrels but more like the music of heaven.

"I love that music."

"Oh, Jenna, you are always saying that. When we sit in the grandstand at the Park and the band plays all that western hoedown, you like that too."

"I do, don't I? But James, can't you hear what these people are singing about? Isn't it about God?"

"Of course, it is," Dad interrupted, then he turned and said no more. I must've said something wrong, why else would he suddenly fall silent. He just wasn't saying anything anymore. Mother listened as intently as I did and then within about twenty minutes the music stopped. A woman with a brimmed blue hat stepped forward, started reading from her Bible. She began to speak about God's saving grace and how God came to save us. I was too thrilled hearing the music to hear the message. I stood there in a daze.   It wasn't a long message but if a pin would have dropped and fallen, it would've sounded like a tree being timbered in the awesome presence of the Holiness of God. I was sure that God's presence was sensed in a very real way with those gathered around to listen. Indeed, God was speaking. My feet were cemented to the ground when Mother and Dad wanted to move on down the street, I couldn't move. Mother suddenly realized I hadn't followed.

When they came back for me the Lieutenant approached asking, "Hello, my name is Lieutenant Warren." She extended her hand to Mother and Dad and then, "We'd love it if you'd bring your family to church on Sunday afternoons. We start at two every Sunday afternoon," she pointed to a red brick building just a few feet up the street, "you can see the building just right here on Hastings Street, is where we meet."

Mother turned to Dad, "Can we take the kids to Church?"

"Okay, go ahead." Even Dad had been melted by this event, or was it the circumstances they now found themselves in? It had been years since we'd seen the inside of a church building and I didn't even have any recollection of ever attending one.

I was thrilled to hear that we could attend church when James said, "We used to go to church before we moved to Vancouver."

"Don't you kids remember attending summer camp?"

"I do, Mother. We used to do all kinds of fun stuff," answered Cam, "didn't we Pete?"

"Yeah, I guess we did, I had fun."

"It's just me, then, I don't remember that stuff."

"I used to carry you in my arms because you were always so sick, Jenna."

"Tim used to say that you had to be allergic to the trees at camp," answered Pete.

Mother said, "I don't believe in that stuff. She had a cold, that's why she was sick."

I wasn't at all interested in the whys of this or that, but just so we were going to be able to attend church made me very excited. My heart warmed with the thought that we would finally be able to learn about

God, and read God's Word. This has to be what I was waiting for—waiting to hear.

We were sitting in the kitchen around the stove trying to keep warm, when Mother was about to make an important announcement. She said, "Dad had his last court date last week and they already announced his sentencing. Tomorrow is Monday when the police will come to arrest Dad. It will be when everyone except for Jenna is in school."

Mother continued to talk, "I hadn't planned on having to tell you this but I was hoping it wouldn't happen. You need to know. Dad has been sentenced to one year in jail and might get off early for good behavior. His sentencing was on Friday. Like I already said, sometime on Monday morning, the police with come to arrest Dad."

Pete asked, "Why are they doing that?"

Dad spoke up, "I didn't want to jeopardize your lives. I can't put any of you in that kind of danger."

Pete answered, "But you don't have to say anything, I can tell them who those men are who tried burning the house down."

"I'm the one responsible. As it is, the police said they would keep an eye on our home."

"Didn't you say there was a cop living down on the other block from us? We picked up a couple of old tires from that guy. Remember, to burn our stump out?"

"I did and yes we did get a couple of tires from him."

"That's why you've been over there so much?"

"We have, Pete. But as it stands, they are not the people to be involved with now and I want to leave it at that."

"Dad thought it was best to take the *wrap* and then we would be safe. Now to talk about what to say when people ask you where your Dad is," Mother continued, "just say he is away for a while. It is none of their business and you don't have to tell them what happened."

Cam complained, "Won't they know from the Newspaper, the Vancouver Sun? It's been in all the newspapers already. I didn't even have to say anything at school and Sam came by and said he heard our Dad was going to jail. I told him I didn't even know that, so how come he thought he knew?"

"Dad will be alright, kids. We can pray for him and maybe I can get you guys to visit him some of the times. But for now, don't worry."

We just sat there in total silence, looking at our toys. Finally, Mother said it was a good idea if we just went to bed early and so we did. Morning came soon enough but we scarcely touched our breakfast before my brothers were off to school. It wasn't long when the police came to take Dad away. When they saw, I was watching, "We don't have to cuff Edgar. Why don't you just come with us, Sir?"

Dad left and I didn't see him for a whole year.

But I counted the days until at last Sunday would come again. Every one of us but Dad were now walking to the little brick building where we could learn about God without Dad's forbidding voice.

This was a new beginning for me but a very hard time for Mother. How was she to pay the bills, keep the house and feed us all at the same time with no money coming into the household budget? I saw Mother in tears, on the phone to the Salvation Army asking if there was anything they could do to help.

Within hours, we had a large box of groceries, clothing and a check for funds to meet our current needs. I saw a smile on my Mother's face as she told me that this was the first time since leaving Russia she ever had to ask for help. While trying to escape from Russia, she was able to find work for her entire family. She was the self-sufficient one who did the helping. A woman that would make it somehow, no matter what and asking for help was not something she wanted to do. Soon she was able to apply for assistance that would keep us until Dad would be home to take over once again.

Cam had a paper route and worked at the bowling alley while the others were finding odd jobs to keep themselves clothed.

Then one day, shortly before Christmas, Cam asked, "Mother, are we going to have a Christmas tree this year?"

"I don't know if I can afford anything this year."

"Can I buy one?"

"We shouldn't worry about that, Cam. Just so we have food on the table."

I dove in, "If you buy one, I'll decorate it for us. We still have decorations, don't we, Mother?"

"They're all very small but we could decorate a tree, I suppose."

"I'll get one then."

Cam brought the tree home, I decorated it. Soon we were involved in the festivities of Christmas at our little red brick church down the road. Then the day came for a special program we would all participate in with a promised Santa Clause that would find his way to the church.

"I don't believe in Santa Clause," Cam complained.

"You don't have to believe in Santa, just enjoy the fun we're going to have."

"Jenna, you make fun out of anything, don't you?"

"What would be wrong with that? What's more, we're supposed to get gifts, too."

"I don't believe they'll give us gifts. We're too new, nobody even knows us yet."

"I'm surprised James, why don't you think they'll give you kids gifts?"

"How could they know what we would like for Christmas, Mother?"

"It's like this, stores donate stuff to them and then the church divides up everything so they can give something to every kid. You'll get a gift, James—you will all get a gift." We finally went to sleep that night even though it was cold with snow already on the ground. I fell asleep enjoying that sense of peace.

That special day came as we all made our way to church to see Santa. After our performances, we sat there singing songs like *Jingle Bells and Silent Night,* until we heard the sleigh bells ringing and someone announced, "Santa has finally come. Look here is Santa Clause with his bag of toys!"

I saw this huge bag of toys as Santa dragged them from the back door to the front of the church, ringing his bell. One by one someone read the names each of the kids. One by one they made their way forward to accept a gift. I started thinking to myself, James is probably right. They won't have our names so we'll just get the hard candies for our gifts.

We just sat there, looking at each other but then all of a sudden we heard our name, "Jenna, Cameron, Peter and James Nedder. Please come up and get your gift." We got up from our seats and made our way to the front of the church and gladly accepted what they gave us. Mother told us to not open the gifts until we got home where we could celebrate Christmas as a family.

I looked over the auditorium to see what the other kids were doing and saw that others were doing the same as us. Probably more fun to have something to open on Christmas morning.

After it was all over, we trekked our way home through the snow, slipping and sliding. Mother made hot chocolate while we sat around the Christmas tree that now had presents under it, all neatly laid there.

"Go ahead, kids. Open your presents, I want to see what Santa gave you."

"I like mine but it has a missing part," Pete said.

"Mine is broken, too. But I'm glad we got these gifts. At least when our friends and our neighbors want to know what we got, we can at least say we got some gifts."

Then Mother said, "We have each other, hard candies and even a gift."

"I had fun, tonight. Did you James?"

"I enjoyed myself. Did you, Cam?"

"Yeah, and my toy isn't even broken."

"Well, you spoiled brat but I'm happy. We do have dinner made, let's have it. The church gave us a turkey and all the stuff that goes with it, so let's enjoy." Mother was up and into the kitchen with all of us following behind.

"So that's what we can smell? It smells so good."

We were very thankful for everything we had been given as Mother reminded us about God's promise, *"But seek first the kingdom of God and His righteousness, and all these things shall be added to you,"* that's Matthew 6:33. Yet, we missed our Dad and at our table of plenty we prayed for him as tears rolled down Mothers face.

Would God now just disappear out of our lives until we needed him again?

Chapter 30

Our God Waits

Life was strange. Living the past down would take years before the neighbors would stop asking, "Where is your Dad?" For now, we would have to live through all our circumstances and that wasn't going to be easy.

As instructed by Mother, I must say, "He's gone away for a while."

They'd laugh at me and say, "Your Dad is in jail for trying to burn down his house!" Then they'd run down the street to play. They had read it all in the local newspapers, but they also knew it said that Dad was spending time in jail for a crime he didn't actually commit. Even at that, I knew there was much more to everything.

This was to be a year of reprieve for me as God was calling me to Himself.

"Jenna." I heard the voice and it was my name. So, I said, "Mother, did you just call me?"

"No, I didn't. Why?"

"I thought I heard my name."

"It wasn't me and there is no one else here."

Then I heard it again, "Jenna, come to me."

"Please God, not now. Oh, I know I promised, but not now. I want to make it on my own. I'm stronger now and I'd like to try it on my own."

"Jenna, I want you for my own. Come to me."

"But God, I've been so dependent for life on everyone else. I've never been able to do anything. It's always been that my total existence depended on other people, even adults who make bad decisions. Finally, Dad will be gone for a while which means no more unreasonable demands, nor conflicts between my Mother and Dad, or whether something is right and wrong. I want to be strong so I can say no to the wrongs in life. If I follow you, I'll just be that *tin soldier* that has to do what she's told to do. I don't want that anymore. Some things are just plain wrong, God. Look at my parents. It was wrong for my Dad to run away with another woman, I'm sure you remember Wilma, God. It was wrong for them to hire someone to burn the haunted house down. I'm not complaining that you took Tim and Grandpa *Home* to be with you. You know what's best. I don't even blame you for anything. But Mother and Dad have never been sure of what was best for them. They can't let go and they have to remind me that I could've died as well. They know who you are yet *they* can't tell us who you are. They even believe your Word, or at least Mother says she does and yet we can't have your Word in our home. Mother doesn't even want me to attend school now even though my health is much better. So, God, just for now, come to me later. Just let me try by myself, see if I can get it right."

Yes, I attended Sunday school, listened to broadcasts on the Radio feeling really guilty but God wasn't giving up. I even memorized Scripture without knowing how to read, memorizing words only. I was proud when we Nedder kids were presented with New Testaments for the verses we learned.

Attending afternoon Sunday School kept me occupied but God wasn't letting me go and it wouldn't be for long because Pete was about to be that persistent brat that would annoy me to death once again. If there was only one thing that irked me to no end it was the relentless nagging and teasing from him. My mind went back to the time we lived in our haunted house and how a neighbor boy loved to tease me. He'd come to the front gate of our home and yell slurs at me, like, "You're ugly or you look funny for a girl." I'd tell my brothers but they'd laugh and walk away. That's when I missed Tim because he would've stood by me. One more time the kid stopped at the gate, yelling, with his predictable, "You look funny for a girl! What're you going to do about it?"

I picked up an open tin can and threw it. I had an aim that couldn't miss and I hit him directly on his nose. He ran like a scared rat being chased by a wild Boar. He came back the next day complaining to my Mother that I had given him a bloody nose. I said, "So, does that mean you leave me alone, or do you want another tin can?" I never heard from him again. Oh, I saw him from time to time, but he wasn't bugging me anymore.

This time it was Pete's turn to be that never-ending bug. I hated bugs to begin with, but he wasn't about to give up. I picked up an opened sardine can and went for my target once more. Yup, I did it again but when I saw the blood flow down the side of his leg, I panicked. This time I was afraid, this was my brother. I had hurt my brother. How could I make a mistake like that?   He got the help he needed from our neighbors.

For me, I was sorry. I ran to stand between two-by-fours of our unfinished home, and pleaded, "Please, God, I didn't mean to hurt Pete, please forgive me." Just like that, God forgave me. Openly on the following Sunday, I professed God as my Savior during the open invitation to invite Jesus into our hearts. As everyone knelt and sang, "Come into my heart, Lord Jesus," I did just that. He was now my Savior.

I experienced lightness in my step with my Savior by my side. I talked to Him because He was always there with me. He was real, so every day we just talked pretty much about everything. He said to me, "I wanted you to choose me. I wouldn't make you come to me but I am here for you. You are not a puppet in my hands but you are my child." No, I wasn't asked to be a *Tin Soldier,* that isn't what God wanted of me after all but He was going to help me all the way.

This wasn't to be the end of the story. I knew that for certain when I heard the phone ring. I answered, "Hello. The phone just went dead, who could that be? Someone calls and then hangs up."

"Don't know, Jenna, do you suppose it's some crazy guy but what would they want with us?"

"It's ringing again but this time let me answer it, Jenna. Maybe someone will talk if I answer. Hello. Who did you want . . . Oh?" It was a couple of minutes before Mother put the receiver back down. For a moment, she paused to catch her breath as she turned away, facing the window.   I knew she didn't want me to see her reaction. Once she gained her composure she turned to me, "Just a wrong number, again."

"How could that be a wrong number? You listened to whoever it was for a long time?"

"The guy wanted to know if we lived somewhere in New Westminster and then when I hesitated he explained some stuff I apparently didn't understand so he hung up."

It wasn't long before Mother made the most wonderful suggestion my ears had ever heard and I had been longing for so long. It may have been a mysterious phone call but the next words from Mother were, "Jenna, I think it's time you attended school and since this is the beginning of spring session, I will take you there and get you started tomorrow. You can come home with your brothers." She turned to talk with my brothers and said, "Remember to bring Jenna home with you. Don't let her be out there waiting too long by herself since she may not know the way back yet."

"Remember Jenna, you will only have been in school for half the year so don't worry that you can't catch up this year. It is alright, we'll just work at it."

Then she continued to talk to all of us, "After I leave Jenna at school, I need to go to town and get some groceries. I'm sure I'll be back before all of you get home. If I'm a few minutes late, you can set the table and I'll be home shortly."

For Jenna, the unbelievable had just happened. For Mother, she was trying to plan out her day for the strange phone call.

The evening came and passed quite uneventfully as all of us sat playing games and listening to our favorite radio shows, but for Tasha, she could no longer concentrate on anything. How could she possible sleep tonight?

Morning came finally came, Tasha quickly made breakfast, and soon the boys ran off ahead as she and Jenna were set for Jenna's first day of school. The preparations went smoothly and were complete in just a few minutes. Tasha said good bye and was off for town.

Tasha made her way to the bus stop just around the corner. She always enjoyed getting out now and then, particularly by herself. It was one of those good days, sunny and cool. Early spring, but it would not be uncommon to come home under drizzling conditions that had been forecasted. Yet, it wasn't cold, so for that she was thankful.

Apprehension was at the forefront. Who was this man on the phone last night? He says he's my brother? He says he visited me in the Hospital. I thought that visit was a dream, a man sent from God who was there to comfort me. He did tell me all I needed to know but was that really him? It was so long ago. Did someone pick up on that and now a pretender who was about to get into my life? Too much has happened and I have no one to turn to but, you God.

Still, Tasha thought, but *Alexei*? How would I know him anyhow and how did he find me? But he knows Abram, the man I've called Dad all these years. How would he know that Abram was my uncle? He had already died in 1944.

Tasha was always very brave and didn't ever back down in fear. She hadn't come this far and all the way through Russia on being afraid to face anything. So, whoever this was, she would just have to face this person. She would have that gut feeling she depended on in the past and just know what to do. God had never failed her in the past and He surely wouldn't this time.

This man who called himself Alexei, said he wanted a safe place for my sake as well as his, to meet. Especially since he said people didn't know who he was either, like me. He suggested meeting at Woodwards Department store. He would be standing at the bus stop in front of the store. He'd be there about 10 am. He would call my name and I would see for myself. I guess I really am afraid.   What if he's some crazy guy that researched my whereabouts? He said he would come alone and I'm not sure that's a good thing.

Well, here goes nothing…this is Woodwards and here I am, getting off the bus. Would I remember him? Tasha had butterflies in her stomach by now. Everything was churning.

She almost dared to breathe a sigh of relief when she saw the bus bench was empty. She didn't see anyone, but looked everywhere. She scanned the entrance to the store. Oh well, I'm not going to wait for him anymore; he's already 30 minutes late. It is okay if I'm late, but he shouldn't do this to me. I need to go in and get a few things, anyhow, I'm not about to waste my time on him. If he was for real, he'd have been here already, waiting.

She'd been shopping for a few minutes stewing over the thought of having such a thing happen. She should've known better than to believe such a foolish story and then to be stood up! The nerve of that guy! If she should see him now, she would give him a piece of her mind. She was about to take a few steps toward the vegetable isle, when she heard, "Anastasia, I'd know you anywhere. You're still my sister!" Without hesitation, he gave her a bear hug until she pushed her way free.

"Alexei, is it really you? I don't know if I can take this. You do remember I always had a heart problem?"

"I remember all too well, but I've always struggled with that blood disease. Somehow I always make it and so will you."

"Please just call me Tasha. How did you find me?"

"Remember, I told you in the hospital to call me Alex. Let's go have coffee in the cafeteria and talk."

"You know, my husband is a very jealous person and when I get home it will be hell for me. But I just had to see you."

"What will you tell him? You can't tell him about me, can you? Have you ever told him anything?

"Never, he can't keep a secret and I'm still too scared to be revealed. But I've watched a few *Lucy Shows*, so, I'll come up with a good one."

"Won't Edgar figure it out?"

"He's too busy being jealous for his own sake. I could tell you stories but I love that man, so what can I say?"

"Let's go talk."

"Alright, but I can't be long."

"You do remember the visit we had at the hospital, right? I told you the plans I had of moving to Vancouver?"

"You said that but after all these years again, I was beginning to think you were just an angel sent from God to comfort me so I wouldn't give up. You said I needed to take care of my family because they needed me."

"I was right, wasn't I?"

"I guess you were. My daughter is better and this is her first day back in school."

"Why so late in the year to begin school?"

"To be honest, when she started getting better, I didn't want to let her go, so I kept her home. When you called, I figured I had to and so I did. I hope I did the right thing."

"I'm sure it was the right thing to do. How is Edgar?"

"Herein is the problem." Tasha told him the rest of the story. "I really don't know what to do these days. We've probably always stayed together because of my insecurities. What would I do? Oh, I can't blame him entirely for what happened since I instigated most of it hoping our lives would become better."

"Do you realize Tasha, that all of your going to find out from fortune tellers, soothsayers, spiritualists and what have you, is why you've made some of these very bad choices?"

"You mean this is how I'm now paying?"

"I know you've always said no one can fool you. That isn't exactly true. Any of us could be in the same situation. God is a very jealous God and He isn't about to share you with Satan. Satan knows that so as crafty as he is, he shoves all the temptation in your way with all the promises he can. You have to remember what he did to Jesus. He promised Him the world if He would just worship him instead of God."

"Alex, God could never do anything like that, you know, but humans? For sure we can, that's easy."

"What Christ went through was for our example. We mustn't do stuff like that."

They enjoyed their coffee together when Tasha looked at the time, "I have to go."

"Not so fast, I'll drive you home."

"You can't, then I'll have to explain everything and I just can't."

"I'll drop you at the bus stop close to your home. Still, I can't just let you go like this. I have a really good Doctor friend of mine and I'm going to make an appointment for you."

"How can I do that? We barely have enough money for food to eat. I don't want money from you either."

"Here's the plan. I want you to meet my maid, and you and she will bring you to my horse racing grounds."

"Alex, I'm not a gambler and I can't afford to lose money!"

"You won't lose money but I'll have someone tell you what to do and you will win a little money each week. You can go home and tell your family where the money comes from. Since you're bringing home money each time, I don't think you will have a problem. Let's at least try that."

"But the doctor, what do I do there?"

"He's taken care of, here's the card and why don't you be there on Thursday after the kids are in school. It'll be for one hour and then you'll be back for them. You just have to let me do this for you."

"I'll try."

"Will I see you next week?"

"Where do you want to meet?"

"Same time, same station?"

"That's a deal!"

Alex drove her close to home and Tasha walked the rest of the way in plenty of time for her kids' arrival from school.

––––––––––––––––––

I don't know what happened but from that time forward, my mother said she was seeing this marvelous Doctor who had her write her story, page by page. She said it was the most wonderful thing she had ever done. Oh, no, she said he never read any of it but it was only for her to get over the past. It did work. Life was calm as we waited the months for Dad to return home.

Life had changed for me as well. Jesus was my Savior and He promised *never to leave me nor forsake me*. I didn't need to look back anymore. He had given me *the right to life*.

Sure, I would have hills to climb and valleys to walk through but He would be there. Human as I was, I would worry about tomorrow and shudder over the past until I read again, "*His eye is on the sparrow, how much more he cares for me*."

Mother would come home sometimes and say that she had won money at the races. "Can't you lose money there?"

"Oh, I never play that way. I always know what to play that's why I come home with money. I wouldn't play if I'd lose."

So, it was, God had answered and now was in the healing business.

THE END

Bibliography

The Shadow   The Cat that Killed

Radio Tape – 1940s
Calling All Cars   Flight to the Desert
Radio Tape – 1940s   Radio Spirits, Inc.

Glossary of Words

Canada   **U.S.A.**

Neilson Chocalate Bar   Chocolate Bar
Chip-rock   Drywall
Ship-lap   Siding
Freshie   Cool-Ade

Hiraku means "expand, open, pioneer" in Japanese. Name used for Japanese immigrant to Canada in the 1940s.

Historical Overviews

V2 Rockets

The V2 launched by Germany against its enemies in WWII was a ballistic missile of relatively short range, but it foreshadowed the development ofa larger liquid propellant rocket engine that was the predecessor of more poweful rocket engines developed for modern space flight. Much of the basic theory used by German scientists in the development of the engine for the V2 came from experimentation by Dr. Robert Goddard in the United States. Post-war American liquid fueled rocket engines evolved directly from the German engine that powered the V2 weapon. Thus it was that the engines eventually used in U.S. Air Force space boosters owed much to the V2 engine and the improvements that followed.

Re: Time Travel Researh Center

The Dairy Wagon

Common practice in Maine dairy farmswas to deliver milk from their own cows tohomes and business in the local area, usually seven days a week. At first they used in containers, then glass bottles with cardboard aps. Themilk was neither pasteurized norhomogenized and contained no additives. This practice was common throughout Canada and the United States in the 1940s.

Horse-drawn milk wagons and bread wagons delivered milk and bread to the door daily as I was gorwing up in the 1940s in Ottawa and Toronto. Upon arrival of the milk or bread wagon, I enjoyed visiting the horses and sometimes fed them apples, or oats if the delivery man gave the the oats. Deliveries were daly. Preservatives of the day did not allow storage of milk and bread for more than a couple of days, and many people had limited or no refrigeration. We had an Ice-Box. Our Ice-Box had two compartments: the top compartment was where the block of ic would be placed, with a ittle room foritems that had to be kept cold.

There was a drain from that compartment to a pan under the Ice-Box to store the water from the melting ice, and had to be emptied daily. The second compartmnet under the ice was dry and cool, but not cold. Ice was delivered 2 or 3 times a week bby the Ice-Man, also with horse drawn cart. No sttop-and-scoop in those days! Horse dung was deposited on the street, and every few days the street cleaner would come alongtowash the dung down the sewer. We had to watch where we walked! Milk was in quart size glass returnable bottles, with a cardboard tab ontop. We bought milk tokens, and placed the number of empty bottles and tokens outside the door for the number of bottles we wanted that day. No one would steal the tokens or milk. The bread man came tothe door toask foryour daily needs or you left a note with bread tokens. Milke was not homogenized: cream settled on top, and we had to shake it to mix it up. Sometimes my parents would skim off some of the cream for coffee, before we shook it up. If we didn'tpromptly retrieve the delivered milk on cold winter mornings, the milk would freeze and expand out the top of a couple of inches, pushing off the cardboard tab which was placed on the top of the glass milk bottles.

Jim Low, "Horse Drawn wagons for mile and bread deliver"
1940s, Ottawa and Toronto, Canada.

Earthquake Sunday June 23, 1946

Vancouver Island's largest historic earthquake (and Canada's largest hirtoric onshore earthquake) was amagnitude 7.3 event that occurred at 10:15 a.m. on Sunday, June 23, 1946. The epicenter was in the ForbiddentPlateau area of central Vancouver Island, just to the west of the communities of Courtenay and Campbell River.

This earthquake caused considerable damage on Vancouver Island and was felt as far away as Portland Oregon, and Prince Rupert B.C. The earthquake knocked down 75% of the chimneys in the closest communities, Cumberland, Union Bay, and Courtenay and did considerable amage in Comox, Port Alberni, and Powell River (on the eastern side of Georgia Strait). A number of chimneys were shaken

down in Victoria and people in Victoria and Vancouver were firghtened—
many running into the streets. Twodeaths resulted from this earthquake,
one due to downing when a small boat capsized in an eathquake-
generated wave, and the other from a heart attack in Seattle,
Washington.

News Report

Yvonne De Carlo

One of Hollywood's Most Radiant Actresses!

Yvonne De Carlo was born with the birth anme of Peggy Yvonne
Middleton on September 1, 1922 in Vancouver, British Columbia. While
some sources have her fist name as Margaret, most agree it is Peggy.
Yvonne was three when her father abandoned the family. Her mother
turned to waitressing in a restaurant to help make ends meet. A rough
beginning for the actress who would, one day, be one of Hollywood's
elite.

Hermother wanted her to be in the entertainment field and enrolled her
daughter in a local dance school and also studied dramatics. Yvonne
was not shy in the least. She entertained the neighborhood with
impromptu productions.

When Yvonne was 15 years old, her mother gathered her up and went to
Hollywood to try her fame and fortune. With no break forthcoming, the
two returned to Canada.

The returned in 1940 where Yvonne would dance in chorus lines at night
while she checked in at the studios by ay in search of film work.

1945 Yvonne landed the title role in the film SALOME, WHERE SHE
DANCED. While the ritics were less than thrilled with this movie, it was,
at long last, a big role, and for Universal Studios, a big success. Now
Yvonne was rolling. That film was followed by FRONTIER GAL as
Lorena Dumont. She appeared In many rolls inher career but with film
roles vanishing, she took the role of Lily Munster in the smash series

THE MUNSTERS which first aired in 1964. Still Yvonne wasn't
completely through with the big screen.

Appearances in films such as THE POWER (1968), THE SEVEN
MINUTES (1971), and HOUSE OF SHADOWS (1976), kept her before
the eye of the movie going public. Yvonne's last big screen appearnace
was 1993's SORITY HOUSE MURDERS. On January 8, 2007,
Miss De Carlo died at the age of 84.

Imdb.com

A BETTER WAY

Romans 3:23

"For everyone has sinned; we all fall short of God's glorious standard."

Romans 6:23

"For the wages of sin is death, but the free gift of God is eternal life through Christ Jesus our Lord."

John 1:12

"But to all who believed him and accepted him, he gave the right to become children of God."

Romans 10:9-10

"If you confess with your mouth that Jesus is Lord and believe in your heart that God raised him from the dead, you will be saved. For it is by believing in your heart that you are made right with God, and it is by confessing with your mouth that you are saved."

John 3:18

"There is no judgment against anyone who believes in him. But anyone who does not believe in him has already been judged for not believing in God's one and only Son."

**All scripture is being quoted
from the New Living Translation of the Bible**

My advice to you: if you do not attend a church already, find a Godly church with a biblical Pastor that can disciple you.

God Bless,

Diana E. Linn
Author